THE SCAM LIST

Because being bad
is just too fun....

KURT DINAN

SARAH —
I hope you
enjoy the
book!

Kurt Din

CRIME SCENE BOOKS

Dedication

For Jen and the kids, always.

Copyright © 2020 Kurt Dinan

Published in the United States by Crime Spree Books
Crimespreebooks.com

First paperback edition August 2020

Book design by Claudean Wheeler

ISBN 978-1-7349127-0-8 (paperback)

www.kurt-dinan.com

Contents

CHAPTER 1

Shakedown Switcheroo

I, Boone McReedy, am an Olympic-level bullshit artist.

It's how I persuade brainiacs that doing my homework would benefit humankind.

Or convince poor suckers to donate money to my beer fund.

Or smile and silver-tongue my way out of speeding tickets.

Lying's in my DNA, transferred to me from my dad, who got it from his dad, and so on down the line. Call it my bullshit birthright. It's a talent that comes naturally, and who am I to fight genetics?

But natural ability can only get you so far. To be a successful conman, you can't just *speak* the lie, you have to *sell* the lie. Not only does whoever is listening have to believe what you're saying, but you have to believe it too. How else could used-car salesmen earn a living? Or the booth owners here at Garbage Mountain convince you to buy shit you don't need? It's all in the sell.

I had a lot of time to think about this back in August while I sat in Dad's hospital room. The goddamn hospice nurse kept talking in this soft, calm voice that made me want to commit murder. When your dad's about to die, the last thing you want is a stranger telling you how peaceful he looks and how he knows you're here with him and how he doesn't have much time left. No, what you want at that moment is an audience with God so you can kick him in the balls for doing to this to your dad.

If you don't know anything about pancreatic cancer, it's pretty much a death sentence with no last-second call from the governor coming to save your ass. In just over three months, Dad went from being a forty-six-year-old guy with a full-on dad bod to a withered, living skeleton. On the day he died, Dad used what little strength he had remaining to wiggle a finger at me. He could barely speak then, and I had to put my ear right by his chapped lips to hear him. His breath was so rank and stale I had to fight not to gag, something I still feel guilty about. I leaned in, and in one of his final moments of life, Dad said...

Nothing.

Because none of that happened. I made it all up, and you believed me because I sold it. See how it works? I'd feel bad for lying to you, but you should have seen it coming. I mean, what were we just talking about? But I promise not to lie to you again. Unless I do. We'll see. It's situational.

So anyway, no, Dad's not dead. He is in prison, though, which is about the same thing. Mom's written him off, that's for sure, but I won't let him off the hook that easily. I'm too pissed. He's been in prison nine months, his sentence coming on the two-year anniversary of Mom making our family the proud owners of the biggest local embarrassment.

The sign out front of this twenty-acre flea market may read "Golden Mountain," but no one calls it that. To the citizens of Batesville, Ohio, the 120 sales booths crammed into one long building is better known as "Garbage Mountain," and for good reason—you name it, we sell it: two-dollar t-shirts that disintegrate on first wash, throwing stars and nunchucks for the budding ninja, velvet paintings of the baby Jesus swaddled in an American flag, six-dollar knockoff Air Jordans…you get the idea. And believe me, if you're going to make your livelihood selling crap, your bullshit gene has to be a dominant one.

So Tuesday afternoon, I'm in the back bathroom at Garbage Mountain plunging away at a clogged toilet and wondering why some people wait an entire year before evacuating their bowels when the door slams open. I lean out of the stall in time to see Billy Gompers trying to shove this scrawny freshman, Andy Alexander, through the tiled wall. We do a little eye dance, Andy's eyes pleading and Gompers' eyes menacing, until Gompers says, "Mind your goddamn business, McReedy."

"No problem here, man."

Billy Gompers has drum-tight, oily skin stretched over an unnaturally lumpy skull that would make even the Elephant Man cringe. Add a caveman's IQ and a great white shark's compassion, and Gompers has a bright future ahead of him. Flashforward twenty years and you'll find him working the graveyard shift at a tow truck company and spending his days euthanizing dogs at the animal shelter for fun.

So I go back to CPR'ing the toilet like I'm trying to save its life and let the little drama play itself out a few feet away.

"I can't get you anymore," Andy says, all blubbery. "My mom actually watches me swallow the pills. I can't palm them like I do at school."

What follows is the loud, telltale *umph* of Andy taking a fist to the stomach.

"Then why the hell did you have me meet you here?" Gompers growls. "I want ten by tomorrow or you're dead."

"How am I supposed to do that?"

"Like I give a shit. Say you spilled them down the drain. Rob someone. Just figure it out."

It's vintage Gompers, not even taking the summer off from his goonery. You see this enough times and secretly hope the Andys of the world will do us all a favor by throwing a lucky punch that accidentally crushes the bully's trachea, but this, unfortunately, isn't the Andy to make that happen.

So in a situation like this, there's only one thing to do: I leave the plunger behind and step out of the stall. Andy's on the floor against the wall with Gompers hulking over him.

"Hey, Gompers," I say, "some advice?"

Gompers snaps my way, looking surprised. Or maybe confused. Like I said, his face doesn't lend itself to careful study.

"Stay out of this, Boone."

I take a step toward them, and Gompers covers the space between us in three quick steps before shoving me hard. Then I'm pinned against the wall, staring at the smiling skull ring on Gompers' middle finger that's curled with the others into a boulder-sized fist.

"I said beat it," Gompers says.

"Okay," I say, "but taking pills from this kid's a waste. It's like robbing a bank and only pocketing the change instead of hitting the vault."

Gompers blinks hard. I should have dumbed things down from the beginning.

"The kid's family's got money, Gompers. Lots of it. Enough for you to buy all the pills you want and have a lot left over. I just figured you'd want to know."

Gompers puts his greasy face inches from mine and breathes on me hard. Now I'll never be able to grow a decent beard.

"Why are you telling me this?" he says.

"Because who doesn't love money? I figure I'm in for a small finder's fee, but since you're the muscle, you keep the bulk of it. If he has any money on him, that is."

Gompers stares at me with dead eyes but lets go of my shirt.

"Or maybe I just keep it all for myself," he says.

"Hey, your call, man. You're the boss. Let's at least see what he's got before we make any decisions."

Andy's doing his best to disappear into the corner, but Gompers smells blood in the water and yanks Andy to his feet.

"You holding out on me?"

"I told you I don't have any pills."

"Not pills. You heard him. Money."

Andy looks at me for help but knows he won't be getting it. He turns his front pockets inside-out to show Gompers they're empty, but Gompers isn't dumb. Well, not completely dumb.

"Turn around," Gompers says, and before Andy can respond, he's face-first against the wall. Gompers shoves a hand into Andy's back pocket, and a second later we're all looking at a wallet with sixty dollars in it.

"That's mine," Andy says.

"Not anymore," Gompers says. Then the cash is out of Andy's wallet and in his pocket. "And if you tell anyone about this, they'll never find your body."

"What about me?" I say. "I'm the one who told you about the money."

"Tough shit."

"No, look," I say, "consider it a payoff. If the kid is dumb enough to tell his parents or the cops, I'll back you up. It'll be our words against his, two against one."

"You'll back me up anyway," Gompers says.

"Why would I do that?"

"Because if you don't, I'll beat your ass."

It's impossible to argue with such sound Neanderthalian logic.

Gompers is on the way out when the bathroom door opens again. Standing in the doorway blocking Gompers' path is a guy who looks like he uses professional wrestlers as toothpicks. He's wearing black jeans and a black t-shirt reading "Kill 'em all and let God sort 'em out."

"Andy?" the man says.

"Dad?" Andy says.

"Shit," Gompers says.

The man steps into the bathroom, and Gompers backs way the hell up. He might be one of the biggest kids in school, but he looks like a toddler next to this behemoth.

"They robbed me," Andy says, pushing past us and standing behind his dad.

"Whoa, wait a minute," I say, holding both hands out. "That's not true. I'm not a part of this. It was all him." I hook a thumb at Gompers, who looks like he's just taken a hammer to the forehead. Not that you could tell if he did.

"No, he tried to take money too," Andy says.

"But only to give it back to you so you didn't lose it all," I say.

Andy's dad takes a step forward, and now it's Gompers and me who are pressing ourselves into the wall.

"Give it to me," the man growls.

Gompers, in a shocking display of rational thinking, doesn't hesitate in handing over the wad of cash. The man then looks at me, his hand out.

"I told you I didn't take any of it," I say.

"No, but you wanted to. So give me what you've got."

"What?"

"Your money," he says. "All of it. Now."

Before I have time to comply, the man's paw closes over my face and I'm shoved sideways along the wall. I slam into the metal garbage can and hit the ground, soggy paper towels and empty food wrappers raining on me.

"Now," he says again.

I rush to give him what little money I have, and then he's vulturing over Gompers. It's a mirror image of Gompers standing over Andy five minutes ago, but this probably isn't the best time for a discussion on irony. Gompers reaches into his front pocket and pulls out a sad five-dollar bill. He hands it to the man, who then gives it to Andy.

"And the rest?" Andy's dad says.

"There isn't anymore," Gompers says.

The man leans in, and it's enough for even someone as dumb as Gompers to surrender. He may be a shark, but even sharks are afraid of one thing—bigger sharks. Gompers goes through all of his pockets, and when he's finished, he's handed over Andy's money and at least a hundred dollars of his own. Who knew being a bullying asshole could be so lucrative?

"Apologize to my son," the man says.

Gompers and I each whimper out a "sorry" while staring holes through the bathroom floor.

"Good," he says, "and if Andy ever tells me that either one of you even looked at him—"

"It won't happen," Gompers says.

"I know people," Andy's dad says. "You will disappear."

"We don't doubt it, sir," I say.

My eyes go wet, and I can almost smell the urine wanting to flood out of Gompers.

"Let's go," Andy's dad says, and seconds later, Gompers and I are alone in the bathroom.

"We need to call the cops," I say.

"No way. That guy'll kill us."

"But he robbed us," I say. "And he assaulted me."

"Jesus, McReedy, and what would you tell the cops? That we were shaking this kid down and then his dad came in and stole from us instead? Don't be so goddamn stupid."

Gompers leaves without another word, and I'm left with heart palpitations and a toilet to finish unclogging. It takes another five minutes of plunging before I'm finished, which is just enough time for the coast to clear. I find Andy and his dad sitting in the food court, risking their lives with fifty-cent corndogs from Brenda's Hot Dog Emporium. They wave their fried sticks at me in salute.

"Did he split?" I say.

"He hauled ass as soon as he left the bathroom," the man says. "I doubt he'll be bothering the kid anytime soon."

"You just saved me years of having to deal with that gorilla," Andy says.

Roadie, the man who played the role of Andy's dad, is a boother here. Among other things, he rides a Harley and is friends with counterfeiters, gun nuts, and master criminals. He's definitely a handy guy to know and was more than willing to help us out with Gompers.

"Did you get hurt when I threw you down?" Roadie asks.. "It was a last-second improvisation."

"No," I say, my ribs still aching, "I've learned how to take a fall. It's a much-needed survival skill."

"I hear that."

We talk for a while longer, mostly laughing about pulling off a Shakedown Switcheroo and hearing way too many thank-yous from Andy. Eventually, Roadie pulls out the roll of bills he took from Gompers and hands it to me. I take my original twelve, give Andy back his sixty, then count Gompers' donation. Once I take my agreed-upon forty-five percent, I hand Roadie the rest of the cash.

"Thanks for the help," I say.

"Anytime," Roadie says before pocketing the money and heading back to his booth.

"That's one scary dude," Andy says. "Do you know a lot of people like him?"

"More than is healthy," I say.

Our business complete, there isn't any reason for Andy to stick around. It's been a good day. I got paid for doing what I do best, Andy has a meathead off his back, and Gompers will hopefully think twice before he messes with someone.

But I doubt he will.

People are stupid.

It's what makes being me so fun.

And profitable.

CHAPTER 2

A Mystery Girl Appears

My reward for successfully saving the life of an easy Batesville target is the privilege of spending the next two hours sweating to death in Bolan, the sixty-five-foot tyrannosaurus smiling down at the entrance to Garbage Mountain. Officially, my job in Bolan's brain is greeting customers entering the building. Unofficially, my job is inhaling the carcinogenic fiberglass particles flecking off Bolan's innards while I watch old movies. "Employee of the Month," here I come.

Working inside Bolan might actually be tolerable if I had a real view of Batesville, or as most of us call it, Masturbatesville. Instead, all I have is the sad scenery of Garbage Mountain's potholed parking lot and its spattering of cars. Well, that and a view of Treasure Palace, the newer, cleaner flea market that opened next door a year ago. Who would have thought one town could support multiple entrepreneurs selling dolls made out of socks and bedazzled hemp purses? The obvious answer is, it can't. A quick car count comparison between parking lots is all the proof you need.

"What do you think, Rock?" I say. "Six months, tops?"

From his hook on the wall, Rockefeller stares at me with lidless eyes.

"Fine, nine months," I say. "But that's the most I'm giving this place."

Rockefeller, a shrunken head the size of a softball, was a gift from Thurman, owner and operator of booth fourteen's Smoke Shop. Thurman says the head was once attached to the body of Michael Rockefeller, heir to an oil fortune who went missing in New Guinea in the sixties and is thought to have been eaten by cannibals. The story has to be bullshit, and I'd ask Rockefeller for the truth, but he's tightlipped about things since his mouth is sewn shut. Still, what Rockefeller lacks in storytelling abilities, he makes up for in judgmental stares, so he's not a completely worthless roommate.

Today, the two of us are busy doing our part to ensure Garbage Mountain's success by watching *The Sting* on a portable DVD player on loan from booth twenty-one's Vintage Tech. Rockefeller's completely engrossed in the movie, unable to take his eyes off it, literally, while I unconsciously practice my one-handed false cut with a ratty deck of playing cards. Despite the heat stroke coming on, I'm feeling pretty good after my little bathroom con an hour ago. But let's be clear, what happened in there isn't a daily occurrence. There are lines I won't cross. I'm not my father. At least I like to tell myself that.

I'm zoned out of my mind when a red Corolla pulls into the parking lot and two long and wonderfully tan legs appear. I fumble the cards onto the floor and lean out of Bolan for a better look. The girl's only one step out of her car, and already she's scoring high on the Boone McReedy Dream Girl List:

Close to my age? Check.

Alive? Check.

End of list.

What can I say? I'm an equal opportunity boy toy.

Add to the fact this girl has dyed-purple hair, is hardcore cute, and is wearing a Titus Andronicus t-shirt, and I'm ready for us to start house hunting. When she reaches the talk box, I flip on the ancient audio system and say, "Well, hello there, young lady. Welcome to Golden Mountain."

Not my smoothest line, sure, but I'm hobbled by having to use my dinosaur voice. When in Bolan, you must talk like Bolan. It's dinosaur law.

Mystery Girl looks up for a sign of life, but there's nothing to see but Bolan's smiling mouth. She should count herself lucky, because if she saw me in all my sweaty glory, her knees would buckle.

"Is that you, Boone?" she says.

I squint into the sun, half-blinding myself. She's not someone I recognize, so she must've searched me out after reading about me on one of the many fan sites set up in my honor. I support myself on one of Bolan's canines, leaning forward and shouting down in my normal voice, "Yeah, it's me."

Oh, Boone McReedy, you eloquent bastard.

"I'm Leyla," she says and gives me this half-smile gut punch-er. Then she reaches into her back pocket and pulls out a pink piece of paper.

"This is from Mo. There's a show tonight."

Mo, short for Mohammed, is a 5'5", glasses-wearing, first-generation American with Iranian parents, a pedigree that would normally get his butt kicked here in moronically conservative Batesville, but Mo's status as a certified rock star protects him. His band, My Demonic Foreskin, plays a vast catalog of pop punk songs largely centered on Mo's inability to get laid. Flashforward twenty years and Mo's probably still tragically virginal but runs an insanely successful recording studio with a twelve-month waiting list.

"He's playing at The Underground at nine," Leyla says. "Are you coming?"

"I'm not sure," I say. "Will you be there?"

Above me, Rockefeller's look says he's not impressed.

"Give me a break," I tell him. "It's been a long day."

"Sorry, I can't tonight," Leyla says. "I'm just helping with advertising."

"Oh, come on, go," I say. "I'll show you the dance moves that won me the International Dance Off in Switzerland last year."

"But then everyone would want a piece of you, and where would that leave me?"

"No, believe me, if you go, you'll have my undivided attention. How could you not?"

She's smiling back now and says, "I can't, really. It's tempting, though."

"Well, how about to sweeten the pot, I promise to share with you the secret to everlasting happiness?"

"And I'm guessing you could only do that in the backseat of your car?"

"I like the way you think, but no," I say. "It is a secret I can only reveal while drinking and dancing."

This time her smile's a full-on blazer that hits me south of the belt. I'm about to render her completely helpless by ratcheting up my flirting to galactic levels when I'm interrupted by a boy, probably six, and his mom, definitely exhausted, coming up the sidewalk. Leyla steps aside, and I drop back into Bolan's mouth.

"Are you the last dinosaur alive?" the boy says into the talk box.

"Yes, and if you eat your vegetables and listen to your mom, you can live as long as me," I tell him.

"How old are you?"

"I'm sixty-five million years old. In fact, today's my birthday."

"You can't be that old. The earth's only been around for 6,000 years."

"Who told you that?"

"My mom."

Now look, like any sane guy, I want the kid and his mom gone fast so I can get back to all that's important and meaningful in life—i.e., talking to my soon-to-be wife, Leyla—but sometimes I can't stop myself. So I say to the boy, "Well, it sounds like maybe your mom needs to study the fossil record a little more closely."

Even from up here I can see the kid double-blink.

"She should read *Dinosaur in a Haystack* by Stephen Jay Gould," I say. "Lara's Book Nook and Bait Shop in booth thirty-three should have it. Tell your mom to buy a copy. And you have a great day here at Golden Mountain."

The mom stares up at Bolan, but I'm well-hidden. Then she grabs the kid's hand and starts dragging him back toward the parking lot. Of course, that's when the two-way clipped to my belt crackles to life.

"Boone?"

Crap.

"Yeah, Opal?"

"If they leave, I'm deducting from your paycheck whatever I estimate they would've spent. Do you understand?"

Mom may own Garbage Mountain, but Opal's the brains behind the operation. She's also a thousand years old and the reason I fully support the Eskimo tribes who once allegedly shoved their elderly out to sea on icebergs.

I give a lengthy sigh before announcing in my Bolan voice, "All little boys entering Golden Mountain today will receive a free ice cream at I Scream, You Scream, located in the food court. Come help me celebrate my birthday."

The boy looks up from the sidewalk, and when his six-year-old brain processes what he's just heard, he's immediately back on his feet pulling at his mom to get inside. Things go epic tug-of-war then, the mom yanking him toward the car, the kid going boneless on the sidewalk, refusing to get up even as his mom's threat-begs increase in volume. Seconds before the kid goes into an all-out tantrum and starts wailing, the mom gives in and heads for the front door. The pissiness is still all over her face, but she's going because he's stopped making a scene.

"One free ice cream—that's $2.95 from your paycheck," Opal says.

"Doesn't sound free to me," I mutter.

Rockefeller grins.

"Oh, shut up."

I look back at the talk box, expecting to see Leyla, but she's halfway to her car.

"Wait, where are you going?"

"Maybe I'll see you tonight," she yells back. "Check out the flyer."

She's weighed the flyer down with a rock on the talk box, and I'm seconds from leaping six-and-a-half stories to get it when Opal interrupts yet again.

"I need you inside, Boone. Maggie dropped a gallon of vegetable oil in Popcorn Perfection."

This is my life.

I grab Rockefeller off his hook and climb down into Bolan's stomach. This space isn't nearly as cramped as upstairs and is big enough to contain a small desk, two chairs, and a lamp. A stack of half-read detective novels from the Book Nook sits near the exit, alongside a plastic container filled with Little Debbie boxes and individual chip bags. Movie posters with Han Solo, Jack Sparrow, and James Bond cover Bolan's insides, and dozens of cassettes from booth six, Everyone Loves Music, lay scattered by an old boom box. Bolan's the greatest secret clubhouse a boy could ask for.

Before leaving, I hang Rockefeller over the table like a grotesque chandelier and exit through the door, which is wonderfully located where Bolan's butthole would be if he were real, and go grab Leyla's flyer. More important than the names of the bands playing tonight is how Leyla's written her name and number at the bottom. My professional handwriting analysis skills tell me she wants me bad.

The Mountain is essentially a massive warehouse but with white wooden panels on the outside to make it a little less military looking. The panels are in desperate need of a paint job, but I'm not about to bring that up. I'd spend the rest of the summer on a ladder with a paint sprayer, hoping for a strong wind to blow me off to my death.

Opal's standing just inside the entrance of Garbage Mountain, scowling at me like I'm late for curfew. She's wearing a blue and white polyester get-up that makes her a walking firetrap. And here I am without a lighter.

"Is she in there?" I say, motioning toward the office.

"Yes, with the lawyers, so don't bother her."

Mom's meetings with Mr. Stuffy and Ms. Stick-Up-The-Butt have been more frequent lately, and it's easy to understand why—Garbage Mountain's bleeding money. Not only are we losing boothers to Treasure Palace, but at least a dozen of our residents haven't paid for their rental space in months. Mom should kick them out, but she's too nice. Real-world business has no room for Mom's overly compassionate heart.

Opal says, "While you were taking your time getting here, Brenda called from The Mud Hut to say they have a clogged sink. But start with the vegetable oil spill. And I need you to do the night deposit tonight."

"But it's not my night. Tuesday is Darby."

"She's unavailable, so you'll do it."

"I have plans."

"Oh, plans," Opal says. "Curing cancer, maybe? Or are you hoping to finish your opera?"

"I—"

"Darby has real plans, unlike your imaginary ones. Be in my office at 7."

Jesus, now something else to waste my time. Night deposit means dropping a cash-filled, padlocked nylon envelope at the bank box with the day's proceeds, which after a good weekend can run up to $20,000. A Tuesday drop is considerably less, though, even if it's matched with Monday's take. Say maybe $2,000. Regardless, it's chimp work, and I'm the head ape.

"Don't forget, Boone," Opal says again. "Seven o'clock."

I walk off without saying goodbye. That'll show her.

The Mountain may be one big warehouse, but the inside is broken into three aisles, each containing forty booths, twenty on each side. Wagon wheel chandeliers hang from the ceiling alongside odd decorative choices like stuffed animals and colored streamers, all leftovers from the previous owner. Boothers, unfortunately, can furnish their stalls however they want. Some have blinking neon signs, others hand-painted ones. Long red carpet mats run the length of each aisle and are supposed to remain free of objects so the customers have a place to walk, but most boothers clog the aisles with sandwich boards plagued with misspellings. Basically, if you're a clean freak, break out in hives at the sight of clashing colors, or suffer from claustrophobia, The Mountain is not for you.

As I make my way across the complex, I'm under constant assault with smiles, hugs, and hellos from the boothers, something easily blamed on Dad. Once he was arrested, I quickly became the adopted child of a community of misfits. The offers came fast and furious:

Stephanie, who spent her teenage years being shot out of a cannon with a traveling circus, told me to stop by her barbecue stand anytime for a free meal.

Dave of Dave's DVD Den said I could borrow from the pirated movie collection he keeps for trusted customers.

Mindy, who has an eye tattoo on her forehead, offered free tarot readings at Miss Mindy Sees All.

Bob the Bargain Man hooked me up with his friend who runs a police car auction, which led to my first car, The Destroyer.

And so on.

The only way I could have stronger role models would be by joining a biker gang.

I spend the rest of the afternoon unclogging sinks, emptying garbage cans, and hating life. I may have felt good after helping Andy in the bathroom, but nothing is more humbling than hours of shit work. After the mandatory two-hour waiting period passes, I send Leyla a painstakingly crafted text of "Hey, this is Boone," and wait for her reply.

I kill the last hour of my shift wandering the stalls, specifically Karen's Nightmare Toys, which sells grinning cymbal monkeys, jack-in-the-boxes, clown dolls, and other toys you can buy if you want to guarantee your kid years of necessary therapy.

Karen's booth is flanked on one side by Adam's Invention Mania, where you can buy such essentials as a tuba-shaped toothpaste dispenser called Tuba Toothpaste, and on the other side by Kerry's Bargain Rock 'n Roll Memorabilia, filled with such unwanted items as signed guitar picks by members of Nickelback and a piece of gum once chewed by the lead singer of The Police. And people wonder why Garbage Mountain is a sinking ship.

A half-hour before closing, I give up on the day and am heading for our small apartment in the back of the building when I see Darby West standing outside her uncle's booth, Ancient Artifacts. Darby's wearing loose cargo pants, a t-shirt, and cross trainers with her hair pulled back in a ponytail. As usual, she looks ready for a fight. When not pulling straight A's, Darby teaches Combat Ready, a self-defense class for girls at her uncle's dojo, where she's raising her own female ninja army. If you see a guy walking around Batesville High with a black eye or busted nose, odds are Darby or one of her minions is behind it. Flashforward twenty years and Darby's either a pit fighter in the Congolese jungle or the warden of a supermax prison.

"You messed up my plans for tonight," I say.

"Then today can't possibly get any better."

"What's so important you can't do the night drop?"

"Not that it's any of your business, but I got hired to do a private lesson at the dojo."

"And that's more important than whatever I had planned?"

"Infinitely."

Darby stares me down, almost begging me to say something smart-assed so she can roundhouse kick me across the building. You might be thinking I should disarm her with the same charm I used on Leyla, but Darby's impervious to my weapons. She wasn't always, but she is now. There's a history there that isn't worth going into at the moment. Let's just say Darby's made it clear she would rather light herself on fire than be around me.

"Don't you think maybe you owe me?" I say.

"For what?"

"For the two weeks of entertainment I gave you."

"If anything, you owe me. No one should have to put up with you for that long."

I leave Darby to her silent gloating and head over to the Coke machine, pulling a special dollar bill from my wallet. I feed it into the slot, and when the machine's credited me, I pull on the packaging tape I've applied to the bill and yank it from the machine. It's a cheap con, not worthy of my talents, but I'm pissy and thirsty, so it's not the time for an ethics discussion.

All around me boothers are shutting down for the night, pulling down gates and turning off their lights. I'm envisioning a sad, lonely night of video games and maybe a movie after my trip to the bank when my phone buzzes.

I'll see you tonight. Can't wait for those dance moves. ;)

And now I have a decision—do the responsible thing and make the night drop at the bank, or blow it off until morning, change into a non-feces-smelling shirt, and drive to The Underground to meet Leyla in all of her hot glory?

I think we both know the right answer.

CHAPTER 3

Bad Night at The Underground

"Okay, here's the bet," I say. "Ten dollars says I can get this dime inside the bottle without touching the dime, the bottle, or the toothpick. And, no, I won't blow on it either."

I'm sitting at the bar in The Underground, the last business standing in the Great Oaks Mega Mall, which once housed over two hundred stores but is now nothing but covered storefronts and emergency lighting. Tonight, the entire place smells of stale beer and B.O. with just a hint of decaying rat carcasses. It's definitely not the place to go if you're overflowing with self-respect. On stage, the opening act is tearing down their equipment, and the soundman's being ironic and playing the goddamn Dave Matthews Band. Next to me is a dope my age who clearly doesn't know who I am because he's listening to my pitch and considering taking me up on it. We're both looking at a dime balanced on a toothpick snapped into an L over the opening of an empty Rolling Rock bottle.

"And you won't touch any of them?" he says.

"Right."

"Is there a time limit? Like, are we just going to sit here until someone bumps into it or something?"

"No, nothing like that. I only get ten seconds."

He leans in toward the bottle, trying to figure out the angle I'm playing. Of course, there's nothing for him to see, but I know the ten I've put in front of me has his greedy mouth watering.

"Bullshit. It can't be done."

"Care to back that up with money?"

The guy looks at me, then at the bottle, then back at me. Inside his head, Logic and Emotion are battling. Logic is telling him to back off, that this is a setup he can't win. But Emotion is whispering how smart he is and how he knows more than I do. It's telling him there's no way I can get the dime in the bottle without touching it. If you're me, you want Emotion to win the debate, and it usually does.

"Okay, fine," he says. "Show me."

"Let me see your money first."

He puts crumpled ones and a five on the bar, and the bartender, who has frizzed-out black hair and translucent skin like she's seen too many Tim Burton movies, rolls her eyes because she knows what's coming.

"Ready?" I say. "Start the countdown."

When he says "ten," I dip my finger into a small pool of condensation on the bar, then drip the water onto the broken part of the toothpick. A second later, the toothpick slowly starts to open, moving the dime closer to dropping. The guy doesn't even make it to four before the dime falls into the bottom of the bottle. Why does this happen? I have no idea. Physics or something. Who am I, Neil deGrasse Tyson?

I reach for the money, but the guy swipes it.

"Don't do that," I say. "Take your loss like a man."

"It was a bullshit bet. I'm not paying."

"Look, I get it. I really do. Losing a bet like that's a blow to the ego. But here's the thing—see that guy over there?"

I point up to the front of the stage where my friend Arlo, a 6'5", 270-pound colossus, stands. Arlo would probably be a Division I football prospect if he wasn't a self-proclaimed pacifist. He also has a Jesus beard and a calm, hypnotic way of speaking that instantly puts everyone at ease. Flashforward twenty years and Arlo lives in a mountaintop monastery teaching others to levitate. But the guy next to me doesn't need to know about Arlo's hatred of violence. He also apparently doesn't need me to explain my overall point, because this time he listens to Logic and drops the money back onto the bar before calling me an asshole and walking away.

"Another, please," I say to the bartender, who pulls a bottle from the cooler and puts it in front of me. She doesn't even ask for my ID, which is a fake, of course. Not that I need it here. You could draw a pirate ship on a Post-it and they'll take it as valid identification at The Underground.

And yeah, sometimes I drink. And my G.P.A is shit. I've even had sex before and will have it again someday, hopefully. What's your point? My dad's in jail, my mom owns a massive junk emporium, and I spend most of my days in a dinosaur. How's your life going?

A girl in a skin-hugging blue tank top passes, and I throw the smile I give when I want to render women helpless. Somehow this girl's impervious to it. The only explanation possible is legal blindness.

I snag my beer and weave through the crowd to the front of the stage where Mo's waiting to set up. Tonight, he's dressed slacker-cool in ripped black jeans and a Fugazi t-shirt. Next to him, Arlo's playing the role of unnecessary bodyguard. Mo may not be safe from bigoted dickheads on the streets, but here in The Underground, he's royalty.

"Holy crap," Mo says when he sees me. "He lives."

"It's like a Bigfoot sighting," Arlo says.

"Speaking of Bigfoot," I say. "Jesus, that beard of yours."

"What? I shaved this morning. I can't help that I have this much testosterone. But your shirt."

I'm wearing an electric blue bowling shirt from booth eighty-one's Monica's Comfortable Shirts that's definitely not to everyone's taste. I used to dress like every other slobby teenage boy in town, but Monica said something to me a year ago that stuck. I had just fixed the gate on her booth when she held up a shirt to my chest.

"I can't wear that," I said. "The guys will light me up."

"Boone, I'm going to tell you a secret most men don't discover until they're well into their twenties, if then. Are you ready?"

I nodded.

Monica's eyes went right, then left, making sure no one else was in hearing distance. Then she motioned me forward and cupped a hand between her mouth and my ear.

"Dress for girls, Boone. Not for guys. Trust me."

I may have been skeptical, but when a woman like Monica—hell, any female for that matter—whispers in my ear, I'm defenseless. And of course, she was right. Guys at school gave me hell at first because of the shirt, but the girls loved it. I've let the women of Garbage Mountain dress me ever since.

"Any setlist surprises tonight?" I say to Mo.

"Just the usual, brother," he says, smoothing down the Against Me! sticker on his guitar. "Shake the walls—"

"—and blow some eardrums," Arlo finishes.

They high-five. I'd like to make it clear that if I'm ever with someone who finishes my sentences, you have my permission to kill me.

"So is Leyla here?" I say.

"Who?" Mo says.

"The girl you had doing PR for the show. She stopped by with a flyer."

"Arlo does all of our promotions."

I look at Arlo, who says, "Maybe she's working with one of the other bands?"

"She said you sent her to me," I say.

"Not me, man," Mo says.

I scan the crowd for Leyla but come up empty. I'm about to get depressed by the tragic realization that this excellent shirt is going to go to waste when two girls walk by. One of them says hi, which is all the invitation I need. I tell the guys I'll talk to them later and follow the two girls to the pinball machine in the back corner.

And before you ask, no, I don't have a girlfriend. Shocking but true. Just between us, I don't want the commitment because I won't risk being dumped. Dad going to prison is enough rejection for a lifetime. Still, it's fun to find a girl as screwed up as me to fool around with, and The Underground is usually littered with them.

The two girls at the pinball machine aren't from around here because I know all the girls in Batesville. I stand close and watch as the short-haired blonde with the stud in her nose loses her first ball seconds after it's in play.

I lean on the machine and say, "Speaking as someone who knows a potential pinball wizard when he sees one, I'm recommending you drop out of school and go professional."

Her tall friend rolls her eyes, but the blonde says, "Funny, I already did that. I'm just in town to brush up on my skills while on my way to the World Pinball Championships at Madison Square Garden."

"And how are you finding the local talent?"

"A little lacking," she says. "And to think we'd heard so much about Batesville boys. Nice shirt, though."

I give her my aw-shucks smile sending her into full swoon. She abandons her game and says, "Do you remember me?"

"Wait a minute," I say, rubbing my chin. "We built houses for Habitat for Humanity together, right? Or was it cleaning cages at the Humane Society? I know it must've been one of those charities that only let the nicest and most giving people join. Sorry if I can't remember. I'm in so many."

She comes closer to me, her hips dangerously close to mine.

"Katie," she says. "Katie Post?"

I pantomime a light bulb appearing over my head.

"Of course! Katie! I remember now."

"You do? From where?"

"From, uh…"

"If you can't remember, drinks on you. Fair?"

Oh, I'm getting out of this one easily.

"Okay, I confess I can't remember," I say. "But that's a me-problem, not a you-problem. I suffered long-term memory loss when I saved those kids in the runaway school bus. Now, as for drinks, do you want—?"

And that's when Katie's arm shoots forward and a tidal wave of warm beer hits me in the face.

"Drinks on you," she says.

I'm not encouraged by their laughter as they disappear into the crowd. I'd be lying if I said this was the first time this has happened to me.

The Underground's bathroom is a clean freak's nightmare and a graffiti artist's dream. A vast assortment of penis drawings and stickers of bands long gone cover the walls, stalls, and most of the ceiling. The floor is wet with what I can only hope is water, but I'm not optimistic. I make a futile pass at the paper towel machine before having to settle for toilet paper to mop my face.

I'm cleaning up as best I can in the cracked mirror when Parker Briggs comes in. Parker's impossibly good-looking and has a nice trust fund waiting for him when he turns twenty-one, which probably explains his reputation of having a loose zipper. But more importantly, his dad, Cullen Briggs, owns Treasure Palace. Parker and I were friends in middle school, but when we hit high school, he veered off on the golden path with other rich kids. There was never an official end to our friendship; we just stopped hanging out, downgrading our relationship status to acquaintances. Things became strained once his dad built the monstrosity across the street from Garbage Mountain. It's hard faking even the slightest amount of friendliness to a person whose dad is trying to close down your family business.

Parker nods to my beer-soaked shirt and says, "Girl trouble?"

"No, why?"

He gives me his fluorescent white smile and says, "Same old Boone," before checking his look in the mirror.

"I watched you pull The Dime Drop on the moron at the bar," he says. "I can't believe he fell for that."

"They always do."

"It was fun when we used to con kids with bets back in middle school."

"Yeah, we won more Little Debbie snack cakes than we could ever eat."

"We sure did," Parker says. "But that was middle school. I'm surprised you're still pulling scams. I figured you'd—I don't know—grow out of it."

"Is that what you did?"

"I don't have time for games anymore. Dad's grooming me to take over Treasure Palace someday. Right now, I'm pretty much in charge of security."

"Wow," I deadpan. "You're, like, really important."

"Laugh all you want, Boone. You have to grow up sometime."

I let him have the last word because there's no winning with guys like Parker. He leaves, and I wait a bit before exiting myself. With no Leyla in sight, I consider bailing, but Mo and the rest of the band are onstage and close to kicking it off. Mo's parents are the only adults here and stand off to the side and far enough back not to embarrass the hell out of Mo. Despite their strict religious beliefs, they've never stopped Mo's musical pursuits. In fact, just one look at their faces as they watch him, you can tell they're crazy proud of him.

Mo says into the mic, "Hi, we're My Demonic Foreskin. Thanks for coming."

After a quick count, the band launches a face-melting version of Cheap Trick's "Surrender." The crowd starts pogo-ing so hard the floor shakes. My bottle's empty, so I go back to the bar where another rube is sitting alone, practically begging me to take his money. I sit next to him and pull a matchstick and dime from my pocket. He watches me as I set them on top of the bottle.

"So here's the bet."

I launch into my quick pitch. They're called bar bets, sucker bets, or proposition bets. Whatever you call them, it's a simple way to make easy money from unsuspecting people. Dad was the master of the bar bet and once told me he'd never paid for a drink in his life. Now he's in prison, where he's probably scamming other inmates for their gruel. Like the guy earlier, this one wants a time limit. I tell him ten seconds.

"That's it?" he says.

"That's all I'll need."

He looks the bottle over again, then puts two fives on the bar.

"Do it," he says, then starts his ten count.

I go to dip my finger into a penny-sized drip of water on the bar when a hand from behind shoots out and wraps around my wrist. I snap my head, and who is standing there determined to watch me lose ten dollars? Darby West.

"You're down to eight seconds," she says.

"You'll do anything to hold my hand," I say.

"You're lucky I'm not breaking it. Five seconds."

It's a lost cause. Darby wants me to struggle, but even if I was a professional arm-wrestler, I couldn't overpower her. I could awkwardly try the water-on-the-toothpick move with my right hand, but I've lost too much time, and there's no point in looking like an idiot over ten dollars. The guy beside me is watching us, wondering if this is somehow part of the bet, some angle he didn't see coming. But it's me who didn't see this coming.

"I think ten seconds are up," Darby says.

The guy reaches for the money, and I don't stop him. A bet's a bet. He gets off the stool and spies us over his shoulder as he walks away, still thinking he's missed something. If I told him it was a private matter between exes, he probably wouldn't believe it.

"You're not one to forgive and forget, are you?" I say.

"Never," Darby says.

"I thought you had a private training session tonight."

"They didn't show. Why aren't you off doing the deposit?"

"Already done," I lie.

Darby stares me down hard for a full five seconds before deciding I'm not worth it and walks off to rejoin her friends. I'm left with a still-wet shirt from Katie, a ten-dollar hole in my pocket because of Darby, and a bruised ego after being stood up by Leyla. It's definitely not my best night with the opposite sex. But I'm no quitter, so I down my beer, and order two more before moving closer to the front. On the way, I bump into a guy who looks like he eats raw squirrels for dinner. He shoves me hard before I sacrifice one of my beers in exchange for my life. Yet another narrow escape for Boone McReedy, tempter of women and tamer of wild beasts.

After forty minutes, I'm worn out from the day and stumbling for the exit when someone grabs a belt loop on the back of my jeans.

"Leaving before my dance lesson?"

I turn, and Leyla's holding two beers and wearing a My Demonic Foreskin t-shirt with a short skirt and black and white striped tights. It's exactly the hallucination I'd see after crawling in the desert for days without water.

"I was starting to think I'd seen a ghost this afternoon," I say, taking the beer.

"I'm a girl of mystery," Leyla says. "Cheers."

We clink and drink.

"I have to say that is one outstanding shirt," she says.

"Thanks, I made it myself."

"Wow, dinosaur ventriloquist and now stylish shirt tailor. Is there anything you can't do?"

"I have a hard time toning down my sexiness," I say. "I try, though. I find it's unfair to the entire species."

"I can see that."

"It's a heavy cross to bear."

We drink more and flirt more, and before I know it, Leyla's dragging me to dance. Not to brag, but alongside my rugged good looks and undeniable humility, dancing is one of the most powerful weapons in my arsenal. Leyla and I drink and dance as Mo flails away on an amped-up version of "Johnny B. Goode." Nearby, Parker dances with his girlfriend, Marlana, who's grinding away on him like she's trying to start a friction fire.

At some point, things get pretty blurry. I know there's more beer and a lot more sweaty dancing. I'm pretty sure Leyla and I kiss too, but I can't be sure. Like I said, it's all one massive haze. Eventually, the music ends, the lights go on in The Underground, and flashforward to Leyla helping me into the backseat of The Destroyer. The last thing I remember before passing out is Leyla kissing me on the forehead.

"You're cute," she says, "and I'm sorry."

Or maybe I dream that.

It's not until the next day I know it wasn't a dream.

It's actually the start of just the opposite.

CHAPTER 4

Introducing My Dad, the Prisoner

I wake up the next morning in the back seat of The Destroyer to world-class cloggers stomping in my brain. The sun's already up, so the inside of The Destroyer's heating up nicely. If I were a dog, someone would probably have already smashed a window to rescue me from broiling, but the mall parking lot's empty, so I have to save myself. In the front seat, I find my keys laid out nicely by Leyla. There's no "Good morning, Sunshine" note or cherry red lipstick kiss on the dashboard, so she must've had to rush home to make curfew.

My car, The Destroyer, a maroon '87 Monte Carlo, gets .2 miles to the gallon and has an ever-growing hole in the floorboard that will soon allow me to stop the car by Fred Flintstone-ing it. On the plus side, it also has the world's biggest collection of dirty Taco Bell wrappers in the back seat, viewable by appointment only.

Because breakfast is the most important meal of the day, I stop at the QuikPik where I devour a breakfast of Oreos and orange Gatorade. My phone's dead, and I don't have my charger, but no big deal. There won't be any panicked texts or calls from Mom. She probably doesn't even know I didn't make it home since the odds are she didn't either. Most nights, too exhausted from the day even to walk to our small apartment inside

Garbage Mountain, Mom just crashes on the couch in her office. We McReedys were likely successful hobos in our past lives.

Back on the road, I mount an unwinnable battle with The Destroyer's tape deck and have to settle for the radio, which fades in and out at its own discretion. I hit the highway and drive out of Batesville, giving The Mountain an enthusiastic middle finger as I pass.

"Sorry, Jesus," I say. "That wasn't meant for you."

I'm talking to the forty-foot bust statue of Jesus outside the megachurch on the other side of the highway. Because it's only his upper body and he's in the middle of a manmade pond with his arms raised to the sky, Jesus looks like he's drowning. There's also a three-foot-tall lightning rod sticking out of the top of his head making him look like he's an alien or a sort of biblical Phineas Gage. I guess the church owners learned their lesson after the last statue of Jesus got struck by lightning and burned down. Was God sending a message when that happened? How would I know? What am I, a theologian?

I don't have to work until later this afternoon, and with nothing to do, I decide it's a good time for my bi-weekly torture session. Perrysburg is only 90 minutes away, but with only my thoughts to keep me occupied, it might as well be on the other side of the planet. To pass the time, I design an exhaustive self-improvement plan and create new obscenities to shout at the idiots driving the speed limit. Or maybe I only do one of those things. I'm sure you can guess which.

One bathroom break and hamburger stop later, I pull into the Perrysburg Correctional Facility parking lot. The prison has visiting hours four times a week from 10:30 to 2:30 with an always painfully long processing line. Today, as usual, the line's a Who's Who of Future Arrestees. If I wanted to fit in better, I should have stopped on the way for a face tattoo or a roll in a muddy ditch. The guy in front of me, who has just enough teeth to make eating an ear of corn an all-day affair, says hey to me, and I give him one back. Then, because now we're best friends, he asks, "So who are you visiting?"

People love treating the processing line like it's a group therapy session where we can open our hearts about our felon family members. It's not a subject I ever get into. Dad's lived his life running short cons to keep his wallet full. The only long con he ever ran was convincing Mom to marry him, raising a family, and trying to live a normal life. But you can't be who you aren't. In my younger years, I inadvertently became Dad's partner-in-crime, spinning sob stories for kindhearted idiots more than willing to give Dad twenty dollars to help us out with whatever imaginary problem we concocted. At eight years old, I figured it was something every family did and enjoyed the one-on-one time with Dad, even if he made me promise never to tell Mom what we were doing. Eventually, though, I grew smart enough to realize he was using me. And while being a dickhead of a dad doesn't normally get you sent to prison, if you attach a card skimmer to the ATM located within your family-owned flea market, then you hit the trifecta— you go to prison, your wife almost loses her business, and your kid hates you. Winner, winner, chicken dinner.

Perrysburg Correctional may be a prison, but it's not likely to be featured on an episode of *Lockup* anytime soon. The prisoners here are more like the JV squad of felonious behavior—not as hardcore, not as talented, but accomplished enough to be on the overall team. Here, upset inmates don't riot; they grumble and write letters to the editor. After a female guard explains the rules to everyone in line, we're all wanded, metal-detected, and frisked before being led into the visitor's room.

If you're not lucky enough to have a close relative in prison, visitations at Perrysburg aren't like you see in the movies. There are no glass partitions and old-fashioned telephones. Instead, this room's like the cafeteria of a small school where all the bad kids are forced to wear uniforms. Two guards stand along the wall lost in thought, probably dreaming about being promoted to the next level in public safety: mall cop. They don't have guns, but if they did, the triggers would've rusted off by this point.

After a five-minute wait, the door opens and Dad steps into the room wearing an orange jumpsuit with his name stenciled in black over his heart. As he walks past the guard, he says something that makes the man laugh. It reminds me way too much of when I pass the secretary at school on the way to Principal Dodd's office. All my life people have been telling me how much Dad and I are alike. If the apple doesn't fall far from the tree, it's a tree diseased with black rot growing mushy apples infested with worms.

Today, Dad looks older than when I came in two weeks ago. He has a ragged beard and bags under his eyes that could carry a week's worth of groceries. It's like time here passes faster than in the real world. Call it Einstein's theory of prison relativity. He pulls out the chair and sits across from me, and I'm looking into the mirror thirty years in the future if I follow in his criminal footsteps. The fact that it's even a possibility terrifies me.

"You're back," Dad says.

"Prison clearly hasn't hurt your power of observation."

Dad smiles and crosses his legs at the ankles before putting his right hand in his pants pocket. It's the same way I'm sitting. Mirroring a person's behavior is a simple way to gain their confidence without them realizing it. It's a trick Dad does unconsciously at this point in his life. I catch myself doing it a lot too.

"So how are things?" he asks.

Like we're friends. Or like he's my therapist. Or like he's not in prison.

"How's The Mountain?" Dad says.

"Okay," I say. "No thanks to you."

"You can't blame that on me. It was on life support long before I got busted."

"No, you only pulled the plug."

Most parents would lose their shit at such outright disrespect. Not Dad. He's never raised his voice at me and probably has never had an intense argument in his life. It's not anything I do myself either. Even when he was handcuffed in front of Mom and me and taken from the house, he was calm, like he'd expected the moment.

"How's your mother?"

It's a question I never answer. Mom and I don't discuss Dad, almost like he never existed at all. After all of his lies came out in court, Mom's barely mentioned him, and as far as I know, she's never visited. Like a former booth owner who's moved across the street to Treasure Palace, Dad's dead to her. She doesn't know I come here, and I'm not about to tell her either. I can guess what her thoughts would be on the subject.

"You don't have any cash on you, do you?" Dad asks.

"Wow, I'm impressed you held out this long. Usually that's your second question, not your fourth."

"I'm working on being patient. So back to the question. My commissary account is running low."

"I'm all tapped out."

"I doubt it. You're smart enough to never let your wallet get too light. Have you been making any plays?"

I don't say anything.

"Of course you have," Dad says.

He's wrong, but I'm not going to argue with him. There's a big difference between saving Andy's life in the bathroom or sucker-betting a guy at a bar and the cons Dad used to run. No one really gets hurt by what I do. What Dad did was cheat people out of thousands of dollars and almost forced Mom into giving up Golden Mountain. I don't come even close to approaching the lines Dad was more than willing to cross.

"So come on, tell me," Dad says. "What have you been pulling?"

"There's been nothing."

"Come on, not even The Lost Dog con?"

I shake my head.

"Or The Grandparent Gouge? You could make a fortune on that one. Batesville has plenty of old folks' homes. Just get the numbers there and start dialing. You could make an easy thousand in a couple of hours."

"That scam's the lowest of the low," I say.

"If I still had my young man's voice, I'd be all over that one."

"Well, I'm not you."

"Oh, you're not? Heck, you were making plays before I even started teaching you. Remember second grade?"

The story of my first scam, The Copier Con, is a family favorite. My teacher, Mr. Barnaby, created a reward system called "Barnaby Bucks"—play money with his face on it that you could turn in at the end of the month for candy or pencils or whatever else he'd picked up at the Dollar Store. Barnaby Bucks were printed on basic yellow paper, and it didn't take me long to figure out I could run copies of the fake money, then sell a single bill of the counterfeits for a quarter to my gullible seven-year-old classmates. It only took me a week to earn thirteen dollars. That's also how long it took for Mr. Barnaby to realize something was up. Having twenty-four students clean out your prize closet in a single day will raise suspicions. My classmates snitched, ending the scheme, but my life as a conman had begun.

"So is that it, then?" Dad says. "Just wanting to make sure I'm still here?"

"That's not why I come. I know you'll be here. Even you couldn't talk your way out of prison."

"I wouldn't be so sure," he says with a smile. "But come on, why did you drive all the way here?"

It's a fair question, especially because all of our visits are just like this one—me not really talking much while he antagonizes me from across the table. So why am I here? One word: torture. For both of us. A big part of me blames myself for Dad's prison sentence. If I'd told Mom about Dad's scams, she might have stopped him. But I didn't say anything, and now he's here. A team of psychologists could probably make a fortune off me.

"You're not going to answer?" he says. "Okay, fine. I'll just ask next time."

"There won't be a next time," I say, getting up. "I'm not coming back."

As I cross the room, he says, "See you in a couple of weeks, Boone."

"No, you won't."

But we both know he will.

The guard opens the door, but before I can get out, Dad calls my name. Because of who he is and the pull he has on me, I can't help but look back.

"You're right about one thing—you're not me," he says. "You've always been a better conman than I am."

On my way out of the building, I stop by the commissary and put twenty dollars into Dad's account. It's the least I can do for him. He's still my dad. Even if there are days I wish he wasn't.

CHAPTER 5

Why Garbage Mountain Hates Me

Two police cars are parked in the lot when I get back to Garbage Mountain, which, considering our clientele, isn't surprising. What *is* surprising is when I'm halfway up the walk, already sweating from the summer heat, Darby West comes stomping out the front door toward me, her hands clenched into fists at her sides.

"Where is it, Boone?"

She stops a few feet away, but I still take two steps back out of the nuclear blast zone of her roundhouse kick.

"Are hellos not your thing?" I say. "They really do go a long way."

"I said, where is it?"

"What's 'it'?"

"Don't screw around, Boone. This is serious."

"What are you talking about?"

Before Darby can answer, Mom, Opal, and two Batesville cops—a man and a woman—appear at the entrance. None of them are holding "We Love Boone McReedy" signs.

"Boone, will you come here a minute, please?" Mom says.

Mom's in a skirt and a short-sleeve, cable-knit poncho sweater, looking professional yet hip at the same time. She'd be Batesville's most eligible bachelorette if Dad had received the death penalty, but we weren't that lucky. Her face shows a combination of relief and worry. Behind her, Opal looks like the stern, biblically old woman she is. As for the cops, I may not recognize them, but I hate them anyway. Call it my natural reaction to anyone in authority, especially one who carries a gun.

"Where have you been?" Mom says.

"Since when?"

"Since you left here last night."

I give everyone the rundown, starting with The Underground and moving on to crashing in The Destroyer before going vague with "and today I've just been running around, hanging out" because I don't want her to know I visited Dad. The cops listen to all of this but write none of it down. I take this as a good sign.

"Why haven't you answered your phone?" Mom says.

"Battery's dead," I say. "Sorry."

Lady Cop pulls out a portable charger from her pocket and says, "May I?"

Every instinct I have says not to give it to her, but Mom's look says I have no choice. I hand the cop my phone, and she plugs it in. I say to Mom, "What's this about?"

"Linda from the bank called a bit ago saying they never received the night deposit," Mom says. "Then when I couldn't reach you—"

"I suggested we call the police," Opal finishes.

Because of course she did. Flashforward twenty years and Opal's still alive at two hundred forty years old, refusing to die until she's made life miserable for every single person on the planet.

"The money's in The Destroyer," I say. "I was going to do the deposit today, but I haven't gotten to it. I've waited a day before. What's the big deal?"

You'd expect my mom to go ballistic at this, her son out all night with a few thousand dollars of boother money, but that's not Liann McReedy. Like Dad, she's never been a hollerer or a screamer. So there's no freak-out, no interrogation, just the weirdly calm and trusting look she always gives but I've probably never deserved.

"Let's go get the money," she says. "We'll all feel better."

The cops come with us, and Darby brings up the rear like a stalking tiger while I get into The Destroyer and reach under the front seat.

And, of course, the money isn't there.

Or in the glove compartment.

Or above the sun visors.

Or anywhere.

Dude Cop gives it a go next, checking the trunk and rest of the car, but comes up empty too. It's not long before there's a nice crowd of boothers standing around The Destroyer glaring at me.

"There was a girl," I say to everyone to begin my defense. I go on to explain Leyla but get nothing but looks of "Bullshit" from everyone.

"What's Leyla's last name?" Lady Cop says.

"I don't know," I say, "but I have her number in my phone."

Lady Cop hands my phone over, and after waiting a painful minute for it to power up, I go to my texts. Everything Leyla-related is gone, the texts sent and received. Even the selfie I vaguely remember we took while dancing is missing. I do a panicked search through my pockets for the flyer with her number, but I can't find that either.

"No, I swear, there was a girl," I say.

"Leyla-with-no-last-name?" Dude Cop says.

"Is she from around here?" Lady Cop says.

And when I shake my head no, the skepticism from everyone ramps up to eleven.

"How much money was in the deposit?" Dude Cop asks Mom.

It's Opal who brings the good news.

"$14,862."

"Wait, what?" I say.

"We had holdover from the weekend," Mom tells me.

Suddenly, I feel worse, which I didn't think was possible. But I see it all now, what's been done to me. I could try explaining it to the cops and everyone else here, but I'd sound like an idiot. All victims of a con sound stupid when they tell the story of how they got taken. Just imagine Gompers telling the story of what happened to him in the bathroom. See my point?

"Your husband's Thomas McReedy?" Dude Cop says to Mom.

"He is."

"And you're his son?" he says to me.

It doesn't take a genius to see where he's going with this. Everyone else gets it too. The cops look at each other, some police mind-reading going on between them.

"What would you like us to do, ma'am?" Lady Cop says. "We can file a report or you can talk things over with your son."

Mom looks at me, then away. I won't plead my lame case again, especially in front of everyone. If they file a report, she knows it'll lead to more questions for me, possibly making me look even worse than I already do. If she has them leave, the police are off my back, but she's almost admitting to everyone I took the money. Obviously, I hope she asks them to leave, but if that happens, there's a damn good chance the boothers will beat me to death here in the parking lot.

"Thanks for your help," Mom tells them. "I think we can handle this."

The police give Mom a card before leaving, and she tells everyone else she'll talk to them inside. As people wander off,

Darby steps in close and speaks in a voice that would make the devil crap himself.

"What did you do with it?" Darby snarls.

"I didn't take it."

"You've ruined all of us, Boone."

"Says the girl who was originally supposed to take the money to the bank but didn't."

Darby shoves me hard in the chest, and I stumble backward, somehow keeping my feet. She tromps back into Garbage Mountain with the others, leaving me in the sweltering parking lot wondering if the money in my savings account is enough to get me started with a new life, preferably where I can rent a house with a pool and a live-in maid. Six hundred dollars should be enough, right?

But joking aside, I'm scared and freaked and pissed. Leyla, if that's even her real name, just conned me out of $15,000, and I'm the idiot who fell for it. Yeah, it's possible a different person stole the money, but it would be too coincidental that on the day Leyla appears, invites me out, gets me drunk, and takes me back to my car, the money disappears and she has nothing to do with it. Dumbass doesn't begin to cover what I am.

When enough time's passed to where I'm confident the boothers are back to their businesses and not lying in wait for me just inside the entrance, I head into the building. I double-time it down the first aisle, expecting Darby to ninja-drop from the ceiling, tearing my heart from my chest and showing it to me before I die. There's a small crowd gathered outside the main office, so I sneak through the back where Opal's at her desk getting off the phone.

"Well, if it isn't Mr. Responsibility. Come to confess your sins?"

The best way to survive an encounter with Opal is to not engage. You'd be better off opening a vein inside a shark tank.

"Before you go in," she says, "do your mother a favor and be honest with her. She's been through too much with you and your father to have this added to her plate. Unless your goal is to give her a breakdown, which, then, you're well on your way."

Opal goes back to click-clacking away on her keyboard, probably creating software to funnel millions from the Make-a-Wish Foundation. When I walk in, Mom's not at her desk or even at the rusty-legged card table she brought from home to impress potential renters. Instead, she's lying on the Goodwill couch with her feet up on the armrest and a hand covering her eyes.

"I'm sorry," I say.

"How could you be so stupid and selfish?"

"I blame genetics."

"This isn't a time for jokes, Boone. What were you thinking leaving that money in the car?"

"I've done it before."

"Which isn't anything I needed to hear," Mom says. "You really think this girl Leyla took the money?"

"Yeah."

"But you don't know who she is, how to find her, or anything?"

"No."

Mom's so quiet and still that for a second I think the universe has saved her from a lifetime of the inevitable headaches I'll give her by gifting her a pulmonary embolism.

"Are you sure there isn't anything you need to tell me?" she says.

I don't take offense. How can she not ask if I took the money? Especially considering I'm satanic Dad's demon spawn.

"I've told you everything," I say. "How much trouble are we in?"

Mom looks at the ceiling doing calculations.

"Well, let's see," she says. "We're losing two boothers a week on average to Treasure Palace, and there'll be more after this.

We're already a month behind on the bank payment, and likely won't be able to catch up this month. And Cullen Briggs is just waiting for us to screw up so he can swoop in and own the only two flea markets in a hundred miles. So how much trouble are we in, Boone? A lot."

"What happens if we can't get the money back?"

"The bank will foreclose on us, and I'm guessing Briggs will be right there to buy the property. I'm assuming it would happen pretty quickly."

"How soon? Three months? Six months?"

"Try one month," Mom says. "Maybe less."

I come close to projectile vomiting on the wall.

"I can find the money," I say.

Mom has no reply.

"No, I can," I say, even though there's nothing in my history that would make her optimistic.

"You can try, Boone, and I'll probably bring the police back too. I was a little overwhelmed out there before. I'm thinking more clearly now."

She climbs to her feet and puts an arm across my shoulders.

"I love you, you know," Mom says, "but you're really good at screwing things up."

"You've always said I should try my best at whatever I do."

"Well, you've outdone yourself this time," she says. "Come on, let's go face the hostiles."

The small group that was gathered outside the office before has officially grown into a crowd. These are the people who may have once been the friendly, we'll-do-anything-to-support-you-Boone boothers who have been on my side since Dad went away, but they're not looking that way right now. At the moment, their faces are a mix of anger and worry. They're not holding torches or nooses, but they might as well be. I probably shouldn't be expecting any free burritos or fashion suggestions in the near future.

"I know you've heard about the money," Mom says to them, "and I'm doing everything possible to make sure it's found."

"But you sent the police away," Lynn Volz says. "That's not doing everything possible."

Around Garbage Mountain, Lynn's better known as "Tat Man" because he runs booth fifty-five's Tats and Tots, a tattoo parlor that also sells tater tots. It's a business model they'll no doubt be discussing at Harvard's School of Business for decades to come.

"I understand your point, Lynn," Mom says, "but it's complicated. Boone doesn't have the best relationship with the police, and if they get involved, that means the press will too, which will bring us additional bad publicity. We all know we don't need that right now."

"So is there a plan?"

This from Monica, she of the awesome shirts I sometimes wear. She also cans her vegetables and doesn't own a TV. Flashforward twenty years and she's likely living off the grid, writing antigovernment pamphlets that her fourteen children hand out at the local farmer's market.

"Yeah, there's a plan," I say.

Monica's looking at me now, along with dozens of other boothers and Darby, all of them with daggers in their eyes. Blood's about to be spilled, and when I see that coming, instinct takes over and I do what I do best: I open my mouth and spew grade-A bullshit. It's all about appearing and sounding confident. Like I said, you have to sell the lie. So let the swelling Hollywood motivational music begin.

"Look, I'll admit I screwed up, and I'm truly sorry," I say, "but I thrive on adversity, and I know all of you thrive on it too. That's why we're all here. We know the people in this town laugh at Golden Mountain. We also know the people would rather go across the street to Treasure Palace. We're real underdogs in this world, but we come here every day, and we work hard anyway. Why? Because we're not quitters; we're survivors. We'll pull together like we always do, and I'll get your money back. But I can only do that with your help. We can't let this pull us apart. What do you say? Will you help me prove to everyone that we won't let the world beat us down?"

The cheering that erupts sets off Richter scales on the other side of the planet. Golden Mountain quakes with high-fives, boothers kissing, and joyous tears from the hardest of men.

Tat Man pumps his fist in the air.

Monica dances and shouts, "Hallelujah!"

Mom weeps.

Even Darby has a smile that could cut glass.

It's glorious.

It's life-changing.

It's beautiful.

And it's all a lie.

Sorry. I know I said I wouldn't do that again, but I can't really control it.

But, man, wouldn't it be great if that's what happened? It's not, though. I said none of that. After telling everyone I had a plan, I felt this epic gut-buster of a pain in my stomach and bolted for the bathroom, where I puked up a day's worth of Oreos, hamburgers, Gatorade, guilt, and nausea. But none of that is nearly as interesting as the lie, right?

So let's just go with my original story and pretend I'm the hero we all know I am, okay?

Good.

CHAPTER 6

A Visit to Enemy Camp

Thursday sucks.

Having to work makes any day bad enough, but now when I walk around Garbage Mountain, the boothers give me the death glare. As expected, there are no offers of a free coffee-sludge drink from The Mud Hut or Lara stopping me outside the Book Nook to show off a first-edition detective novel she just scored. Maybe if Mom gets arrested like Dad, everyone here will return to feeling sorry for me. Would framing her for murder be too extreme?

I spend my workday completing odd jobs around The Mountain—emptying garbage cans, taping a plastic bag over a broken window in the back of the facility, etc. Not that I don't put in any effort to finding Leyla. I search every social media site I can think of and come up with nothing. I send texts to everyone I know, but no one knows anything. I even download my phone bill and find the number I used to text Leyla, but when I try it again, it kicks the message back, saying the number doesn't exist. It's all what I expect. I can look for Leyla until my eyes fall out, but I'm not going to find her. She set me up, took the money, and pulled a perfect blow-off. Dad would be proud.

So I don't know what else to do except maybe chalk it all up as part of the evolutionary plan for Garbage Mountain's painful death. Survival of the species and all of that. Who am I to go against Darwin?

I'm ducking and weaving my way through the building, watching out for bricks thrown my way, when Roadie stops me outside his booth, America Rocks!

"Hanging in there?"

"Barely."

Roadie's in his normal uniform of black jeans, black boots, and a Harley Davidson shirt. The only way he could look any manlier would be if he was eating nails while wrestling a bear. His booth is easily the most popular booth at Garbage Mountain because the world can never have enough rolls of toilet paper with the president's face on it or pictures of a vengeful bald eagle shitting on whatever country we hate this week.

Across the aisle, Jim Marcum, owner of Bumper Sticker Bonanza (just in case you want to lie about your kid being on the Honor Roll), stands with other boothers, all of them mentally trying to light me on fire.

"We should get you out of here before they bring out the tar and feathers," Roadie says.

"What do you have in mind?"

"I think it's time to infiltrate enemy lines."

A short time later, after unsuccessfully arguing we should first pick up some beards and sunglasses from booth sixty-one's Kay's Costumes, we're stepping onto Treasure Palace property. We're not even inside the building, and it's clear why we're getting destroyed in the flea market wars:

They have a smooth parking lot; we have a minefield of potholes.

They have a shuttle taking people to the building; we have shady figures ready to shank you between the cars.

They have an actual castle facade at their entrance, complete with two guys being broiled alive inside suits of armor; we have a paint-chipped, smart-mouthed dinosaur.

Draw your own conclusions.

"Look, actual lines painted on the cement showing you where to park," I say.

"Yeah, but on the other hand, this place can't promise you tetanus like we can," Roadie says.

"It's a customer favorite."

The inside of Treasure Palace is even more depressing—cleaner booths, better lighting, non-sticky floors, and actual smiling people. I quickly realize we're not in competition with them at all. We're not even in their league. This isn't a flea market; it's more of an upscale shopping mall pretending to be for down-to-earth people so they don't feel guilty for blowing large wads of cash. Hell, they even have a bathroom that's won design awards, something I didn't even know existed. The entrance is a port-a-potty door, but it opens into a bathroom so clean and pleasant-smelling that for a second I consider licking the floor to see if it's made of candy.

"The Mountain's in a lot of trouble," Roadie says later as we sit in the crowded food court. We don't buy anything because we won't support the enemy, but the cinnamon roll place nearby has me thinking of turning traitor.

"We'll be okay," I say. "People have been coming to us longer."

"Customer loyalty will only get you so far," Roadie says. "Eventually, the new bright and shiny things win. We have to offer something different or we'll go the way of Great Oaks Megamall."

Four teenage girls walk by smiling and laughing, which I'm pretty sure I've never seen customers at Garbage Mountain do. And that's not counting Mr. Hayes, who wears a clip-on tail and constantly mumbles at his shoes.

"Do you remember what I told you right after your dad got arrested?" Roadie says.

"Yeah, that if I needed anything to come to you."

"And have you?"

"Sure, lots of times," I say, thinking of my fake ID, Roadie helping me wire Bolan for electricity, and the countless rides he's given me when The Destroyer's being a dick and refusing to start.

"And I'm happy to keep helping you out," Roadie says, "but I think it also earns me the right to talk to you honestly if I feel the need."

"Oh, god."

"No, don't 'Oh, god' me," he says. "I'm only doing this because I like you and your mom and The Mountain too much not to say anything."

I don't have to be psychic to know I'm not going to like this at all, but Roadie's right; he's earned the privilege to say whatever the hell he wants.

"Fine, what is it you want to tell me?" I say.

"That it's time."

"For what?"

"For you to put on your big boy pants and start justifying your existence on this planet."

"Harsh."

"Necessary," Roadie says. "Your mom needs you. The Mountain needs you. It's time to step up and play a bigger role."

"Mom's strong enough to do this by herself," I say.

"Oh, you're right about that, but she shouldn't have to. Not when you're fully capable of helping. She's trying to keep the place afloat, Boone, but it's a sinking ship, and you just torpedoed it. More owners are talking about leaving. Even Kay, who's been there for over twenty years, is thinking about coming over here and setting up shop. What are you doing to help?"

"I do a lot."

"Being a dick to incoming customers from your dinosaur doesn't count."

"Yeah, but it's funny."

"Funny doesn't keep a business alive. But you're right; you do a lot. You could be doing more, though. We both know that. Seriously, man, and I say this as a friend, it's time for you to be a grownup."

"How much of a grownup can I really be? I still make my gummy bears 69 before eating them."

"Yeah, I do that too."

And this is why, despite the dressing-down I'm currently getting, Roadie and I are friends. A guy my age pushes a broom past our table, a task I've done a thousand times at The Mountain. But this guy actually looks content, not zombie-moaning through the job like I do. I swear they must be pumping methamphetamine through the ventilation system.

"I didn't take the money," I say.

"I never thought you did," Roadie says. "But what are you doing to try to get it back?"

"I'm going to figure out what happened," I say, but even I hear how weak it sounds coming out of my mouth.

"What have you done so far?"

I tell him about my failures, then add, "You're the one with the criminal buddies. Can't you figure out a plan?"

"If we were younger, maybe. But now everyone has a family and a real job, and none of us are willing to risk prison. Screw that."

"Where were you with that attitude when my dad was messing things up?"

"Telling him in private he needed to knock it off," Roadie says. "Not that it helped."

We fall into people-watching, which is a radically different experience here than it is at the Mountain. The people walking into the food court here look like they've actually held a job for more than a month at a time and may actually have money to pay for their food. The Mountain seems to have an invisible tractor beam that only draws in people who spend whatever money they have on tattoos and weight-gain pills.

"Enough business talk," Roadie says. "Just how capable are you of keeping a dark and terrible secret?"

I follow his eyes and say, "Cinnamon roll?"

"I won't tell if you won't."

Minutes later, our fingers sticky with icing, we're both afterglowing so hard we need cigarettes. I say, "You're right, Garbage Mountain is in serious trouble."

"We sure as shit are."

We're suavely licking our plates clean when a man in cowboy boots and a chaotic shirt struts up to the table. I've known Cullen Briggs for years, long before he opened Treasure Palace, because of his son and my former friend, who's right beside his dad looking down with contempt.

"Visitors from Golden Mountain, welcome," Mr. Briggs says. "I hope you're having a nice visit."

"I'm considering filing a lawsuit against this place for unfair business practices," Roadie says.

"The cinnamon rolls?" Briggs says, smiling.

"They're downright criminal," Roadie says.

"All's fair in business."

I've always liked Mr. Briggs, even if he's doing all he can to put Mom out of business. He has a smooth confidence and friendliness that's hard to deny. Of course, I'm naturally suspicious of overly friendly people. That's Conman 101: Act like you're someone's best friend and they'll believe whatever you say.

"Boone, it's been a long time," he says. "I miss seeing you around the house. I always liked those little bar bets you did."

"Parker knows a lot of them too," I say. "He even taught me a few."

Parker smiles, but it's a political one. We likely won't be sitting around a campfire and singing "Kumbaya" anytime soon.

"Why don't I give the two of you a tour of our facilities here?" Mr. Briggs says to us, then to Roadie, "Maybe I can convince you to bring your business over here."

"Sure, why not?" Roadie says. "We've got time."

Roadie would never set up shop here, but it's good to know what the competition has to offer, even if they don't view us as a real threat. With Mr. Briggs leading the way, the four of us head deeper into Treasure Palace. The farther we go, the more depressing it gets. I'll need to revise my original prediction with Rockefeller when I get back. Golden Mountain might not even last the week.

"I heard through the grapevine you had a little trouble the other day that called for a police visit," Mr. Briggs says.

My stomach drops.

"It's all been straightened out," Roadie says.

"So the money's been located?" Mr. Briggs says. "My sources say it was a considerable amount."

"Like I said, it's been handled," Roadie says.

If only.

"Well, let me show you something you might find interesting," Mr. Briggs says, and we follow him to a nearby booth where a college-aged girl in a striped red and white vest with a Treasure Palace patch on the pocket is talking to a customer.

"Lorri, could I borrow that from you for a minute, please?"

"Of course, Mr. Briggs."

Lorri hands over a silver device the size of a cellphone. From the number pad and screen, you might even confuse it for one. But this has a thin swipe panel on the side to read credit cards, along with a slot at the bottom to insert them if needed.

"Parker, since it was your idea to bring these here, why don't you explain this to our guests?"

The smug bastard stands a little taller at that and says, "We don't have money go missing here at Treasure Palace because we don't deal in cash. It isn't safe. Instead, we have roaming checkout clerks helping people purchase their products. We've found if you approach a customer holding a product and ask them if they're ready to check out, they're more likely to buy it than if they have time to second-guess themselves. All of our transactions are done through these credit card readers, which are top of the line and serviced through Profit Protector. They're an up-and-coming security company, the strongest of the strong. We do all of our surveillance and transactions through their local office."

"Wow," I deadpan.

"'Wow' is right," Parker says. Tapping his phone, he adds, "I call, and they come."

Mr. Briggs puts an arm around his son and says to Roadie, "I'm proud of the responsibility Parker's taken on here. He understands all of the technological things that confuse an old guy like me. It makes this building as safe as it can be."

As much as I don't like Parker, I have to say I'm jealous. He seems to have a good relationship with his dad, something I wish I had with my father. Maybe I did at one point, but not anymore.

It's nothing I sit around thinking about too much because if I did, I know I'd get depressed.

"Well, we won't keep you," Mr. Briggs says, reaching into his pocket. "Here, take a couple of these for the next time you visit."

He hands Roadie two business cards before saying goodbye and walking away. Parker returns the credit card reader to Lorri, then gives me a pompous smile before catching up with his dad.

"What did he give you?" I ask Roadie.

He holds up two cards for free cinnamon rolls.

"Man, that's playing dirty," I say.

"The dirtiest."

"It'd be too bad if someone was to make a thousand copies and spread them around town."

"All's fair in business," Roadie says.

Five minutes later, we're back on Garbage Mountain property, where my day gets much worse when I see Gompers leaning against his crappy silver Mustang. He's in cutoff jean shorts, a black, baggy Insane Clown Posse t-shirt, and combat boots. The glare he's giving me is strong enough to extinguish the sun. The only thing missing from the picture is him holding a bloody hatchet, but he'll probably be able to separate my head from my body using only his bare hands and raw aggression.

"Looks like your friend figured things out," Roadie says.

"Can you, um…?"

"Yeah, give me a second."

Roadie walks over to Gompers while I courageously back him up from thirty yards off. The puff in Gompers' chest deflates the closer Roadie gets. I guess even animals at the top of the food chain recognize when they're outmatched. After a short conversation where Roadie does all the talking, Gompers climbs into his car and drives off.

"Wow, that guy sweats hate," Roadie says a minute later. "You can smell it on him."

"I have that effect on people."

"You certainly do, man," he says. "You certainly do."

CHAPTER 7

Change-Raising Racists for Fun and Profit

"I'm not really up for this," I say.

"Come on, man," Mo says. "It'll cheer you up."

"God knows you could use it," Arlo says.

It's 4:30 in the afternoon, and the three of us are sitting in The Destroyer outside Dewey's Beverage Barn, a convenience store on the Batesville county line. A massive banner over the front door reads, "We speak ENGLISH here!," which is just a small taste of the bigotry you can find inside. The owner is Dewey Hoffman, who, when not selling beer and cigarettes, spends his time writing angry editorials to the local paper about what he calls the "immigrant scourge." Every two years he launches an unsuccessful campaign for school board, running on a platform of lowering teachers' salaries, cutting all sports and clubs, and demanding all students say the Pledge of Allegiance before every single class. Some people just need to be lit on fire.

"Let's go, Boone," Mo says. "You need this, so get in there."

"Fine. Who's making the call?" I say.

Arlo holds up a finger.

"Of course," I say, turning to Mo, "because you'll be—"

"—possibly getting killed," he finishes.

"You guys are good friends."

"Yeah, we're the best," Arlo says. "Now quit stalling and go."

I make sure I have enough cash in my wallet and pop in a piece of gum before heading into the store. Chewing gum gives me swagger. When in doubt, chew gum. It's also a good way to hide nerves, and I have plenty of them at the moment. The short con Mo and Arlo want me to do is beyond stupid, one my dad used to have me assist on. I've never run it without him. In fact, I haven't really done anything dangerous like this since his arrest. Excluding pissing off Gompers.

The doorbell rings as I enter the Beverage Barn. Dewey's at the counter, probably daydreaming about launching nuclear missiles against all foreign-speaking countries. Today he's wearing a white t-shirt with a handgun printed on it. No words, just the gun. He looks up and scowls, not taking his eyes off me as I head for the candy aisle. To him I'm not a paying customer; I'm a potential shoplifter he may get lucky enough to shoot.

I play the dumb teenager, browsing all my candy options until finally deciding on a Snickers bar. On my way to the counter, I also grab a bag of Cool Ranch Doritos. I don't want to give this bigot too much of my money, but I don't want to look too suspicious either. A white index card on the cash register declares, "We need singles," which is the best thing I can see.

Dewey doesn't give me a "Hello" or a "Will that be all?", which I'm not expecting, but it's important to get him talking. The busier his brain, especially numbers-wise, the less chance he'll realize what's happening.

"It's sweltering outside," I say, "but nice and cool in here."

"Until you let the hot air in," Dewey says, scanning the candy bar and chip bag. "$2.88."

"Yeah, it must be almost ninety outside," I tell him. "What do you have it in here? Seventy?"

I hand him a ten, and he opens the register, getting out the $7.12 he owes me.

I put it into my pocket, and that's when the store phone rings.

He reaches for it, and I say, "Hey, I have singles here if you want them."

"Dewey's," he says answering the phone and nods to me.

I pull out nine singles and a five for a total of fourteen dollars but purposefully tell him, "There's ten."

He cranes his neck, looking out the window, and says into the phone, "Unleaded's $2.56," then after a pause, "Premium's $2.86."

On the other end right now, Arlo's no doubt about to ask the cost of a carton of Camel Lights or a twelve-pack of Diet Coke, anything to get Dewey to be thinking of more numbers. He pulls a ten from the register and hands it to me. I immediately put it into my pocket and point to the pile of singles on the counter. He starts counting the singles and gets to the five at the bottom, holding it up to me, showing me I've overpaid, while he's still listening on the phone.

"No, we're located at 1380 Stone, not 1830," he says to Arlo.

"Oh, duh," I say, taking another six ones from my pocket and tossing them on the counter. "Why don't you just give me two tens instead? Then you have a bunch of singles."

A moment of confusion flashes across Dewey's face. He knows something's wrong, and there is. He's about to give me a twenty when he only owes me ten since he already gave me a ten I put in my pocket. But he isn't focused; Arlo's making sure of that. It's called change-raising, and it's a time-honored tradition of the con artist. Dewey's not new to this job, and no doubt knows the scam, but he can't think straight right now. Most cashiers would never fall for a trick like this, but Dewey's so arrogant he doesn't think anyone's smarter than him, especially a dumb high school kid. He takes a twenty from the register and puts it on the counter.

This is precisely where I should take my money—or, more accurately, Dewey's money—and leave before he catches on. That would be the safe move. I'm not exactly the safest person, though. It's possible I may have a deeply ingrained death wish. But my friends want to cheer me up. Besides, what's better than separating an asshole from his money? So that's when Mo walks in.

As I mentioned earlier, Mo's parents are from Iran, so to a prick like Dewey, Mo shouldn't be in this country at all, and he sure as hell shouldn't be in this store. Legally, Dewey can't kick him out—he knows that—but he can make it clear he doesn't want him here.

"Bathroom?" Mo says.

"For paying customers only," Dewey says, then to Arlo on the phone, "It's—I don't know—$3.50 or whatever. Look, I'm busy right now."

"I'm going to buy something," Mo says. "I just need the bathroom."

"Buy something first," Dewey growls.

While Dewey's brain is jumbled, I take the two tens Dewey's given me and add them to the cash on the counter.

"Here, let's just keep it simple," I say. "Just give me two twenties. Then you have plenty of change."

Dewey's hardcore glitching now. From Arlo rambling in his ear to Mo wandering the aisles suspiciously and me tossing money around, I'm surprised Dewey hasn't had an aneurism.

"For two twenties," I say, pointing to the money.

And he gives it to me.

I once saw Dad take a clerk at a movie theater for ninety dollars doing this. He had me call her asking movie times while he bought a ticket and change-raised her. I could probably bleed Dewey dry, but instead of pressing my luck, I grab my candy bar and chips and head out of the store, spitting my gum in the trash. A minute later, Mo exits the store empty-handed. He quickly jumps into The Destroyer and we blast out of the parking lot, all of us laughing.

"You didn't buy anything?" I say to Mo.

"He's never getting any of my money," Mo says. "Nice of him to contribute to our beer fund, though. What'd we get?"

"Thirty, minus the $2.88 I spent."

"Not bad for five minutes' work," Arlo says.

Don't understand what just happened at the Beverage Barn? I'm not going to break it down for you. Who am I, your fifth-grade math teacher? But trust me, don't try what I just did. It's stupid and, more importantly, highly illegal. It's also Dewey, though, who deserves what he gets since he's so hateful. Am I justifying bad behavior? Absolutely. I never said I planned on being the pope when I grow up.

After stopping by the QuikPik to buy a twelve-pack at a nonracist convenience store, we drive to Penetration Point, a dead-end dirt road flanked by cornfields on both sides. It's still daylight, so we have the place to ourselves for now. Tonight though, there'll be at least one car parked here, its shocks getting a good work- out, making the place's name perfectly clear to even the dumbest person. Mo and I are leaning against The Destroyer with our beers, which have already gone warm in the sun, while Arlo sits on the ground up against a mysteriously placed school crossing sign. All around, the ground's a battlefield of crushed and faded beer cans from the last decade.

"It's too bad our state doesn't pay a dime a can," Mo says. "You could easily make up the fifteen grand you lost."

"Thanks for reminding me," I say. "You're doing a nice job making me feel better."

"Any luck on the girl?" Arlo says.

"I've tried everything I can think of, but there's no point. She's gone."

"How did she know you had the money in the first place?"

"Yeah, no one gets that lucky," Mo says.

"No, she knew what she was doing. I'm just not sure how," I say. "She lured me there, got me drunk, then took the money. Perfect execution."

I finish off my beer and chuck the empty can into the corn-field, making a promise to send ten dollars to an anti-littering campaign tomorrow. Arlo tosses me another from the box at his feet, sending one Mo's way too.

"So is this the end of Garbage Mountain?" Mo says.

"Unless I can come up with that money, and I don't see that happening."

"You could sell a kidney online. I hear people give thousands for those."

"I'm probably down to only one functional kidney at this point, so that's a no," I say. "I was thinking maybe I'd start one of those sex cams so people can watch me."

"Yeah, you'd make at least six dollars," Arlo says.

"All from your mom subscribing," Mo says to him.

"No, Arlo's mom wouldn't subscribe," I say. "She'd be my co-star."

After that, it's a lot of pointless brainstorming on how to make a lot of money fast, but in the end, I decide opening an illegal gambling den, Airbnb'ing our apartment, or charging people five bucks to punch me in the face aren't doable.

Finally, Mo says, "You should just punk rock the money back."

"What does that mean?" I say.

"You know, invest in yourself. Most bands don't get signed by a major label; they post songs online, hop in a van, and travel around playing shows. Get out there and do what you do best."

"Being handsome and charming?"

"No, being conniving."

"I'll take that as a compliment."

"You should," Mo says. "Look at how much money you just made in five minutes."

"I can't change-raise $15,000."

"Right, but I'm sure you know other ways to make money."

"I'm not going to do what my dad does. Or did," I say, correcting myself. "I won't steal innocent people's money."

"Then don't con the innocent. There are dozens of assholes all over this town who deserve karma. Target them."

I'd be lying if I said I hadn't thought of this before. Dad's taught me plenty of cons I could run to pull in decent money. But to make up $15,000 I'd have to pull more elaborate cons, which would take time and the right partner, neither of which I have. Mo and Arlo might be helpful in running diversions like they did today, but that's nothing like what I would really need.

"I'm shocked to say it," Arlo says, "but I do think Mo's got a good idea."

"No, I'd need someone who was either trained like I've been or had a natural gift given to them by the criminal gods."

"What about—?" Mo says.

I hold up a hand.

"Don't say it," I tell him.

Arlo says, "Why? You know as well as we do that she—"

We're interrupted by a dull roar and look up to see Gompers' Mustang kicking up dust as it drives toward us. Dad once told me no matter how south things may go during a con, you have to remain calm and not appear rattled. It's advice I try to apply to daily life too. But as Gompers' car gets closer, I can't help planning my escape into the corn.

"What's he doing here?" Mo says.

"Maybe he has a girl with him?" Arlo says.

"There's not enough chloroform in the world to make that happen," I say. "He's here for me."

The Mustang skids to a halt, and Gompers climbs out. He's not wearing a shirt because of course he isn't. He stomps our way, a finger pointing at me.

"You owe me eighty bucks."

"Look, I'm sorry, but I told you penis enlargement pills don't work for everyone. There must be doctors out there you could see or—"

"Laugh it up, but your uncle, or whoever that guy was earlier, isn't here to protect you."

"No, but Arlo is."

Arlo gives Gompers a two-fingered salute.

"Everyone knows he won't fight," Gompers says.

"That's not entirely accurate," Arlo says, getting to his feet. "It's not that I won't fight; I just choose not to. There's a big difference."

Arlo doesn't say anything else, but the implication's clear. We all stand there not moving. The summer sun beats down on us, but even harder on the shirtless Gompers. Maybe I can just wait him out until he dies from melanoma.

"How'd you find out?" I ask him.

"That dumbass kid posted about it online," he says. "I'll be visiting him next."

"Cut him a break, Gompers. It's me you're pissed at."

"You're goddamn right, McReedy. And at some point, I'm going to catch you out alone. When I do, you're dead."

For maybe the first time in his life, Gompers is right. And as much as I'd like one, a perpetual bodyguard isn't in my budget. Today's going to end in a standoff, but eventually Gompers will get me. I need to buy time.

"Okay, look, I understand you're angry," I say. "Hell, who wouldn't be? But you have to admit, taking advantage of someone smaller than you? You're better than that. A kid like Andy's small time. There are opportunities out there better suited to your, shall we say, skill set."

"Opportunities like what?"

"I don't have anything specific in mind right now, but they're out there. I'm guessing you were selling those pills you were taking from Andy? That's worth, what, ten, twenty dollars a week?"

"What's your point?"

"That's chump change. Give me a day or two and I'll plan something where we can make some real cash. You know I can do it."

Gompers stares at me, thinking it over. With Arlo here, he knows he can't pound on me, and the promise of big money should be enough to save my life for a while, but Gompers is unpredictable. I need sweeten the deal. I take my portion of the money scammed from Dewey's and hold it out. Call it a small investment in my future safety, even if I have no intention of working with Gompers. I may be crazy, but I'm not stupid.

"You took a lot more than this from me," Gompers says, snatching the money.

"It's all I have right now, but more will be coming. Trust me. Guys?"

Both Mo and Arlo nod.

"Boone's the best," Mo says.

"But you need to keep your hands off him," Arlo warns with mild menace in his voice.

"Fine," Gompers says. "But you'd better not screw me over, McReedy, or I'm beating your ass."

"Of course," I say.

As soon as Gompers gets in his car, Mo says, "He's going to beat on you anyway."

"Yep," I say.

"Any idea what you're going to do?" Arlo says.

There's only one thing I can do. To save Garbage Mountain I'm going to need a partner-in-crime, and to protect me from Gompers long-term, I'm going to need a hardcore ass-kicker. The good news is I know someone who can handle both jobs. The bad news is she hates my guts.

But like they say, desperate times call for desperate measures, so I guess it's time to swallow my pride and go see Darby West.

CHAPTER 8

A New Partner and a Kick to the Groin

Three hours after leaving Mo and Arlo, I park The Destroyer outside Yin's Dojo, the karate place owned by Darby's aunt and uncle. In a competition between me and Darby for who has the most screwed-up family, she's the clear winner. Back in fourth grade, Darby's aunt and uncle took custody of her from her parents, who were eventually charged with child endangerment. Shortly after the custody change, the two nominees for Parents of the Year left town. I'm no psychologist, but I'm guessing this probably explains Darby's violence against the world in general and assholes in particular.

Inside the dojo, Darby's leading a class of over a dozen young girls. Parents in folding chairs sit along the wall watching their miniature ninjas in white uniforms follow Darby's lead, grunting and growling as they chop and kick at the air. Darby's every movement is completely controlled with no wasted energy. An assistant walks the perimeter, stepping into the rows occasionally to correct bad form, but Darby's the one in charge. She's creating an army here, and when the country's attacked by an unarmed force under three feet tall, Darby's tiny warriors will be ready to meet them.

On the other side of the room, Bill West, Darby's uncle, frowns when he sees me. If he comes over to ask about the missing money, all he's going to find is the vapor trail I leave as I zoom out the door. Once the session ends, Darby smiles and laughs with the girls. They look at Darby with wide eyes, idolization at its finest. For Darby's part, she gives hugs and high-fives and tells them she'll see them next week. It's about as far removed from her high school life as you can get, where a smile from Darby means she's probably about to send you into orbit. When most of the girls have finally left the dojo and she sees me, Darby's smile goes back into hibernation. She walks over, looking both relaxed and explosive at the same time.

"What?" she says.

"Still no hello, huh?"

Darby gives me an "I'm waiting" face.

"You have your own assault force here," I say. "If you ever want to stage a coup at the elementary school, you won't have any problem."

"Girls have to know how to protect themselves."

"No doubt."

Darby stares at me, waiting for a joke that doesn't come.

"Why are you here?" she says. "You're not planning on robbing us again, are you?"

This is turning out to be even more painful than I expected. I was raised to be independent, which sounds good on paper, but also makes asking for help darn near impossible. I don't know how to start, so I just standing here looking stupid. Darby's looking at my blank face, probably thinking I've just come from electroshock therapy.

"Ten seconds," Darby says.

I'm not sure if she means ten seconds before she walks away for good or ten seconds before she throws me through the window. It's best not to find out.

"I want to earn back the lost money, and I need your help."

"My help?"

"You're the only one who can help in the way I need."

"And what way is that?"

I smile and double-bounce my eyebrows.

"Not a chance," Darby says, walking away.

"Come on," I say, following her. "You, me—we can make that money up in no time."

"Forget it, Boone."

"You can't deny what you are, Darby."

"And what's that? I can't wait to hear this."

"You're a natural grifter. You have the best instincts I've ever seen, and not only that—"

"Just stop," Darby says as she spins around on me. "What about trying to find the money? Have you thought of that?"

"The money's gone."

"And how do you know?"

"Because that's how it works. We both know it," I say. "Has anyone ever called you on any of the plays we made? No. And they won't because we were too clean."

"Don't change the subject."

"I'm not changing the subject. Leyla conned me out of the money, and she's gone for good."

"You're still sticking with that story?"

"It's not a story."

"Tell me, Boone, you're a smart enough guy. What's more plausible—some mystery girl who no one knows took the money, or you did?"

"Look, if I did take the money, why would I be here right now?"

"I don't know, guilty conscience? Trying to throw people off the track?

"That would require a deeper level of planning than I'm capable of."

"Well, that's definitely true," she says, and after a moment, "So assuming for a second you're telling the truth—and that's a big assumption—what is it you want exactly?"

"For you and me to team up to save The Mountain, one con at a time."

Darby's eyes narrow as she cocks her head.

"Boone, why did I break up with you?"

"I don't know; you never told me. You just ghosted me until I got the point."

"Right, because I don't want to be around you."

"Why?"

Darby just walks away and starts stacking chairs. You're probably thinking I must've used a Jedi mind trick to get Darby to go out with me in the first place. I understand the skepticism; we're not exactly a natural fit. Where I'm lazy, partying, and—how should I put it?—romantically active, Darby's athletic, clean-living, and pretty much virginal. But sometimes the universe likes to play matchmaker just to watch the ensuing chaos.

"Look," I say, "if you don't want to help me, just remember you'll be helping The Mountain. I mean, if we don't do this, who's going to save that place? Besides, in case you haven't realized it yet, it's sort of your fault this happened in the first place."

"Excuse me?"

Now I've done it. Darby's coming at me with an I-hope-you've-enjoyed-your-brief-life look in her eyes.

"You're blaming this on me?"

"Not entirely," I say, backing up. "But none of this would have happened if you hadn't gotten conned to start."

"How did I get conned?"

"The person who called for a private lesson and then never showed up? That was to make sure someone responsible like you wasn't depositing the money."

Darby looks at me skeptically.

"But how would they know you would be the one to take the money then?"

"Well, how would you find out that information if you wanted to know it?"

"Research," Darby says.

I nod.

"So what do you say? I need your help."

Darby thinks before shaking her head.

"It's just not going to happen," she says.

"Why not?"

"Because I don't like you, Boone. I can't trust you."

"What? You can trust me."

"Saying it doesn't make it true."

"What have I done that makes me untrustable?"

"'Untrustable' isn't even a word. You mean 'untrustworthy.'"

"See, you're helping me already. We're a great team. You know it's true."

Darby's face is blank, but I know her brain's processing at light speed. She won't be the valedictorian next year, but Darby's one of the smartest people in our class, people skills notwithstanding.

"Well, if we're being honest, why don't you admit part of this is you wanting me to protect you from Gompers?"

"You know about that?"

"Everyone knows, Boone."

"Okay, sure, it's a definite plus to have muscle around. And who knows where all of this leads—you may get to beat up a person or two."

"That's not all I am," Darby says.

"But it'll come in handy if needed. Come on, give me a chance to prove myself."

Darby goes back into computer-processing mode, her eyes soon lighting up as they fall on a girl with fire red hair pulled back in a ponytail who's practicing moves in front of the mirror.

"You know what, Boone, fine," Darby says. "If you want me to help you, you can start by helping me. Kimberly, can you come here, please?"

As if summoned by Wonder Woman herself, Kimberly races across the room to us.

"Kimberly, Boone here wants to be a helper," Darby says. "Remember earlier you were asking about when you'd get to try out the moves on real people? Well, I think Boone would be perfect. Do you want to show him what you've learned?"

Kimberly nods a little too enthusiastically for my liking. She's probably ten years old, four-feet-nothing tall, and weighs seventy pounds soaking wet. She may have dreams of being like Darby one day, but she's not Darby yet. She's just a little girl, and if she comes at me, I'm putting her down.

"I don't think this is a good idea," I say.

"Why? You said you wanted to help," Darby says.

"I do, but…"

"But what, Boone? Just say it."

I'm on thin ice here, which seems to be the only ice I'm ever on.

"She's a girl," I say.

"At least you'll admit it," Darby says. "Kimberly, are you ready?"

The girl bounces on her toes, sizing me up. She reminds me of a demonic poodle that hasn't been fed in a week and I'm the guy standing here covered in steak sauce.

"Okay," Darby says to her, "turn around and walk away like we talk about in class. Boone, you come up from behind and try to pull her to the ground."

"I don't like this," I say.

"What are you, chicken?" Kimberly says.

Jesus.

Darby gives me a "Well, are you?" look.

"Fine."

Kimberly may be a little girl, but in ten seconds she's going to be a crying little girl. She turns and walks away, a little bounce in her step like she's coming home from a good day at school. Nearby, the remaining parents and kids have gathered to watch Kimberly's humiliation. I just hope they don't blame me when we're all drowning in her tears.

"Go on," Darby tells me.

"Shouldn't it be a surprise? She knows I'm coming."

"It won't matter."

"Whatever."

I'm sure you can guess what happens next. I'm about a foot from Kimberly when I put a hand on her shoulder. Then there's a blur and a howler monkey screech before the room flips upside down. When I look up, I'm struggling for air and Kimberly has her shoe hovering inches over my crotch. She looks at Darby, who tells her, "Treat every situation like your survival depends on it."

So Kimberly stomps my crotch.

I'll say this—I've taken my share of punches to the face, but nothing compares to the pain inflicted on me by Kimberly's bionic foot. Flashforward twenty years and I'll still have blurred vision and a bag of frozen peas stuffed down my pants. I stay on the mat in the full-fetal position until the nausea finally passes, which seems to take an hour. The humiliation, however, will last a lifetime. By the time I stagger to my feet, Kimberly's leaving, probably thinking of ways she can provoke someone else so she can enjoy more groin stompage.

"That was brutal," I say.

"I could teach you how to do that," Darby says.

"You could?"

"But I'm not going to."

Darby studies me for a second, and I throw my million-dollar smile at her. It has no effect.

"So does this mean you'll help me?" I say.

"I have rules," she says.

"Fire away."

"First, I get final say on the marks. I don't want any innocents involved. If we're taking money from people, they have to deserve it."

"You see us as, like, vigilante conmen?"

"Right, we're only targeting the guilty," Darby says.

"Guilty of what?"

"We'll know it when we see it."

"Whatever you want."

"Good," Darby says, "Second, we don't stop looking for Leyla. I know you think she's gone, but that doesn't mean she is. You're just being lazy."

"Fine," I say, which it isn't fine—it's really just a waste of time—but if it'll get Darby on board, I'll go with it.

"Next," Darby says, "don't lie to me. I hate that more than anything."

"But that goes against every instinct I have."

"I'm not kidding, Boone. If you lie to me, this is over."

"Understood," I say. "Is that it? Or should I go get a notebook?"

She looks at the ceiling, and then says, "There is one more thing. It's probably the most important, actually."

"Now I'm really curious."

Darby takes a step forward and puts a finger in my face.

"Don't touch me, Boone. Whatever happened between us in the past is over. I also don't want any of your touches on the arm or those dreamy looks you throw at every girl who passes by, or, really, any flirting at all. None of it. Do you understand?"

"What about a celebratory slap on the butt when we make back all the money?"

"Only if you want to spend the rest of the summer in a coma."

"It may be worth it.

Darby looks away and shakes her head.

"So we're clear, this doesn't mean I trust you."

"I get that."

"Or even like you."

"I get that too."

Darby says, "You let people down, Boone. Don't let me down."

"Or you'll sic Kimberly on me?"

"Worse."

"I'm not sure that exists."

Darby looks past me like she's reconsidering and says to the air, "I'm absolutely going to regret this."

"See, I told you that you have great instincts."

Darby doesn't say anything, but instead rolls her eyes so hard I'm surprised they don't fall out of her head.

It's a look I should probably get used to.

CHAPTER 9

Darby Tries to Get Me Destroyed

The next day at The Mountain I'm given the privilege of doing battle with a hornets' nest on the loading dock. Instead of the recommended suit of armor, I risk dehydration in the suffocating summer sun by wear black garbage bags, leather gloves, and a welder's helmet from booth sixty-three's Vernon's Tool Shed. After beating the nest down with a broom, I douse it with gasoline and light the flying bastards' home on fire. Boone 1, Hornets 0. I'm comfortable with you calling me a hero.

Shortly before lunchtime, I stop by Roadie's booth where he's watching a baseball game on an ancient black and white portable TV the size of a toaster. I hand him my junior yearbook, telling him what I need.

"No problem," Roadie says. "Want to tell me what this is about?"

"I'm taking your advice."

Thankfully, Roadie's not a gloater, because if he was, this exchange could've been torturous. Instead, he taps the yearbook and says, "And she's going to help?"

"God help me."

"From what I've heard, even God watches his ass around her. Give me twenty minutes."

I leave Roadie to his work and head off for aisle two. I fall in behind a group of college-aged girls who must have lost their sense of smell because they're not responding to the pheromones I naturally emit. I'm considering this troubling scenario when I hear my name. Mom's moving much faster than anyone else in the whole building, which would make most people think something was wrong, but turbo is Mom's default speed. If sheer force of will was all it took, Garbage Mountain would be a Fortune 500 company. She gives me a too-tight Mom hug and kisses me hard on the cheek.

"How's my youngest?"

"You mean your only, right?"

"As far as you know," she says. "Come on, walk with me."

Mom puts an arm around my waist, and we're off at light speed.

"How have the numbers been this week?" I say.

"What I expected, unfortunately," she says, "but I did a webinar yesterday on growing your customer base that had good ideas. We'll see what happens."

"Anything I can do to help?"

"Have any dynamite for the building next door?"

"Let me talk to Roadie."

"I'm kidding, Boone."

Parents just don't know how to have fun.

We stop at booth thirty-nine at the end of the aisle, Taco Bob's, and Mom orders us two burritos and drinks from Gwen, aka Mrs. Taco Bob.

"Are you getting enough to eat?" Mom says. "I know I need to get to the grocery."

"No, I'm fine."

"And making good decisions?"

Which is Mom's way of asking, "You're not injecting heroin into your eyeballs, are you?" because she knows I drink. She doesn't give me too much grief about this because she has her own questionable teenage history, something Gigi, her mother, once filled me in on, much to Mom's irritation. And look, Mom came out of all her teenage bad behavior okay. Or okay-ish. We McReedys try not to throw stones at glass houses.

"Everything's good, Mom, seriously."

"Found my money yet?"

"I'm trying."

"And you don't think I'm a bad mom for not being around much?"

"Of course not. You're a great mom."

"Good answer," she says, "even if you are a bad liar."

Her face softens, and suddenly she slips out of business mode and looks like a guilty mom. Mom's never learned to walk the line between letting your kid be independent and helicoptering over them. It's one extreme or the other, and fortunately she's picked the one that lets me do what I please most of the time.

"I'm heading for the office. What's your plan?"

"I need to see Miss Laverne about some clothes."

"Do you need any money?"

"Absolutely."

"Me too," she says. "Slip me some if you find any."

She stops at the intersection, and before we split up, she puts me in a python grip.

"Be careful, please," she says.

"I will."

"You're a good kid, Boone. A little too much of your dad in you, but a good kid." She lets me go and adds, "I know you have things to do, but…"

I unconsciously start to grumble, then stop myself.

"What do you need?"

Mom rattles off a to-do list I mentally memorize and prioritize. Then she's off to save Garbage Mountain from impending doom. I devour the burrito, which will probably have me running for the bathroom within the hour, before spending thirty minutes knocking out the small jobs Mom's given me. I get to Miss Laverne's Classic Clothing in booth ninety-four as she's unpacking a box of clothes that look like they might be popular with the world's most famous drag queens.

Miss Laverne is a big woman with a big heart and an even bigger reputation. Nowadays she directs local theater, but in the nineties she worked costume design in Hollywood. To hear her tell it, she slept with all the major stars of the time. Considering her confidence and mega-level flirting, I don't doubt it.

"Did I ever tell you about the long weekend I once spent with Russell Crowe?" she says as a conversation starter.

"Many, many times," I say.

"You remind me of a young Russell, minus the accent, of course. The accent lowered my defenses."

"I'll practice my Australian accent."

"You don't need the accent, Boone," Miss Laverne says, playfully running the back of her hand over my cheek. "Now to what do I owe this pleasure?"

"Anything new you think would look good on me?"

"Ooh-la-la," Miss Laverne says. "Big date?"

"Just updating my wardrobe."

Miss Laverne hugs me until my ribs beg for mercy.

"Oh, sweetie! I'm so happy I might cry!"

The next twenty minutes are spent playing dress-up doll for Miss Laverne as she holds up shirt and pants combinations in front of me. She once told me to play the part, you have to look the part. If I'm going to go full-on conman, I might as well look good while doing it. By the time Miss Laverne's finished, there's a large pile of rejects on the floor and a hook holding the keepers.

"This should get you started, honey," Miss Laverne says. "I have others in storage, so come back tomorrow."

"This is enough for now," I say. "My wallet's a little light."

"What's money worth?" she says, waving me off. "You take these and get out of here."

"Miss Laverne, I'm not letting you give me these clothes. You're struggling for business as it is. And I've already lost enough of people's money around here."

"I'm not taking no for an answer, Boone," she says. "Listen to your elders. Family is more important than money every single time. Remember that. Just stop by and tell me if these clothes help you get lucky. I want *all* the details."

I don't argue. Sometimes it's best to graciously accept a gift before things get awkward. Inside Bolan ten minutes later, I change into black jeans and a white t-shirt, then add a black denim jacket to give it a test run. After tying on my new-to-me black and white wingtips, I check myself in the small mirror. I'm not going to say I look good, but okay, I look good. Really good. Even Rockefeller gives me a look that says he wishes he had hands so he could give me thumbs up.

It takes me five minutes of ferreting around Bolan's stomach before finding the small black case I'm going to need tonight before driving across town to pick up Darby. The two of us know each other from our Batesville Elementary years, and even as a dumb little kid, I knew something was up with her. I specifically remember how in fourth grade Darby would sit in class quiet and unmoving, turning in work with such precise handwriting you'd think she was secretly typing it. But during recess, Darby was a different animal. She played aggressive games of tag with seriously freaked-out kids or attacked the blacktop with sidewalk chalk, scribbling furiously like she was releasing whatever part of her was being forced down during class. The fights didn't start until fifth grade when the elementary schools combined at the intermediate building and kids who didn't know better made the mistake of making fun of her. After a long string of no-shows by her parents to disciplinary meetings, a guidance counselor at school called Children's Protective Services. When CPS showed up at the Wests', they found a filthy house, two drugged-out parents, and a ten-year-old girl doing her best to keep everyone alive. That's when Darby's aunt and uncle took custody and she started training at the dojo, a safe place to release the hurricane inside of her. And thank God, because without an outlet of controlled violence, every Batesville citizen would have perpetual black eyes.

I pull up in front of Darby's house just as the streetlights go. She's sitting on the curb in black workout pants and a tight Tap Out t-shirt, her hair back in a ponytail like she's prepared for a steel cage match. She climbs into the passenger seat, and as I drive off, she says, "I don't see the point in this."

"Hi to you too."

"We could just do this over the phone."

"If we're going to be partners, we need to act like it. Planning calls for one-on-one interaction," I say. "Besides, I got you a present."

More precisely, Roadie made Darby a present. I hand it to her, and she inspects the card in the fading sunlight.

"A fake ID? Really?" Darby says.

"You'll need it tonight."

"Where are we going?"

"It's a surprise."

"This is such a mistake."

"And yet here you are."

The Destroyer rumbles underneath us as we drive west through town. Plenty of people have sat exactly where Darby's sitting, but unlike them, she's not being bounced around like a tennis ball in a dryer. No, Darby's simply watching out the passenger window, unmoved by the turbulence, almost like the car is afraid of pissing her off. I try and retry the radio, but The Destroyer's choosing to make me suffer.

"Did you do tonight's homework?" I say.

"Of course," she says. "The better question is, did you?"

"Did I do what?"

"The homework?"

"Wait, we had homework?"

I smile at Darby. She's not impressed.

"You love the sound of your own voice, don't you?" she says.

"I'd just rather talk than sit here like this."

"You know, some people enjoy quiet."

"And I am not one of those people."

"Yet another strike against you."

"How many strikes is that?"

"I lost count a long time ago."

I hand Darby a small, blue spiral notebook with THE SCAM LIST written on the front cover in my dad's handwriting. The inside pages are filled with cons and bar bets he's learned or created over the years. Initially, the collection was a simple list, but as he added to it, he transferred all of his knowledge to this notebook. Most of the cons he taught me directly. Others I learned from swiping the notebook from his bottom desk drawer in his office when he wasn't home. If Darby and I are going to have any chance of earning back the missing money, The Scam List is our best hope.

"Some of these are really complicated," she says. "Are you even sure you understand these?"

"Are you calling me dumb?"

"If it looks like a duck…"

"Maybe this *is* a mistake."

"You can always take me home."

"Too late," I say, pointing to the rundown building up the road. "There it is."

Darby takes a look at where I'm pointing and scowls.

"Seriously?"

"I thought you might be rusty."

"I told you I get to pick the marks," she says.

"You do. I'm just choosing the place tonight."

Darby sighs but doesn't argue. I take this as a good sign.

"What's the play?" she says.

"The Moneybox Bamboozle."

She flips to one of the earlier pages in The Scam List and reads the con's explanation

"No one's dumb enough to fall for that," she says.

"I respectfully remind you where we're going."

Darby looks at the approaching building and shakes her head.

"Fine," she says. "But let's make this fast. My IQ's dropping already."

Technically, Strut isn't a strip club, although I have no doubt people have stripped there. And it's not a biker bar either, although there are plenty of bikers there too. Strut's a lone-standing building located on the Batesville county line, so it draws only the shadiest of our citizens, and also those from neighboring Preble, a dry county. When I pull into the parking lot, there's a circle of people under a vapor light watching two guys beat the hell out of each other.

"You want to go challenge the winner?" I say.

Darby looks them over like she's considering it. Then she's out of the car and heading for the building. I grab the black case from the backseat and catch up to her. The sun may be down for the night, but the air hasn't cooled much. We're halfway to the door when we both spot the five-dollar bill lying on the ground. I pick it up, we both look at it, then each other.

"That's found money," Darby says. "It's bad luck if you don't earn it."

"What are you talking about?"

"Exactly what I said. If you don't earn that money, you're asking for trouble."

"I wouldn't peg you as superstitious."

"It's not superstitious if it's true. You either earn it or give it to me since you already owe my family thousands."

"No, go ahead; I'm not afraid of you," I say. "What's the bet?"

Darby looks over at the building and smiles at what she sees. I already know what she's thinking. Like The Underground, Strut has a bouncer at the door checking IDs. Unlike The Underground, though, this bouncer's a six-foot-plus Amazonian who probably spends the day chopping down trees with her bare hands.

"We'll keep it easy," Darby says. "Ask her if she'll meet up with you after she gets off work."

"This is all about seeing me get beat up, isn't it?"

"I'm honestly shocked it doesn't happen on a daily basis."

This is going to take two sticks of gum.

Strut's wraparound porch somehow isn't bowing under the giantess's size. She's standing in the light of the red and white neon Rolling Stones lips sign and watching the fight as I hold out my ID to her. I play it safe and give her my hundred-dollar smile. Her eyes go from the ID to my face and back to the ID. Then she gives me a brief wave forward. I should just go inside and count myself lucky, but a McReedy doesn't back down from a challenge, especially one involving money.

"So my friend here thinks I'm in desperate need of a beating," I say to the woman, "but I don't agree."

At this, the bouncer looks at me, actually seeing me for the first time.

I continue, saying, "See, what I think I need is a strong female role model in my life."

"Oh, you do, do you?"

The smirk on her face could be taken as either vaguely amused or the start of irritation. I pray the former.

"Yeah, my mom left when I was three, and my sister ran off with the lead singer of a Motley Crüe tribute band. So I clearly have abandonment issues that manifest themselves in anti-authoritarian behavior. But if a woman could show me not all females will leave me, that women can be trusted, well, I'd probably live a much cleaner life. Maybe a woman like..."

I let it hang there and try to decipher her face. Bouncers, by nature, aren't the easiest reads.

"A woman like me?" she says.

I immediately throw up my hands, waving her off.

"Oh, god no," I say. "Not you. Definitely not you."

She squints hard at me, her smirk growing into a smile.

"I'm not ready for a woman like you," I say. "Baby steps and all. Eventually, sure, a confident woman like you who doesn't take crap from anyone and can look after herself. But for now, no, definitely not you. You'd eat me alive."

She's full-on smiling now, but it's a smile that says she knows I'm full of shit, just having fun.

"But, you know, maybe, in fact, I should just go right to the top of the mountain," I say. "Life's short, right? So, yeah, okay, maybe a woman like you. But only if you think I could handle it. Maybe we could talk about it after you get off work tonight?"

The woman holds my eye for a second, then looks down at the black case I'm carrying.

"What's in there?"

"Bottles of my sexiness waiting to be auctioned off to the highest bidder."

The woman frowns and says to Darby, "Is he like this all the time?"

"It's exhausting."

"I'll bet."

She looks back at me, and there's still a chance Darby's going to get her wish and see this woman whack-a-mole me.

"Your name's Boone?" she says.

I nod. "And you're...?"

"You have yourself a good night, Boone."

I don't push my luck. Darby holds out her ID for the woman, who doesn't even glance at it. We walk toward the front door, Darby handing me the five as we go.

"You're ridiculous," she says.

"What can I say? People find me charming."

"Eventually that charm is going to run out."

"If only I had a nickel for every time I've heard that."

CHAPTER 10

The Moneybox Bamboozle

Inside Strut we're hit with a full-frontal assault of bass and drum. This is the moment I'll be telling my doctor about next week when I'm being fitted for a hearing aid. The band on stage is a three-piece who must've been excited yesterday when they touched musical instruments for the first time and decided to start a band. They're murdering a Tom Petty song, but at least they're doing so without the additional pain of a lead singer. I don't know what they call themselves, but I suggest Instrumental Anguish.

We weave our way through the thin crowd, a diverse mix of meth heads and unshaven drunkards with nothing better to do on a Friday night than be at Strut. A woman in jean shorts practically cut at the waist and wearing a red, white, and blue bikini top passes, accidentally brushing my arm.

"And now you've got hepatitis," Darby says to me.

"Don't be silly," I say. "You can't get hepatitis if you already have it."

We grab a spot along the wall where we can survey the whole bar. There's a booth open near the bathrooms, but it's a high-traffic area, and we don't want too many looky-loos as we work. We're looking for a nice balance of public and private with just the right person nearby to dupe.

"What about him?" I say, pointing to a sad-looking guy with three empty shot glasses in front of him.

"Too easy," Darby says.

"Why make it hard?"

"The artistry is in the challenge."

"Are you even speaking English?"

"You said this is about getting the rust off."

"Who do you suggest then?" I say. "Her?"

I nod at a woman Mom's age, whose life has eroded Grand Canyon-deep wrinkles in her face.

"No, not her," Darby says. "Let's make it him."

I don't have to ask why. *Him* turns out to be sitting at the end of the bar in a softball jersey, shaking an angry finger at the crying woman beside him. I recognize him from high school from when I was a freshman and he was a senior. His name's Chet or Wayne or Darrel…one of those names that guarantee you two ex-wives and years of unpaid child support by the time you're thirty. When the crying woman gets off her stool, he grabs her arm and whispers menacingly into her ear. A second later, the woman walks past with a dead look in her eyes.

"Do I get veto power?" I say.

"No, he could use a massive ego correction."

"Yeah, but he's also an alpha male asshole."

"Which means he'll underestimate us."

"Or stab us."

"Then make sure he sits next to you."

We walk along the bar where people with an arsenal of empty bottles in front of them are watching the Reds' bullpen implode on TV. As we pass our mark, I get a better look at his softball jersey. Ironed on the back is the name *Chad* because of course it is. Chad looks up as we pass, his eye lingering way too long on

Darby. Oh, please, please, please let him reach out and grab her butt. I've always wanted to witness someone have his still-beating heart ripped from his chest.

The trick to roping a mark is to make him think he's noticed us first, so we sit in an empty booth close enough where Chad can see us if he turns but far enough away he can't hear us. I open my case and take out a small contraption with lots of exposed metal gears and thick rollers. The device has a thin slot at the top and another at the bottom, and on the side is a hand crank with a wooden handle. I put a six-inch stack of black paper wrapped in rubber bands on the table alongside a brown bottle with an eyedropper on top. Now, all we have to do is wait.

"So your homework?" I say.

"No, you first," she says, "because once I start, we'll never get back to Leyla, and I'm not giving up on her like you."

I take out the folded piece of notebook paper I've been scribbling on after talking with Darby last night. I look at it for a second, hoping for last-minute additions, but Darby takes it from my hand. It's not a long read.

"This is it?" she says. "You can't remember anything else about Leyla?"

"Our relationship wasn't really based on baring our souls."

"Have you ever had a relationship that is?"

"Well, you and I—"

"Stop."

While Darby rereads my list of what I remember about Leyla, I put a piece of the black paper in the top slot of the device along with a squirt from the eyedropper and turn the crank. The gears and rollers turn, drawing the paper inside. Seconds later, a damp ten-dollar bill appears out of the bottom slot. I remove it and lay it on the table.

"Is there a chance anyone else could have taken the money?" Darby says.

"I don't see how."

"Well, did anyone know you had the money?"

"Normally, no one would have known."

"Normally?"

"I possibly may have mentioned it while I was drunk."

"Possibly?"

"Okay, definitely."

"God, Boone."

A waitress stops by and asks us what we're drinking. I fully expect Darby to order water, but she surprises me.

"I'll have a rum and Coke," she says.

"Huh?" I say.

"And he'll have water since he's driving."

The waitress nods and walks off.

"I might as well get my use out of this ID," Darby says to me.

"You drink? How did I not know that?"

"That's part of your problem, Boone. There's a lot you don't know about me."

"What do you mean by 'a lot'?"

Darby leans in and whispers across the table to me, "I've seen and done things that would melt your brain. You just find it easier thinking you've figured people out instead of getting to know them."

It's going to be one of those nights. I put another black piece of paper into the machine and turn the crank. It's another ten.

"Can you think of anyone who might have wanted to target you?"

"I do have my critics."

"But anyone specifically? What about girls you might have hooked up with? We have to start somewhere—let's write them down."

"We're going to need a lot more paper than this."

"You sound proud."

"I mean, I'm not exactly ashamed of it."

Darby makes a sour face.

"You're just so gross," she says.

"Why do you hate me so much?"

"I don't hate you, Boone. You're just not nice to girls, so I don't like you."

"Wait, what in the hell does that mean?"

"Exactly what I said—you're not nice to girls."

"But why would you think that? Because I think I'm really nice to girls. I love girls."

"No, you love girls as physical objects."

"Totally."

"But you don't love them as actual, real people. There's a big difference."

"I love everything about women."

"Really? What's the longest you've gone out with anybody?" Darby says. "Come on, Boone. How long?"

I hate arguing with people who are clearly better at it than I am.

"I happen to believe variety is the spice of life and tying yourself down at this age isn't healthy," I say.

"Or it could be you go out with a girl a couple of times, make out with her or god knows what, and get bored fast because you don't really know anything about her so you move on to the next girl."

"They don't complain," I say. "Well, at least not many of them do. Anyway, that's not what happened with you at all. I thought we were doing okay."

Darby's mouth pinches, and she looks away.

"I'm not getting into this with you," she says.

"Why not?"

"Because I'm not, and if you ask again, you're on your own with this dumb plan."

Well, if she won't get into it, then I will. Here's the short version of my even-shorter relationship with Darby: After a long day of listening to Darby laugh at me as I shocked the shit out of myself while trying to fix Ancient Artifacts' lights, I asked her out. Knowing we're opposites in a million ways, I was surprised as she was that I did it, but for some equally inexplicable reason, Darby said yes. We went out exactly three times, and on those dates, Darby's true hustler nature showed itself. We pulled cons together and most nights ended up making out in my car afterward from the adrenaline of it all. Then suddenly she stopped returning all of my calls and texts and avoided me at work. And now here we are. The end.

I can hear you right now thinking, *There must be more to the story, Boone. What aren't you telling us?* But, honestly, there's nothing else. There are no dark corners of that story I'm not revealing. We went out, had fun, she blew me off for unknown reasons, and that's it. She apparently has a different take on things, but since she won't talk about it, I get to write the history book on this one.

The waitress drops off our drinks, and I churn out more bills, laying them at the end of the table where Chad can see. Darby's watching him and, playing her part, constantly looking at the door.

"I'm not giving up on Leyla," she says. "There has to be something we can do there."

"I'll keep thinking about it," I say, and to keep her talking, change the subject. "Who'd you come up with?"

Darby takes out her phone and opens her notepad app. She puts it on the table for me to see her potential marks. I'm hoping for a long list of people that when added together equals $15,000. But no.

"One person?" I say.

"I don't dislike many people enough to take their money. It's just types of people. I know them when I see them."

"And this Vance Reid guy?" I say, pointing at the phone.

"Him, I hate. And his wife. They're the worst."

"Who are they?"

Darby starts in on how Vance Reid runs a competing dojo in nearby Asheville and is a macho jerk who teaches karate the wrong way. It's all starting to sound like the plot of *The Karate Kid*, and Darby doesn't even get into specifics on why she doesn't like the guy when her eyes flash over to the mark and back to me.

"He's coming," she says.

"What's the angle?" I say.

"Concerned sister, tardy buyer."

It may be nothing we've ever discussed before, but I instinctively know what she means.

"Oh, and there's one other thing," Darby says. "You're mute."

"Huh?"

"No, you can't even do that. You're completely silent. Good luck."

Before I can argue, our mark's standing at our table, smiling down at Darby. I act like I don't see him and put another black piece of paper into the machine and turn the crank. Then I pretend to notice the guy and wrap my arms around the machine, pulling it toward me.

"Are you him?" Darby says. "You're him, right? Oh, thank god."

"What?" Chad says.

"Quick, sit down. Hurry, before anyone else sees."

Chad does what Darby says, sliding in next to me. I push into the side of the booth, my arms still wrapped around the machine.

"I didn't think you were going to show," she says to him. "Did you bring it? Reggie'll let go if I tell him to."

Great. Reggie. Just the name I've always dreamed of having.

"What's going on?" Chad says, confused.

"This is all that's left, but it's enough," Darby says, and then switches to me while pointing to the stack of black paper on the table. "You promise that's all of it, right?"

I stare and grip the machine tighter.

"No, we've talked about this," she says. "You're giving it to him tonight before we get in trouble. I don't care how much money you've made."

The guy's confused but becoming clearer on things. It just goes to show how damn good Darby is at this. Because right now, she's not Darby anymore, she's a panicked girl trying to protect her brother. She's not just playing the part, though; she believes the lie, and because of that, this guy's starting to believe it too. My theory is she's so good at this because she grew up having to pretend like everything was fine when it really wasn't.

"Did you bring the money?" Darby says.

"Um, yeah," Chad says.

I shake my head so hard I almost pull a muscle in my neck.

"You're giving it to him, Reggie. That's all there is to it."

I drive a finger at the money on the table.

"It doesn't matter. This isn't safe. We need to be happy with the thousand you already made."

"A thousand?" Chad says.

"That's what he's gotten from it so far, yeah," Darby says. "But I'm fine with selling the machine to you for five hundred because I want it gone. You're still up for taking it, right? Please say you haven't changed your mind. You can have all of it. There's even a whole other stack of black money in the bag. Everything's yours. Please say you're not backing out."

Darby's on the verge of crying, and if the guy wavers, I have no doubt the tears flow.

"Where did you get this again?" Chad says.

Clarity crosses Darby's face.

"Oh my god, you're not him, are you?" she says.

"No, I am but—"

"You have to go."

"No, it is me," Chad says.

Darby leans out to look at the front door, then back to the guy.

"Please leave," she says. "He's going to show up and see you and get scared off. We have to sell this and be done with it. Reggie's going to get arrested if he doesn't stop."

Chad reaches out and touches Darby's arm, which under normal circumstances is a good way to lose a limb.

"Hey, it's all okay," he says. "I'm the guy."

"You are?"

"I am. I swear."

Darby lets out a big sigh.

"Oh god, you scared me there," she says. "I thought I'd already told you the story."

"You did. I guess I was checking to make sure you were for real."

The smile Darby gives him isn't one I've ever seen before. It's a smile that simultaneously lets the mark know she believes him and lets me know that we 100% have him. It's also a smile that says Darby's having a blast.

"Reggie doesn't have a lot of friends, so he spends a lot of time playing by himself and, unfortunately, with himself," Darby says. "He was out by the highway last week where there was that big pileup and found the bag with the black money in it. We read online that when the treasury discontinues money, it's dyed first before being shredded at a place in Iowa. This money must've been on its way here. Reggie might not be smart about most things, but he is about science stuff. He made this contraption, and the solution in the bottle for it too before I realized what he was doing. Go ahead, Reggie, show him. We can trust him."

I take another black piece of paper off the pile and crank it into the machine. Chad doesn't blink as the paper disappears inside and comes out the other end a wet twenty-dollar bill. We're screwed if he asks for another demonstration because I only loaded the first few bills with the black glaze that easily washes off with the vitamin C solution inside the machine. The rest of the pile is only made up of blank paper that he'll spend the rest of the night inserting and reinserting into the device, wondering why he's only getting white paper in return. Eventually, he'll research online and realize he's been scammed. By then, we'll be miles away and fast asleep.

"You said there's another of these piles?" Chad says.

I pull the bag to me, and Darby gives me a hard look that makes the guy laugh. I dig out the other fake money stack and put it on the table.

"How much is in each pile?" he says.

"You only find out after it goes through," Darby says. "But like I said before, Reggie has a thousand dollars at home. He only washed about seventy bills, and there's probably at least another two hundred black bills left."

"And we agreed to…?"

"Five hundred dollars," Darby says. "I'm so glad you're going to help us. I want this away from us before Reggie gets us in trouble. And he will. Do you have the money here?"

Chad looks at me, and I try to look like I frequently put table knives into electrical sockets. I drool a little, and his eyes lose focus. He's probably dreaming of a softball bat he can buy for a thousand dollars to help him relive his glory days.

"I'll be right back," he says and gets up from the booth. I don't watch, but Darby does.

"Did he?" I say.

"Right to it," she says.

The guy returns from the cash machine a minute later and hands Darby the money. The relief she fakes is a thing of beauty.

"Thank you so much," she says. "You've saved his life."

I throw one final small tantrum before handing over the bag. Chad leaves fast, as all marks do when they think they've gotten away with something. I can practically hear him laughing in his car as he's driving away, the moron. Darby and I leave soon after, and once we're out of the building, away from all the noise, I say, "You were amazing."

"And you thought I might be rusty."

That's when Darby executes her most surprising move of the night—she smacks my butt.

"I thought we had a no touching rule," I say.

"That applies to you, not me," she says. "She who makes the rules can break the rules. Always remember that."

CHAPTER 11

The Klepto K.O.

Saturday is always Garbage Mountain's busiest day of the week. The entire complex has a rodeo feel and smell to it like at any moment everyone might break into a spontaneous line dance. I spend the better part of the day mopping up Slush Puppy spills and fighting a losing battle to keep the bathrooms above slaughterhouse-level cleanliness. On the bright side, with the workout my immune system is getting, one day I will make an excellent Ebola hot zone doctor. The only real fun I have all day is when Opal radios we've got a shoplifter.

"Oh, thank God," I say. "Location?"

"Brainy Sarah's got him," she says. "Tall guy in jeans and a blue jacket."

"In summer? Could he be more obvious?"

"Go get 'em, Boone."

Shoplifters are the lowest form of criminal. I couldn't care less about the stealing part; it's the lack of artistry I find offensive. At its core, shoplifting is shoving merchandise down your pants when no one's looking. You know your life's on the wrong track if you haven't evolved past a scam pulled by six-year-olds in the candy aisle. Most businesses call the cops on shoplifters. I'm sure that's what they do over at Treasure Palace. But at Garbage

Mountain, we handle things a little differently. Here, we like to run a variation on The Mustard Scam we call The Klepto K.O.

Brainy Sarah owns booth seventy-two's Word-O-Rama, which sells dictionaries in every language imaginable. With an inventory like that, you'd think the store would have tumble-weeds blowing through it, but for inexplicable reasons, Brainy Sarah does shockingly well. My pet theory is people like having books around because it makes them look smart, even if they never read them. When I come into her booth, she's behind the counter catching up on her Portuguese while Mr. Hot Hands is in the dead languages section.

"What did he take?" I say.

"A pocket-sized Latin dictionary."

"So a literate criminal?"

"*In flagrante delicto.*"

The idiot in question doesn't look anything like you're proba-bly picturing. He's not a scruffy, twenty-something McDonald's-cook-for-life guy. No, this guy's in his mid-forties, clean-shaven, and walks with an attitude that says he probably bosses people around their cubicles all day. I know the type because we get them here all the time—bored people wanting to inject a little excitement into their lives by stealing what they have no prob-lem affording. Unfortunately for this guy, he's picked the wrong flea market to prove to himself he's not a total yawn.

"Did you mark him yet?" I ask.

Brainy Sarah holds up an unopened mustard packet from Bingo Buddy's Burgers.

"This is going to be the best part of my day," she says.

"Probably for all of us."

She walks off, opening the packet as she goes. Our shoplift-ing friend sees her coming and tries to act natural, cracking yet another dictionary and flipping through its pages. Brainy Sarah approaches and as she passes squirts a nice glob of mustard on the back of his blue jacket, marking him—hence, intended scam victims being called "marks." There, you've learned something. You're welcome.

Now we just have to wait for the mark to leave, which he doesn't right away. He's probably thinking the longer he browses, the less suspicious he looks. Like I said, shoplifters aren't the brightest.

When Sarah gets back I say, "Can I ask you a question?"

"Sure."

"Do you think I'm bad to girls?"

"Why on earth are you asking that?"

"A girl might have accused me of that last night."

"And do you think she's right?"

"I don't want to think so."

"Well, who would?"

Definitely not me. In fact, what I remember about my outing with Darby isn't the $500 we hustled or even Darby's flirty smack on my butt. It was her telling me I don't treat girls well. It was those words going through my head as I went to sleep, and the first thought I had when I woke up this morning. But let's get down to it, shall we? Do I have a lengthy list of girls I've gone out with? Sure. And are most of those relationships short-lived? Okay, yes, but not as many of them as Darby likes to think. And since we're on the topic, yeah, I get it—I can be a little smug. Some judgmental people might even call me arrogant. I prefer to call it confidence. Do I know deep down inside not every girl wants me or finds me irresistible? Of course. I'm joking when I say things like that, at least usually. But what's the alternative? To be incredibly self-conscious and down on myself? That sounds miserable. I think it's important to bet on myself because no one else is going to. So, okay, maybe I can cool it a bit with the fake smugness. Maybe I'll even give it a try. But deep down, I think I'm a good guy. At least my mom would agree with me.

"Boone, here's the thing," Brainy Sarah says. "I'm not around you enough to know if the girl's right. I think only you can answer that. But there is a good test you could apply."

"I'm afraid to ask what it is."

"If someone treated your mom—or your sister, if you had one—the same way you treat girls, how would you feel?"

I consider Brainy Sarah's question as I leave her behind and follow the shoplifter further into The Mountain. If I'm really being honest about things, I wouldn't be happy with a guy acting toward my mom the same way I do with girls. It's gross enough picturing a guy fooling around with Mom, but then the guy not talking to her the next day or ignoring her texts, well, that just pisses me off. And if I found out he was going out with other women at the same time he was seeing Mom? Well, let's just say it's a good thing this state has a three-day waiting period to buy a gun.

For his next stop, the shoplifter gets in line at booth sixty-six's Noodle Revolution, which if truth in advertising laws were upheld would be called Noodle Revulsion. I continue my tail by standing across the aisle, just inside Kay's Costumes.

Opal may be Garbage Mountain's oldest inhabitant, but Kay has been here the longest of any booth owner. She's done wardrobe for every performance by all area schools in a twenty-mile radius, dating back to when President Lincoln had his disappointing evening at the theater. Halloween is Kay's most lucrative time of the year, but she's found year-round revenue as a cosplay seamstress. Today she's dressed as Storm from the X-Men. I say a silent thanks to the universe Kay didn't choose to dress as a saggy Mystique.

"Boone, to what do I owe this pleasure?" Kay says.

"Can't a guy just show up to say hi?"

"Men never just say hi. There's always another motive, usually one driven by sex or money. Am I wrong?"

"Actually, today you are. I'm following a klepto," I say. "But while I'm here, I did want to ask if you'll consider staying here at The Mountain instead of going over to our evil neighbors next door."

"So it is about money," Kay says. "Who told you I might be leaving?"

"Word gets around. What are they offering you to make the switch?"

"You mean besides more customers, cheaper booth rental, nicer facilities, and money that doesn't mysteriously go missing?"

"Right, besides all of that."

Kay gives me a weak smile and pushes the white hair of her wig away from her eyes.

"Boone, this isn't personal; it's a business decision. Even your mom understands that. The lost money last week was just the final straw."

"But you've been here longer than anyone. Do you really want to give that honor to Mr. Hubbard and his booth dedicated to professional wrestling memorabilia? That'd just be embarrassing."

"Like I said, it's business."

Which leaves me no other option but to bullshit as much as possible.

"What if I can get your money back? With interest?" I say.

"How would you do that?"

"And what if I could increase your sales by, say, twenty percent in the next thirty days?"

"I'd say you should go into used car sales. You can't make good on those promises."

"But if I could?" I say, as pathetically as possible.

Kay's still looking at me hard, but her shoulders drop. It's all the opening I need. Time to go in for the kill.

"Look, you're one of The Mountain's founders. You've been here since before I was alive," I say. "You could have left anytime before now, but you haven't. That's because you're loyal. Just give me a week to make this better."

Kay's no dummy. She knows I can't deliver. I also know she's no pushover, something I'm proven right about a second later.

"Okay, fair enough," Kay says. "I'll give you a week. But what can you do for me in the meantime?"

"You're bartering with me?"

"Boone, at my age I'm going to use whatever life I have left to get my way. So, yes, I'm bartering with you."

"What do you want?"

Kay looks me up and down slowly, then does a twirl with her finger. I spin, once, twice, and then am told to stop when my back is to her. If Kay asks me to show up at her place tonight at eight and bring a bottle of wine, I may not stop running until I get to the Atlantic Ocean where I will promptly drown myself.

"You're a little slope-shouldered and lacking in the backside, so butt pads will be necessary," she says.

"What are you talking about?"

"I need a new model," Kay says. "Not all the time, but for busier days. You'll be outfitted in a costume and will walk the aisle talking to customers, directing them to me when they show interest. Let's say two shifts a day for the next week."

"How about one shift?"

"Only if you want me calling over to Treasure Palace right after you leave."

Remind me to ask Roadie to forge me a power-of-attorney document so I can have Kay sent to a retirement home, one so full of abusive nurses *60 Minutes* has done investigative reports on it.

"Fine," I sigh. "Now can you help me with this shoplifter, please? Or do you want to charge me for that too?"

"Shoplifter revenge is always free," she says. "What's the game today?"

"The Klepto K.O."

I point out our mark standing in the aisle eating his noodles and watch and listen from the booth as Kay steps up behind him.

"Oh, sweetie," she says, "you've got something all over your jacket. Let me clean you off."

Before the guy can react, Kay's taking off his jacket.

"I don't think—" he says.

"It looks like it might be mustard. You can't go walking around with that on you."

She has his jacket off now, wiping at it with a napkin and slathering the mustard all over the back. He's watching her work, which should make the pull difficult, but then Alvin from Noodle Revolution steps into the aisle, and with theatrics that would win him a Tony Award, spills chow mien down the front of the man's shirt.

"Oh my god," Alvin says, "I'm sorry!"

The guy snaps his head around, and it's all the distraction Kay needs. In one smooth motion she swipes his wallet from his jacket. Without breaking stride, I pass her in the aisle, where she hands me the wallet. I put it into my front pocket as I head away from the excitement. Inside the wallet's fifty-four dollars, which goes to prove my point this guy's not stealing out of need.

Inside America Rocks!, Roadie's busy bartering with a woman who's modeling what only the most fashionable of potato farmers will be wearing this fall, and when he catches my eye, I pull on my earlobe. He excuses himself from the woman and comes over. I toss him the wallet and say, "Chop job."

He nods and wheels out the paper shredder from behind his counter. Before feeding in the guy's license and credit cards, he pauses.

"You sure? You could probably make up the fifteen grand with these."

"Too easy to trace," I say. "I'm not dumb like my dad."

Roadie nods and drops the cards in one by one, the metal teeth grinding as they devour the guy's life.

"Can you set me up with some boxes for tonight?" I say.

"Auction Hustle?" Roadie says.

"It's an easy few hundred dollars."

"You're going to need to come up with a con bigger than that."

"I'm working on it."

"How many do you need?"

"Maybe fifty?" I say. "A variety would be good."

"I'm sure the people around here will be more than willing to help."

In the five minutes since I've left him, he's also had a chocolate milkshake spilled on his head. At the front door, one of Batesville's finest is waiting for him. After some words are exchanged, the guy goes looking for his now-destroyed wallet. He goes into full panic mode, searching around, and that's when the dictionary from Word-O-Rama falls out. Soon, he's being patted down, and it doesn't take long for the cop to find the switchblade Kay slipped into his jacket pocket. He starts the usual "That's not mine!" all of our shoplifters whine as they're being led to the squad car. If the police know the revenge scam we're running, they've never said anything. All I know is we've never had a repeat offender. Like they say, it takes a village.

I spend the rest of my day keeping busy by emptying garbage cans filled with half-eaten hotdogs and Styrofoam cups filled with flat pop. When Mom spots me near the food court, she comes over and hugs me. I take the fifty-four dollars from my pants and hand it to her.

"A generous citizen made a donation," I say.

Most moms would lose their minds over this, but not Liann McReedy. She married Dad for a reason. She just grew out of his bad habits. Mom counts the money and says, "Only $14,808 to go."

"It's a little less than that. I've been busy."

"I don't want the specifics," she says.

"The less you know, the better."

"I better not have to learn the visitation schedule at the juvenile detention center."

"You won't."

Mom gives me another hug and says, "I feel like we haven't had any quality time in weeks. You're probably in need of a good home-cooked meal. When are you free?"

"Make an appointment with my secretary," I say.

"I'll get back to you."

Over Mom's shoulder, I see a young couple in regrettably matching tank tops and blue-stained lips coming our way, neither looking happy.

"Complainers approaching at five o'clock," I say.

Mom kisses me on the cheek and tells me she loves me before smiling and turning to greet what will probably be grumbling about the lack of quality snow cone flavoring at Ice Ice Baby in booth nine.

I finish my shift, shower up, then text Darby my plan for making money tonight. I take a picture of a page from inside The Scam List to give her the details. She gets back to me in a little over a minute. She's down with the plan like I knew she would be.

Moonville, and hopefully a bunch more money from an Auction Hustle, here we come.

CHAPTER 12

Darby Attacks!

Instead of going into the dojo to pick Darby up, I wait in the parking lot in case that rabid monster Kimberly from Thursday is hoping for an encore performance. If I'm lucky, by next month my urine will blood-free again. The Destroyer's radio is feeling masochistically charitable tonight, allowing me to hear stations, but only the non-commercial ones. I have the envious choice of Jesus music, classical, or a guy on NPR begging for donations so he can continue comatizing the listeners with his gentle voice. I concede victory to The Destroyer and shut off the radio. It's 7:10 when Darby exits the dojo with her uncle. He spots me but doesn't automatically scowl. I consider this a small victory.

Darby gets into the car and says, "Any luck on Leyla?"

"Still no 'hello,' huh?"

Darby waits. I turn right out of the parking lot and head for Moonville, which is a good twenty-minute drive. With no tolerable radio choices, we're quickly into awkward silence territory. We all know how well I do with those.

"Fine," I say. "Yes, I did some searching and came up with nothing. Like I said would happen."

"What did you try?"

"You don't want to take my word for it?"

Darby waits again.

"Okay," I say, "I posted her name and description on every social media platform I could think of. If any of my followers recognize her, they'll let me know."

"So that reached eight people," Darby says.

Apparently, Butt-Slapping Darby has gone back into hibernation.

"And if you must know, I checked every online yearbook from all high schools in the area," I say.

"Good thinking."

"Was that a compliment?"

"Anything else?" Darby says.

I could tell her about how I'm considering reaching out to the millions of members in the Boone McReedy Fan Club. Or Googling "Criminal mastermind Leyla who lives close to Batesville." Or show her the schematics of the time machine I'm hoping to build. But I don't think Darby would appreciate those avenues of investigation.

"That's all I've got," I say. "You?"

"I asked girls around the dojo today but came up with nothing."

"Again, like I said would happen."

"Something will come to me."

"Not me?"

"I'm not holding my breath."

Some people might be offended, but not me. The thing is, nothing is a bigger turn-on to me than banter. I mean, sure, a girl throwing herself at me turns me on, and if I'm telling the truth, I'm all about a girl wearing a white button-up. But a girl who'll verbally joust with me, giving as good as she gets? Man, that's a killer. I love not knowing if the girl is teasing me because she likes me or if she really doesn't like me at all. That's probably what drew me to Darby in the first place. And still draws me to her. Does that make me a masochist? Or is it sadist? Why are you asking me? Who am I, Noah Webster?

"So I've been thinking about what you said last night about me not being nice to girls."

"And?"

"I'm not sure I agree."

"Of course you don't."

"But I am willing to entertain the idea."

"How's that going to work? You thinking about it for five minutes, deciding I'm wrong, then moving on with your life?"

"For your information, I talked to someone about it at The Mountain today."

Darby turns in her seat, facing me.

"Really? Who?"

"Brainy Sarah."

"And what did she say?"

"To ask myself if I was okay with a guy treating my mom the same way I treat girls."

"And what did you come up with?"

It takes some time for me to get out the words.

"That I might—just might—have a problem with a guy doing that," I say.

"Wow, Boone. I'm…I don't know what to say."

"How about I'm amazingly introspective and wise beyond my years?"

"Or that you really know how to ruin a nice moment," Darby says. "The big question is, what are you going to do about this revelation?"

"I have no idea."

"Aren't you 'amazingly introspective'?"

"Maybe you can offer a solution?" I say.

"I'm not sure that's my job."

"So you're one of those people who's happy to light the fire but won't help put it out?"

Now it's Darby's turn to be quiet. We leave Batesville and head into the country. I wasn't being a smartass when I told Darby I had no idea what to do with my newly discovered problem. At least not at this moment I don't. It's all new to me. Maybe in another decade or so I'll have a solution.

"Okay, since you asked, maybe there is one thing I can suggest," Darby says.

"I'm all ears."

"Since Brainy Sarah got through to you with a question, I'll ask one too."

"Fire away."

"What do you know about me?" Darby says.

I don't hesitate because I know all about Darby. I launch into a quick history of how she came to live with her aunt and uncle, her work at the dojo, her natural abilities as a con artist, and an estimate of her GPA. It's a fairly decent summary if I do say so myself.

"Yeah, but those are things anyone knows about me, minus the con artist part," she says. "What about what I want to do after high school? Or what I want to be when I grow up? Or even if I want to live anywhere outside of Batesville? Things like that."

"I've got nothing."

"But don't you find that strange?" she says. "You've really made no effort to know anything about me. I wonder how many other girls you've been with would say the same thing?"

It's not a question I want an answer to, and suddenly I'm regretting bringing up the topic at all. Darby's not finished turning the knife, though.

"And how about this? What do I really know about you?" she says.

"How am I supposed to know that?"

"I'll tell you what I know—not much of anything. And it's not because I don't try. You just make everything into a joke."

"What about the bet you made with me last night with the bouncer? Isn't that joking around?"

"You seriously don't see the difference? That was for fun. But when we went those other times, it was all fun and nothing personal. Girls don't really like that. At least I don't. You're like a diet made up entirely of sugar. It's enjoyable, but you can't live on it. Heck, you never even talk about your dad."

"That's nothing I want to talk about with anyone. It's not just you."

"It's just an example, Boone. I could give you a hundred more."

"But it couldn't have been a surprise to you. I've always been that way. Why even agree to go out with me in the first place?"

Darby's looking out the passenger window, not answering me. I could keep bugging her, but it would be embarrassing having to explain to the paramedics how I was thrown out of my car.

There's no one working the entrance to Royer State Park, so we blast past the guard shack and into the open mouth of the waiting trees. We drive deep into the park, taking poorly marked side roads and ignoring "Staff Only" signs. The roads here are all unpaved one-laners, and the gravel beating on The Destroyer's underside sounds like a hailstorm.

"Do you have any idea where you're going?" Darby says.

"To hell if I don't change my ways."

"I'm pretty sure I'm already there."

Darby may think we're lost, but I know exactly where we're going. Before Garbage Mountain devoured my life, I lived out here. I'd bribe an upperclassman for a ride, then hang out for hours before begging a ride home since my original chauffer was usually long gone. Ironically, now that I have The Destroyer, I don't come out here as much. As we go deeper into the park, Darby is doing a spot-on impression of a silent, dead-eyed hitchhiker foolishly picked up outside a mental hospital.

Five minutes into the park, we turn a corner and see dozens of parked cars straddling the ditch on the side of the road. I'm forced to pull way to the left if I don't want to hit the two guys carrying twelve-packs of Pabst Blue Ribbon. Emerging from the backseat of one car are a couple with disheveled clothing who hopefully were paying attention during the safe sex lectures in health class.

"Why are there so many people here?" Darby says.

"How is it you've never been here before? Partying at Moonville is a Batesville rite of passage. Besides, where else would people go on a Saturday?"

"Um, let's see, bowling, to a friend's house, to the movies, a coffee shop, shopping—"

"You lead a sad existence."

"Yeah, I get the feeling I'm about to see what sad really is."

I drive slowly by the line of cars looking for a place to park. Near the turnaround I see two skinny guys I don't recognize leaning over the hood of a white Ford Focus. They look like they'd be a lot more at home playing Dungeons and Dragons in a basement rather than here at Moonville. As we drive by, Darby's head turns, her eyes lasered in on them.

"What the—?"

Darby jumps out of The Destroyer while it's still moving, hitting the ground running before I can see what's she's talking about. I throw The Destroyer into park in the middle of the road and get out. By the time I get to Darby, one of the dorks is on the ground looking dazed, and the other's facedown on the Focus's hood with Darby's forearm on the back of his neck.

"Christ, let me up," he's whimpering.

"Former boyfriend?" I ask.

Darby's breathing heavily through her nose and says, "Look at the car."

I step back for a better angle to see what's set Darby off. Sharpied on the hood is a fairly accurate portrayal of Heidi Hicks, a classmate, on her knees performing an act on a guy that would get her arrested in most Southern states.

"I wouldn't be expecting a call from Marvel Comics anytime soon," I say.

"It wasn't us," the guy on the hood says.

Darby grabs his hand while continuing to press on his neck. She twists his arm so hard I step back to avoid the inevitable arterial spray.

"Wasn't you?" she says. "Then what's this?"

Poor da Vinci's fingers are covered in Sharpie. This will not end well.

"Okay, it was us. Is that what you want? Just let me go."

The scrawny guy on the ground gets up, rubbing his chest to see if there's a fist-sized hole in it. He doesn't make a move to run or help his friend. Clearly, he's the smarter of the two.

Darby says, "You, get over here."

He takes a hesitant step forward, looking at me with desperate eyes.

"You're on your own, man," I say.

He's close to the car when Darby cobra-strikes, her arm shooting forward and jerking the guy out of his shoes. A half-second later, he and his friend are face-to-face on the hood, inches from kissing, with Darby holding them down by their hair.

"Do you know who I am?" she says.

"Darby West," one of them says.

"Why did you do this?"

"Ink said he'd pay us."

"Ink?"

"Yeah, he tweeted about it the other day."

"Boone?" Darby says.

I pull out my phone. Moonville's not a hub of top-notch cell phone reception, so it takes a few seconds to bring up Brian Murrin's, aka Ink's, Twitter. I scroll through a bunch of tweets about video games and say, "There's nothing here."

I don't see exactly what Darby does, but whatever it is causes both guys to yelp a sound usually only hear by dying animals.

"Not his normal account, the other one," the guy half-screams.

"Which one?" I ask.

He tells me a handle I've never heard of, and I type it in. When it comes up on my screen, I say, "Uh oh."

"What?" Darby says.

"Look," one guy says, "that's his account, not ours."

"I hope you told your parents you loved them before you left the house tonight," I say.

"It's not us," the other one begs. "We swear."

I show Darby the phone as I scroll through tweets. They're all about Heidi's weight, her looks, and Photoshopped pictures of her having acrobatic sex with farm animals. The most recent tweet is a picture of her car and license, along with a reward for the first person to tag it.

"This is funny to you?" she says to them.

"We told you, it's Ink's account, not ours."

"But you're the ones standing here."

"Look, we're sorry, okay? We'll pay for it. Seriously."

Darby takes a breath so deep I'm surprised her lungs don't explode. She exhales slowly through her nose with her eyes closed, and when she opens them again, she's a different, calmer person.

"I'm going to let you up now," she says. "Don't run."

The guys nod so fast it's like they're having seizures.

Darby lets go of their hair and steps back. They stand up in front of Heidi's car and smooth down their clothes, hopelessly trying to regain a portion of their self-respect.

"Boone, take a picture," Darby says. "Make sure you get the hood."

After positions the guys in front of their artwork, I shoot pictures. The light being what it is, these shots won't be winning me any photography contests, but they do the trick.

"Two things," Darby says to them. "One, you have a week to get $500 to Heidi so she can get this repainted. If you don't, I'm taking this picture to the police."

"But it wouldn't cost $500 to repaint this," a guy protests.

"Two," Darby says, "you'll get a thousand dollars to Boone. Got it?"

"What's that money for?"

"Protection."

"Protection from what?"

"Have you forgotten who you're talking to?" Darby says.

They shake their heads.

"Then you know not to disappoint me."

The guys deflate to nothing. Along with a girl who can banter, I'm also heavily turned on by a woman who radiates possible violence. I'm sure a psychotherapist would have a field day with me. As the two vandals slink off, Darby's still staring at the car hood, clenching her jaw and shaking her head.

"That someone would think it's okay to do this…"

"I admire your restraint," I say.

"I need more of it."

"I may not be good to girls like you say, but at least I'm not those guys."

"I'm not sure that's where you should set the bar."

The air smells of the obligatory bonfire burning down the hill. Off in the distance we hear the competing radios and the general teenage commotion that happens at any party. We stand there awkwardly for a second, then Darby's back to shaking her head.

"Come on," I say, "Let's head down and get to work before you change your mind and want to leave."

CHAPTER 13

Auction Hustle

Moonville's a ten-minute walk from the road, and we use our phones' flashlights to avoid falling ankles-over-ass. We hike along a well-worn trail littered with beer cans, chip bags, and a lumpy, brittle mass that might be a used condom. I don't get out my Sherlock Holmes magnifying glass to verify. The woods are alive with a million crickets chirping away almost loud enough to drown out the partying below. To show I'm capable of taking Darby's criticism about not really trying to know a girl, I bring up a topic I've wondered about for years.

"So what's it like?" I say.

"What's what like?"

"When you lose control like that back there? You were all over those guys."

"It's awful."

And nothing else. Maybe right after someone experiences a major adrenaline surge isn't the best time to ask personal questions.

Eventually, the woods give way to rusted train tracks. Ahead, trees and weeds have started to cover the entrance to the old train tunnel. Flashforward twenty years and you'll have to machete your way through a tangle of branches to get to Moonville.

"I seriously can't believe girls walk through there at night alone," she says. "I can't imagine a place more dangerous."

"The people who come here aren't like that."

"No, of course not. Alcohol, drugs, an absence of adults—I'm sure everyone's on their best behavior."

I've been to Moonville enough times I could make this journey blindfolded, which is good because when we get in the tunnel, we can't see a thing. The tracks in here were removed long ago, so we walk on loose stones where every step we take echoes off the walls, giving it all a slasher-film vibe. Mid-tunnel, we hear enthusiastic grunting. A quick flashlight beam sweep reveals a guy and a girl rutting away against the filthy tunnel wall. And to think some people say romance is dead.

"You really want to know what it feels like to lose control?" Darby says.

"Absolutely," I say.

"Well, like I said, it's awful. I lose all rational thought and just lash out. And I can't really see anything except what's right in front of me. There's this fight-or-flight thing going on that makes me want to fight. I just hate it so much."

I don't say anything, not because I don't know what to say, but because I've learned sometimes it's better to keep my mouth shut.

Darby says, "I used to be worse. I'm better at controlling it now, but not like I want to be."

"How do you want to be?"

"I want to be in complete control. I don't like giving any of it up."

"Well, you have complete control over me."

Darby actually laughs at this.

"It's nice to know someone does," she says.

Out of the tunnel, we climb a short rise on the right leading to party central. During the daytime, it's a popular hiking destination for the weirdoes out there who enjoy nature, but once the sun drops, high-schoolers take over, sometimes as many as a hundred, like tonight. In the middle of the clearing, there's a bonfire so big it would give Smokey the Bear a heart attack. Kids chug from red Solo cups and vape and drag on joints like a killer meteor is hours away from destroying the planet. We spot Mo and Arlo just past the bonfire, the two of them waiting to be paid for now guarding the pyramid of boxes they picked up from Roadie earlier today.

"You're still okay with this?" I ask Darby.

"It skirts the line, but at our age you shouldn't think you can get something for nothing."

I agree with Darby about this skirting the line. It's the type of thing Dad would pull. Hell, he's the one who taught this to me. But we have to make money, and who am I to question Darby's moral guidance?

"Thanks for playing security guards," I say to Mo and Arlo.

"You forgot dock workers," Mo says.

"And truck drivers," Arlo says.

"And don't forget co-conspirators," Darby says, giving both guys smiles.

"Saving the best for last," Mo says, and he and Darby high-five.

I probably haven't given you the most complete picture of Darby. She's a beast, to be sure, but she also has plenty of friends and gets along with people, Mo and Arlo included. It's just she's mostly known for her primary characteristic, which is her ability to tear you to shreds. Is it my fault I see her that way or her fault she presents herself that way? I don't know. What am I, a psychotherapist?

"Do you guys know what to do?" I say to Mo and Arlo.

"What you told us," Mo says.

"Exactly," Arlo says.

"See?" I say to Darby. "Some people listen to me."

"And to think I respected you two a minute ago," Darby says to them.

I hand Mo and Arlo ones and fives, and they leave to keep the curious from getting too close while Darby and I finalize plans. As we're doing our last-minute strategizing, Darby loses focus, her eyes wide, zeroing in on something over my left shoulder. I turn and see Parker Briggs coming our way.

"Oh my god, are you swooning?" I say to Darby.

"Me and every other girl in the tristate area," she says. "And a few of the boys too."

"You complain about me and girls—well, Parker's been in the Hotel Honda so many times, they might as well name it after him."

Darby gives me a look, and I say, "There's a broken-down car in the woods over there couples use for privacy."

"And now I have herpes just from hearing about it," Darby says.

"Remember, his dad is trying to shut us down."

"That's business, Boone. It's all about the personal when it comes to Parker."

"You're going to hurt my ego if you keep that up."

"I'm pretty sure your ego can take the hits."

Parker, ever the politician-in-training, ignores me and goes right to Darby, saying hello and giving her a hug she welcomes with more eagerness than any self-respecting person should allow.

"Boone," Parker says, finally seeing me, "when I saw this little box sculpture, I thought it had your name all over it. And it turns out I was right."

"Nothing gets past you, Parker."

"Not much."

"Want to help?" Darby says.

I turn my head at her so fast I'm surprised it doesn't twist off.

"Sure, sounds fun," he says.

Darby gives me a spot-on imitation of my double-bouncing eyebrows, and I almost puke out the bonfire.

"Fine," I tell Parker. "Just buy if no one's showing any interest. Help stoke the crowd."

"That's it?"

"Nice and easy."

"Just like old times."

I don't need to give Parker money for this like I did Mo and Arlo. In fact, he should probably be bankrolling us. Hell, his family could probably support the entire economy of a small Caribbean nation if needed. I'm ready to climb onto my tree stump and begin, but first pull the wrinkled five from my pocket and flash it at Darby.

"Now?" she says.

"Can you think of a better time? Unless you want to concede defeat."

"Never. What's the bet?"

Before I answer, let me explain my philosophy on making bets with friends. To make betting the most fun, the challenge has to be one of two things: A. difficult but doable; or B. really embarrassing but doable. There isn't much Darby *can't* do, but there are plenty of things she wouldn't *want* to do. So with that in mind…

"As you work the crowd, you have to give everyone a pet name," I say.

"Like what?"

"Sweet Cheeks, Doll Baby…you know what I'm talking about. The more obnoxious, the better."

Darby looks out at the growing crowd and says, "I'm not sure my mouth can say words like that."

"Just pretend everyone's Parker."

"That's actually good advice."

I climb onto the tree stump and look at the pile of boxes from Garbage Mountain. It's a nice-sized pyramid with the most expensive items—the latest PlayStation console, two iPhones, and a pair of noise-canceling wireless headphones—displayed prominently on top for all to see. The stump has me three feet higher than anyone else, and I hold my arms out, taking in a deep breath because I need to be louder than the music.

"Everyone gather around for this very special giveaway tonight from Golden Mountain!"

Darby wades into the crowd of kids nearby and ushers them forward. Many I recognize from school; others I don't. It doesn't matter. My reputation won't matter tonight. Even if it did, it's nothing I can think about. Again, to sell the lie, you have to believe the lie.

"Come on in, everyone," I say. "No reason to stand in the back. You're going to want to see these offers."

It doesn't take long for me to have thirty kids in front of me, including Darby and my three confederates, Mo, Arlo, and Parker. I keep calling people in though, building anticipation.

"What's this about, McReedy?" Dave Hickey, a senior, says.

"Patience, Dave. Those of you here from the start will be rewarded."

"With what?" says a girl I don't recognize.

"Are you really ready to find out?"

"Yes," she says.

"What about the rest of you? Are you ready to see what riches I've brought you from Golden Mountain?"

The response is louder than I expect. Alcohol is a wonderful assistant when it comes to cons. It loosens people up, making them willing to do what they might not normally do. But even more importantly, it deadens any real critical thinking and ability to step away from a situation to see things clearly. I point to the small pile of items at the base of the tree stump that Darby and I agreed would be a good starting point.

"In hopes of showing you all we offer at Golden Mountain, I'm here with extra special offers on select pieces of merchandise from some of our dealers. These are bargains you can't find anywhere else. Items of the highest quality. I'm going to start small and build up to deals you will not believe."

With this, I point up to the high-end electronics at the top of the pyramid. A nice, expected murmur goes through the crowd.

"Now this item," I say, holding up the small box, "comes from Adam's Inventions. How many of you have ever been sitting in class or at work, and you move your arm, and suddenly, wow, you realize you don't have any deodorant on. Who's had that happen? Because I know I have. Raise your hand if you know that embarrassment."

A dozen or so put their hands up, and I say, "Wow, from the smell of it, it seems some of you are dealing with that problem right now."

Now, laughter. It's almost sad how easy they're making this.

"And what happens when the smell hits? You realize, 'Oh my god, I don't have any deodorant,' right? And you're stuck having to walk around the rest of the day with your arms pinned at your side, worried someone's going to smell you. Well, let me show you what Adam invented," I say and pull a credit-card-sized object from the box. "This little lovely here can fit in your wallet, your phone case, or even in your back pocket to save you embarrassment."

I hold up the thin deodorant, pull off the tiny lid, and show everyone how it works. People aren't bowled over with excitement, but I don't need them to be. I just need their continued attention.

"Now, each box contains five deodorants and sells at Golden Mountain for a measly ten dollars. But tonight, as a special promotion, and to show you the great bargains we have going on every day, you can have a box of these lifesavers for just one dollar. I know, crazy, right? But one simple dollar. Who's in?"

No one makes a move, and I hold the box up higher.

"One dollar is all it takes," I say. "This is no scam. These really work. One dollar."

"I'll give you a buck," Mo says, and steps up to the stump.

"Of course you will," I say. "You'd be stupid not to. Darby, help him out, please."

Darby, who's holding six stacked boxes, hands one to Mo, who gives her a dollar.

"Thanks, Sugar Bottom," she says, and people nearby chuckle.

"That's right," I say. "Buy anything tonight, and as a special gift, Darby will call you something special. It's a deal no one can turn down. Who else wants one?"

"I'm in," Parker says from the other side of the crowd, and exchanges a dollar for a box with Darby.

"You enjoy, Mr. Gorgeous," Darby says, and I'm not entirely sure it's part of the bet for her.

Now that the buying's started, it doesn't stop until Darby's sold boxes to the newly named Darling Dimples, Lips O'Luscious, Mr. Kissable, and Suzy "Hips That Don't Quit" Gomez. Others raise their hands for a box, but I shake my head.

"I'm sorry, but you'll have to act faster next time," I say. "Those of you with your purchases, does this rock? Say, 'This rocks!'"

"This rocks!" all six say.

"I'll show you how much it rocks," I say. "Darby, give each one of these people their money back. It's a gift for believing in Golden Mountain."

It sounds like a line, but it's not. Darby quickly moves through the line handing dollar bills back to the buyers. Mo and Parker knew this was coming, but they act as excited as the others about the returned money.

"Now, just wait, because we have deals coming up you will not believe," I say, pointing to the electronics again. "But I'll be rewarding customers who get in on the bottom floor early first. They get first dibs on items from here on out. So if you want a chance at the bigger bargains in a bit, get onboard soon."

Darby hands me the next item, which under normal circumstances would get zero play out here, but a good conman learns to take advantage of important upcoming events.

"Here in my hand, I'm holding a Miracle Shaving Kit, complete with razor, three cartridges, shaving gel, and cologne. The perfect gift for Father's Day, which is when?"

"Next Sunday," Arlo answers.

"Exactly," I say. "At The Men's Mansion, located in booth forty-six at Golden Mountain, this set goes for twenty-two dollars, but tonight I've been given the go-ahead to offer it to you for only five dollars. Five dollars! Buy it now. You'll have all your Father's Day shopping out of the way and first shot at our upcoming bargains of a lifetime. Do any of you who bought the deodorant box want one of these? You're first in line."

As planned, Mo and Parker beg off, but the others gladly buy kits. We also sell the remaining boxes to Fun Size, Captain

Cupcake, Chunkie Wunkie, Boogabear, Snookie Britches, and Winky Dink. When she finishes with the names, Darby looks wonderfully close to vomiting.

"Are you guys happy with your purchases?" I say.

"Yes!"

"If you are, shout, 'This rocks!'"

"This rocks!" they all answer.

Again, I take the wad of cash in my hand and wave it over my head.

"You know what, Darby? Let's give them all their money back!" The people in the crowd actually cheer this time as Darby hands out the money. Soon, they'll be naming their firstborn after me. I'm drenched in sweat and chewing my gum like a maniac when I spot Gompers watching me from the middle of the crowd, his eyes angry. I can't let his obvious desire to destroy me be a distraction, so I move on to a small box of earbuds. I launch into my spiel, explaining how expensive they are in a regular store, what they sell for at Garbage Mountain, and how I'm selling them tonight for only ten dollars. I start with the ten people who bought the earlier items, and eight of them buy. The other twelve boxes we've brought go just as fast.

"Are you all happy?" I shout.

"Yes!"

"Say, 'This rocks!'"

"This rocks!"

"Darby," I say, "I can't believe I'm going to do this, but give everyone their money back!"

Darby returns to the buyers and hands back their ten dollars. Everyone's having a great time. Who doesn't love free stuff? But what I've done here is create a pattern, and people love patterns.

It tells them what is going to happen next. Or in this case, what they think will happen next. But it won't.

"Okay, everyone, we have the bargains of a lifetime at Golden Mountain," I say, pointing to the electronics at the top of the pyramid, "and here's a great bargain available to you tonight. Darby, if you will."

Darby holds up a box not much bigger than the last, but the response is a lot of ooh-ing and ahh-ing, which was the plan.

"This item needs no introduction," I say, "but just in case you've been hibernating for the last five years, Darby, would you do the honors?"

She hops onto the stump beside me, holding the box over her head. I'm surprised a golden light from the heavens doesn't shine down on it.

"I can't believe we have these tonight," Darby says. "I argued with Gina, the owner of All Things Electronic, that this was too much to give away, but she said if it supported The Mountain, she was willing to take the hit. How many of you know what these are?"

Everyone cheers. God bless beer and the desire for free stuff.

"Then you know Pulse's Portable Cell Phone charger is the best out there. No more worrying about your phone dying. No more worrying about missed texts. Just plug into this, and your phone's back to a full charge in ten minutes."

Everything Darby said is true. The Pulse Portable Charger is top of the line. This isn't a Pulse, though, and Darby never said it was. The item she's holding is a Pluse, a Japanese knockoff with the same box as a Pulse—color, font, and all. They'll get close, but not exact results for about a week before the device dies.

"How much is it?" a girl yells.

"How much are they normally?" Darby yells back.

"About eighty dollars."

"Right, but tonight, and tonight only, you can have this portable charger for only twenty dollars. Isn't that crazy?"

So crazy that people immediately start pooling their money together to buy one. So crazy we sell fifty of them in under ten minutes. So crazy I don't even care Darby has to stop with the nicknames to keep the line moving. And so crazy when I yell, "Does this rock?," the response that comes back almost knocks me off the stump.

"That's it for tonight," I say. "Thanks to everyone for supporting Golden Mountain. I hope you're happy with your purchases."

I hop down from the stump. Most people are wondering when they'll be getting their money back like the other three times, but it's not coming. No one asks outright, though, because they understand it's a dumb expectation. Besides, they're happy with what they've gotten tonight. A lot of them have gotten four things for only twenty dollars. And the people with only the charger for twenty dollars are happy too. They're so happy they're not even asking about the boxes of high-end electronics I've been pointing to all night. Boxes that are, by the way, empty and will soon be going into the bonfire. For those of you math nerds out there, Darby and I just sold over eighty items, which in reality only cost about $150, to make a thousand dollars. Not bad for an hour's work.

I pay both Mo and Arlo fifty dollars for their labor, but when I try to give Parker ten bucks for helping, he waves me off.

"No need, but that was fun," he says, and then turns to Darby. "So what do I have to do to convince you and your family to come set up shop over at Treasure Palace?"

"Make an intriguing offer," she says.

"Well, I'll tell you what. I'm having a party at my house on Tuesday. You should come. We can negotiate."

"Thanks. Maybe I'll do that," Darby says, and I don't look too closely to see if she's blushing, because if she is, I'll be throwing myself into the bonfire along with the boxes.

"Oh, and you too, Boone, of course," he says.

"Sure, man. I'll see what I can do."

As Parker walks off, I say to Darby, "He invited me first, the other night."

"You sound jealous."

"I'm just saying he invited me first."

"You must be proud," Darby says.

"Don't you mean, 'You must be proud, my darling dumpling'?"

I give Darby her hard-earned five dollars and clean up our mess. Nearby, a group of underclassmen break into a raucous and heinously off-key chorus of Neil Diamond's "Sweet Caroline." There's no smack on the butt this time, but Darby does take my hand to have me spin her to the terrible singing. I don't think it's a coincidence she's being flirty right after one of our successful cons. The adrenaline rush that comes from a con is a nice jolt to the hormones.

"Do you have time for another stop?" I say.

"Yeah, why?"

"Because I have a great way for us to celebrate."

CHAPTER 14

Meet Ink, a P.O.S.

If food-stained menus, sticky floors, and crusty ketchup bottles make your mouth water, then Holtzmiller's Diner, aka The H, is the restaurant for you. During mornings and early afternoons, The H is lousy with old people eating dinner as early as possible so they can get back to the business of dying. From three o'clock on, though, Batesville High students invade to drink flat pop and down French fries packed with sawdust filler while staring at their cell phones. It's a richly gratifying, five-star Zagat experience.

"You know what?" I say, pulling into The H. "I just realized you never swear. Why is that?"

"Because it's a sign of low intelligence."

"So you're saying you'll drink but not swear."

"Yeah, that's what I'm saying."

"But not even a *shit* or *dammit*? You should really give it a try. It's so goddamn satisfying."

"Not going to happen."

Through the front glass window, we can see Ink, the guy we've come for, sitting in a back booth by himself with his face buried in his laptop screen. Ink got his name from the purplish stain running from his right cheek and down his neck to the elbow. Most people might easily misidentify this as an out-of-control birthmark. But for Brian Stamper, aka Ink, it's a cautionary tale on the importance of caution when handling indelible ink.

"I feel gross coming to him," Darby says.

"I get it, but we need to make bigger money fast, and Ink can help. Plus, now he'll have to do it for free."

"Which is right in our budget."

"Exactly."

Before we enter, Darby points to the waitress and cook talking at the counter, both of whom look like the universe leaves a galactic-sized turd in their cereal every morning.

"Five bucks if you can get them to make you a steak," Darby says. "For free."

"Holtzmiller's doesn't have steak.

"Yeah, that's the challenge, Einstein."

"I'm starting to think these bets are so you can see me get beaten up."

"A girl can dream, can't she?"

Inside, Darby heads off for Ink while I go sit at the counter directly in front of the waitress and cook, neither of whom looks at me or stops their conversation. Who knew a debate over superior cigarette brands could be so mesmerizing?

"Excuse me."

Neither looks up, probably because they aren't aware of just how handsome I am. I tap my finger lightly on the counter and say, "Sorry," which earns me identical scowls. His nametag says *Frank* and hers *Ruby* because state law demands every diner has a Frank and Ruby working there.

"Sorry to interrupt," I say, "but do you see that girl who I came in with?"

I point to the booth where Darby's slipped in beside Ink. He's doing his best impression of the guy from *The Scream* painting while Darby's digs her talon-like fingers into his shoulder.

"That's my friend Darby, and she has hyperwursterosis," I say. "Do you know what that is?"

Frank and Ruby both shake their heads and watch as Darby stands up, increasing the pressure on her grip. Ink's eyes are close to popping out of his skull.

"It means she has a protein deficiency that causes her to fly into rages if her Janiwicz levels drop," I say. "An hour ago she found out she's pregnant by the guy she's talking to. Who knows what the chemicals in her body are doing to her brain right now."

Darby's releases Ink, who's slid halfway onto the diner floor, which probably hasn't been mopped since 1981.

"I'm going to sound like a jerk for this, but you don't happen to have steak or anything like that, do you?"

"I might have a Salisbury in the freezer," Frank says. "Would that work?"

"Anything classified as steak is good."

"I'll get on it. We don't need another murder in this place."
Another?

Frank disappears into the back, and Ruby says, "This is where you're going to tell me you don't have any money, right?"

My mouth drops open so far I'm lucky I don't swallow any of the flies dive-bombing the counter.

"This is a little game you play with the girl?" Ruby says.

It's always humbling when you realize you're not the smartest person in the room. It's especially humbling when there are only a total of five people in the room.

"We're just having fun," I say.

"Is she your girlfriend?"

"No, nothing like that."

"But you like her?"

I look over to the booth where Darby's released Ink's shoulder, but all the fingers of his left hand are currently trapped under his laptop lid with Darby pressing down hard.

"What's not to like?" I say.

"Then what's the problem?"

"I'm not exactly sure."

"You should work on that. I think she'd be good for someone like you."

"And I'd be good for her?"

Ruby gives me the once-over and says, "I'll box up your steak when it's finished."

Everyone's a critic.

By the time I get to his table, Ink's fingers are still trapped in his laptop. He's looking so pale it's possible Darby's drained all of his blood. I sit across from them and almost reach for one of the uneaten Buffalo wings on Ink's plate, but stop myself because I've seen Ink's fingers in his nose almost as often as I've seen them out.

"How are things, Ink?" I say.

"Call her off," he says.

"You're implying I have any say in what Darby does. I can assure you that will never happen."

"You've got that right," Darby says.

"I wasn't doing anything wrong. I was just playing Universe of Thunder."

Darby looks at me.

"It's a thing," I shrug.

"Yeah," Darby says.

Darby eases off the laptop, and Ink jerks his hands back, inspecting his mangled fingers. He tries to stop Darby when she reaches for the laptop, but she bats his hand away. The scowl on her face when she opens the lid and looks at the screen is all I need.

"I'm guessing not Universe of Blunder?" I say.

Darby turns the screen my way. On it are four separate windows, each showing different Twitter pages, all made to look like legitimate accounts for girls in our school, even using their actual pictures. But these accounts are filled with Photoshopped images of the girls in various sexual situations with tweets that would make the most hardcore pornographer blush.

"Not good, Ink," I say. "Not good."

"I can explain," he says.

"This ought to be good," Darby says.

"Okay, I can't really explain, but what's the big deal?" Ink says. "I'm just trolling. It's fun."

Darby raps her knuckles so hard on the laptop the screen inside has probably cracked.

"Fun?" she says. "Calling girls 'ugly bitches' is entertaining? Putting their heads on porn stars' bodies is no big deal? You're nothing but a bully."

"Ironic, you calling me a bully while sitting here hurting me."

He shrinks back as he says it, but I give him credit for speaking at all when Darby looks like she wants to punch him into next week.

"Yeah, well, at least we're talking to you face-to-face," Darby says. "You're hiding behind a computer screen."

"Why the sudden concern for people you probably don't even know?" Ink says. "You see me getting pushed around in the halls and don't say a word. So spare me the judgment. I'm a victim too."

"And that makes it okay to have people vandalize Heidi Hicks' car?" Darby says.

Ink looks like he wishes he could suddenly teleport into any of the 1,500 active volcanoes in the world.

"Maybe I went too far with that," he says. "I didn't think anyone would do it."

"But they did, Ink," I say.

"Right, *they* did, not me."

"Semantics aren't going to save you," Darby says.

"Look, Heidi's not innocent here," Ink says. "She owes me."

"Owes you?" Darby says. "I can't wait to hear this."

Ink shifts uncomfortably in his seat.

"Okay, look," he says. "She came to me to fix her laptop, and I did it. It took me two whole days. Then when she picked it up, she said she didn't have the money to pay for the stuff yet but could get it. I told her maybe we could go out instead and call it even, and she looked at me like the idea was stupid. Like *I* was stupid. She said she'd get me the money, that she just needed a little time. So when she didn't pay at all, yeah, I took it personally. I told you I was sorry."

Darby gives a short nod, then leans into Ink closer than any female ever has.

"Boone," she says, "please get Ink more napkins."

I hold up a hand to signal Ruby.

"Why do I need napkins?" Ink says.

"Because a broken nose gushes a lot of blood," Darby says.

No one in human history has ever moved as fast as Ink does. He throws his hands over his face and jams himself into the wall so hard the impression will be there until the day the health inspector inevitably orders The H torn down.

"Look, I was wrong. I see that now," he says. "And I'm going to delete everything and won't do it again. But do you have any idea how hard it is to ask someone out? Then to have her say no and act like she pities me when she does it?"

"You're Photoshopping girls having sex with dogs, Ink," Darby growls. "You offered a bounty if someone tagged Heidi's car. You're not getting my sympathy."

"No, no, of course not," Ink says. "And you've made me see what I was doing was shitty. I was just having fun and—"

"Fun?" Darby says.

"Okay, poor choice of words, but I'll stop. I'll never do it again."

"You're sure?"

"One hundred percent. I swear to God."

Darby holds his eye a long time, then looks at me and says, "He's all yours."

On the drive over here, Darby and I discussed our next move. In just over twenty-four hours, we've made $1,500, but that's not close to what we need. I had an idea for our next scam, but was reluctant to offer it up for a lot of reasons, the main one being we're venturing into felonious amounts of money. Shockingly, Darby agreed to the con, and even suggested the perfect victims for us to target. To make it happen, though, we would need to trust Ink, and who in their right mind would do that? Because let's be clear, Ink's a piece of shit. It's not debatable. He has a good family and a head start in life most people would kill for. So he can't use a tortured home life as an excuse. The purple ink stain doesn't help, but he was a shithead before that happened. Flashforward twenty years and Ink's probably writing fake news for right-wing extremist websites and hacking celebrities' phones for sex pics. But he also has certain skills and abilities that could help us here, so we're going to hold our nose and force him to work for us.

"Do you know what penance is, Ink?" I say.

"Like punishment?"

"Yeah, except it's a way to help make things square again, sort of clean the slate."

Ink frowns and says, "What do you want me to do?"

I slide him a piece of paper with three numbers on it.

"I need you to set up a phone number from this area code and a call-in charge of $19.95 with a $9.95 per minute rate."

"Who would ever call that?" Ink says.

"That's not your concern. And I need it done tonight."

"That's easy," Ink says.

"Well, the area code's in Jamaica; that'll make it harder. And I need you to set up an untraceable account where the fees will automatically be deposited. Does that make it harder?"

"It makes it impossible. We're talking Bitcoin, PGP encryption, Dark Web knowledge…"

"Penance is never easy."

"And you owe us," Darby says. "Don't forget that."

Ink sighs so hard the walls might crumble.

"Okay, I'll have it ready in a couple days."

"No, tomorrow," Darby says.

"Fine," Ink says. "Any other impossible tasks you'd like me to perform for you?"

"Well, now that you mention it," Darby says.

"Oh god, what?"

"Since you're Mr. Computer, I need you to get all the security footage from Great Oaks last Tuesday night. I want to see anyone who went in and came out of The Underground."

"But I'd have to hack into whatever's left of their security system."

"And your point?"

"For one, it's illegal. And two, who knows how old that system is? It'll be next to impossible."

"You like that word, don't you?" Darby says. "But 'next to impossible' doesn't mean 'not possible,' right?"

"No, it's possible. It's just a gigantic pain in the ass."

"Worse than spending the rest of the summer in a full-body cast?" Darby says.

Ink's such a beaten dog now he just hangs his head.

"Fine."

"We're trusting you here, Ink," Darby says.

"Oh, you can trust me. Anything for you two."

Darby gives him a hard look like she might change her mind, then slides Ink's laptop in front of him, the screen facing me.

"Boone," Darby says.

I pull out my phone and tell Ink, "Say, 'I'm a creeper'" before taking a picture of him in front of his fake Twitter accounts.

"Erase all of them," Darby tells him. "If not, Boone's sending this to your mom and every girl in school."

"Sure, absolutely," Ink says. "The second you leave, these accounts are gone."

"And if I hear about you trolling girls again, or talking bad about girls, or even giving a girl a dirty look behind her back…"

"No, I get it," he says. "You're like a one-woman social justice machine."

"The world's changing, Ink. You need to be on our side."

"What side is that?"

"The ass-kicking women side."

Darby and I both get up to let Ink stew in his urine. I tell him, "You might want to learn how to play Universe of Thunder with your toes, just in case."

As I pass by Ruby at the cash register, she hands me a Styrofoam box.

"Good luck with the baby," she says to Darby, and winks at me.

Darby rolls her eyes, but on the way out of The H hands me the five. Back in The Destroyer, I say, "That was good thinking about the security cameras."

"I told you I wasn't giving up on Leyla."

"You certainly did."

"But I feel like I need a chemical shower after tonight."

"Gross feelings aside," I say, "it was all sort of fun, right?"

Darby doesn't respond, which isn't surprising, but out of the corner of my eye, I swear I see her smiling.

CHAPTER 15

I Come to a Terrible Decision

"See, I told you you'd be back."

Dad's smile isn't of the shit-eating variety, but there is a smugness to it. Today he's in his orange jumpsuit that will keep him safe from hunters if prison officials allow him to go for a walk in the woods during deer-hunting season. He's also sporting a black eye this time, and I want to thank who did it. If I sent a cigarette gift basket addressed to "My Hero," would prison officials know who to give it to?

"How did you get that?" I say, pointing to his eye.

"I got caught palming an ace in the rec room," Dad says, laughing. "I'm out of practice."

"You just can't play a clean game, can you?"

"Where's the fun in that?"

I'm not exactly sure why I'm here. Wednesdays are my usual visiting days, and it's only Sunday. And like he was quick to point out, I did promise I wouldn't be back. But when I woke up this morning, I had this urge to see him, which isn't unusual for me. I mean, he's an asshole, sure. An asshole who destroyed our family. But he's still my dad, the guy who was a huge part of my life for fifteen years, even if most of our relationship was based on playing accomplice to his cons. I just miss him sometimes, even if I hate him too. It's complicated. Today is one of those Miss Him Days, so arguing isn't on my agenda. Not that he might not give me a reason to change my mind.

"I hear you're out making plays," Dad says.

"Where did you hear that?"

"I may be in prison, Boone, but I'm not completely cut off from the world. Fill me in. You wouldn't believe how unbelievably boring this place gets."

So I tell him all of it—about change-raising Dewey, the Moneybox Bamboozle, and last night's Auction Hustle. He gets the biggest kick out of Darby's having me play a mute at Strut, and soon we're both laughing. I have to admit, it's nice.

"How much have you made back?" Dad says.

My face is all the answer he needs.

"What's next then?" he says.

"I've set up a Phone Fleece that should pull in good money."

"Do you have the number set up?"

I nod.

"And an offshore account?"

I nod again.

"How did you manage the phone banks making the calls?" he says. "That's what always stopped me from trying it."

A quick lesson in phone scams—most people don't answer calls from numbers they don't recognize. But enough people are curious enough to then return the call to find out who it was. What they don't realize is they might be calling an international number, usually one in Jamaica or the Dominican Republic that looks like an area code in the United States. The phone laws in those countries are notoriously lax, and smart scammers can set up instant charges to your phone just for making the call, then siphon more money out of you per minute. What stops most people from running this con is you need a phone bank out of the country to make the initial random calls giving the marks the number to call back. It didn't take me too long to come up with a workaround, though.

"I don't need a phone bank," I say. "Dave Wheeler, a guy I know in Asheville, posted the number on H8Box for me."

"H8Box?"

"It's a site where people share news and pictures and stuff. Dave posted the number in a room where guys drool over high school girls. Then he locked down the thread so no one could comment or warn others."

"So the people will be calling the international number directly instead of you having to contact them first," Dad says.

"Yeah, twenty dollars per call, and if they don't hang up immediately, they'll go through a series of recorded instructions to keep them on the line longer."

"And Darby agreed to this?"

"Only because of the room we posted it in. She figured only creepers would be in there. To her, they're asking to get scammed."

Dad leans back in his chair and smiles hard at me.

"You're really good at this," he says.

I don't like the implication.

"I'm only hitting people who deserve it," I say. "And I'm doing it to help The Mountain. You were conning innocent people. There's a big difference."

"Whatever helps you sleep at night," Dad says. "You know, your mom used to be a hell-raiser too. She just moved on from that after you were born."

"Then why didn't you?"

"I can't be who I'm not. Just like you can't be who you aren't."

I realize now why I'm here today. It's more than about missing him. Ever since I understood who my dad is, this itch has been scratching at the back of my mind. If you've ever read about the psychology of conmen—and I've read a bunch on it, especially after Dad went to jail—the word *psychopath* comes up a lot. At first, I thought that meant a serial killer, but quickly learned a psychopath is a person who lacks any empathy or compassion. It turns out a lot of CEOs of companies lack compassion, which is how they can shut down stores and fire people without any regret. Or how a conman can scam thousands of dollars from an old woman or any unsuspecting person and walk away without thinking about them again. Which is what Dad would do. Am I capable of that too? He seems to think I am. And if I am, that means…well, I don't want to complete the thought.

"Do you ever think about the people you scammed?" I say.

"Why complicate things?"

"Not even Mom?"

"I don't think it's fair to say I scammed your mother. She knew what she was getting with me."

"But did she really? Did she know what a liar you are? Do you even know what this has done to her?"

"I can guess."

"No, I don't think you can. She's not the same. She always looks one step away from going off the edge. You did that to her."

"Things weren't great between us even before Golden Mountain came along," Dad says.

"But what you did made any problems a thousand times worse."

"There's nothing I can do about any of that now."

"That's sure convenient."

I push back in my chair and stare at a weird black stain on the ceiling that's probably mold. I didn't plan any of this out, so

I'm not sure where to go with it. I feel like someone dumped a 5,000-piece puzzle with no edge pieces on the ground in front of me and told me to get started.

"She's going to lose The Mountain," I say.

Dad nods.

"And it's your fault," I add.

"You're the one who lost the money, but I understand what you're saying. Buying that place was a risk to begin with. Your mom and I both knew that. But you're right; I didn't help the situation."

"That's putting it mildly."

"I actually argued against buying the place, but she said it was worth the gamble."

"So this is her fault?"

"It's nobody's fault, Boone. That's not what I'm saying. I'm just telling you the facts."

"It's about time."

On the other end of the room, an inmate sits with his wife and two young daughters. The family's smiling and talking like they each had a trash bag of cotton candy for lunch and washed it down with a case of Red Bull. I want to remind them they're in a prison, not the amusement park, but why ruin their delusion?

"I'm going to give you some advice," Dad says. "You can take it or leave it."

"This must be 'The Summer of Give Boone Advice,'" I say. "You might as well join in."

"I like what you're doing with Darby, trying to help Golden Mountain and all. It sounds like you're making progress. But even you have to know it won't be enough. Little cons are good for walking-around money, but not for saving someone's livelihood."

"Then what do you suggest?"

"You need to be hitting everyone, and hitting them hard. You can't be choosing your marks based on an idealistic view of good versus evil. That's just you trying to make yourself feel better. You're not Robin Hood. This is about family, and you're on a tight schedule. This is no time to be showing mercy to anyone."

"Darby and I don't work that way."

"Is that a rule both of you have? Or maybe just her?"

I don't say anything.

"That's what I thought."

I leave shortly after feeling more confused than when I got here. But I still stop by the commissary and put forty dollars into Dad's commissary account, which he didn't even ask me to do. Like I said before, our relationship is complicated. And it seems to be getting more complicated by the day. Or by the hour.

Because as soon as I get back to Garbage Mountain, who's stepping out of the front office with Mom? Cullen Briggs. Both are chatting like old friends, but Mom has the smile on her face that she gets when she's trying to be nice to a customer who's complaining $1.50 is too much to pay for a corndog and Coke. The two of them shake hands goodbye, but instead of heading for the exit, Briggs turns down the aisle toward the stalls, probably to poach some of our renters, the bastard.

I follow Mom into her office, where she's sitting at her desk, a hand to her forehead.

"What did our sworn enemy want?" I ask.

"He offered to buy me out."

"You can't."

"He has good points."

"Why would he even want this place? He already has his own flea market to run."

"I asked him that too," she says. "It's the land he wants, not the building."

"So he'll just tear the whole place down and build, what, a hotel or something?"

"Or something."

I don't like any of this. I don't like how my mom looks so exhausted and beaten. I don't like the sound of defeat in her voice. And I sure as hell don't like Cullen Briggs coming here and adding to her stress.

"You told him no, right?" I say.

"I told him I'd think about it."

"You'd *think* about it?"

Mom leans back in her chair and sighs, and now I'm the terrible son adding to her stress. But I'll say this about Mom—she's never dismissed my questions, even when I was an obnoxious six-year-old. Even now that I'm seventeen and more obnoxious than ever, she still answers me.

"Boone, there are a lot of things to consider. We're steadily losing business and renters, and not having your dad's salary isn't doing us any good either. We don't have long before the bank takes over, and once they do, we'll have nothing. If I sell to Briggs, at least we'll have money at the end of this."

"But this place was your dream," I say. "You just can't give up on it. Not yet, at least."

"I'm not giving up; I'm being realistic. If things continue going the way they are, selling is the only option. Believe me, I don't like it, but it's a fact."

"So we need more customers and more renters? That's what'll save this place?"

"You make it sound so simple, but yes, more of everything would help."

"But mostly more money?"

Mom ignores the question, but I know I'm right.

"I keep running the numbers hoping I'm miscalculating, but they always come out the same."

"You're a math head; you wouldn't mess up the numbers. You always say they don't lie."

"This is the one time I wish they did." She's quiet for a long time before saying, "I just don't know what to do."

It makes me sick to hear that, and just as sick because of what it means for me.

Because Mom may not know what to do.

But I do.

Dammit.

CHAPTER 16

The Raffle Ruse

"You seem off. What's wrong?" Darby says.

"Nothing. I'm fine."

"No, you're not, but whatever the problem is, get over it. I've been looking forward to this for a long time."

We're in The Destroyer outside Viper Strike Mixed Martial Arts studio, waiting for their last session of the night to end. Darby's intuition is scary good because she's right, I *am* off after visiting Dad today and my follow-up time with Mom. The rest of the day wasn't as drama-filled, but it was work-filled, including:

Gluing pipe cleaners onto fifty black-Sharpied ping-pong balls to make spiders for Grandma's Curios.

Taste-testing Brenda's experimental atrocities at The Mud Hut, including the perfectly named Defecake, which put me on the toilet every fifteen minutes for the next two hours.

Hallucinating from the toxic incense fumes as I sorted aromatherapy soaps at Peaceful Kingdom.

And electrocuting myself while helping Jim fix an old VCR inside Vintage Tech.

On the plus side, I sprouted an impressive set of blisters and paper cuts on my hands from all the work, and if all breaks my way, doctors say the feeling will return to my electrocuted arm before I'm seventy.

My humiliation continued when I stop by Kay's Costumes, where she dressed me up as Kodo the Grizzly, a genetically altered, sword-wielding bear with a fish head and human face. I made the rounds in the fuzzy costume, posing for selfies as I snarled and growled at kids. Not all of it was acting.

I ended my afternoon by doing something you can file under None of Your Business. Let's just say I reluctantly took a bit of Dad's advice to heart and leave it at that, okay? And let's also just say it involves something Darby would never allow me to do from The Scam List. But I didn't feel good about it. In fact, I feel like a huge dick. But family first, and this will help save The Mountain. Am I justifying terrible behavior? Absolutely. And it's why I probably won't sleep tonight.

Now Darby's her usual quiet self, sitting in the passenger seat and watching the lesson going on inside her aunt and uncle's biggest competition. I fiddle with the radio and come up empty, then check my appearance in the rearview mirror to make sure I'm still staggeringly handsome before I finally start tapping on the steering wheel with my thumbs. I'm about two bars into redefining thumb drumming for generations when Darby's hand shoots out and covers both of mine.

"Seriously," she says, "what's up with you? I've never seen you like this. You're acting all nervous."

"I'm not nervous. Just antsy."

"More like annoying. Come on, tell me what's going on. Remember our talk the other day about you never offering anything about yourself?"

Outside, the lights in the parking lot are coming on for the night. We have another fifteen minutes before it's showtime, and there's no way I can stall that long. I don't want to get into the conversation I had with Dad today since most of it was Darby-related in one way or another. But at the same time, he's someone I need to talk about, and the reason for the state I'm in.

"I saw my dad today," I say.

Darby turns in her seat and folds a leg underneath her.

"How did it go?"

"About as well as every other time I've gone."

"Then why do you do it?"

"Because I can't not go, if that makes any sense."

Darby's face softens.

"It makes total sense," she says. "You and I both have been let down by our parents. I don't know about you, but as angry as I get at mine, I still wish I had them around."

"That's exactly it. I don't want to go see him, but I find myself driving there anyway. And after I leave, I hate myself for going. But I go back anyway. It's pathetic."

I can't keep Darby's eye. Inside the studio, the session's wrapping up, but not nearly as fast as I'd like it to.

"If you want pathetic, I'll tell you about the last time I saw my parents," Darby says. "It was back in ninth grade. I hadn't seen them in two years and they showed up by surprise. They looked great and said they had turned their lives around. They told me they were looking at apartments in town, had leads on jobs, and said we would all be living together as a family again soon. Their stay lasted longer than it ever had before, and it was all very normal, sort of like how I always pictured it should be. In private, my aunt told me not to get my hopes up, but I did anyway. Then, a week later, I came home from school and my aunt and uncle were waiting for me. They said my parents had taken a bunch of money and jewelry and had left. I didn't want to believe them at first, but I knew they wouldn't lie. The worst part is my parents took $300 I'd saved up from working at the dojo."

"That's some A+ parenting right there," I say.

"That's when I ran away, but only for the night. I actually just went to the dojo, pounded on one of the practice dummies until I was exhausted, and slept in the back room and cried. How pathetic is that? I think my aunt and uncle even knew where I was. I went back home the next morning after swearing to myself I'd never be fooled by my mom and dad again. My therapist says it'll probably happen anyway."

"Why?"

"For the same reason you'll keep going to see your dad. Because they're our parents and we need them. I'm really trying to be the better person and work on forgiveness. I think you're trying the same things, even if you won't admit it. Plus, you and I are good sons and daughters, even if they're not good parents or even good people."

I'm not sure I can be categorized as a "good son," but it's not the time to get into it.

"Now, is your head clear enough? Because it's time to go," Darby says.

People are exiting the studio for their cars. In true bad guy fashion, all the students here are in black uniforms. Darby's leaning forward in her seat watching the building closely. Inside, two people about the age of Darby's aunt and uncle are standing near the door waiting for the last students to leave.

"Tell me again why we're hitting these people?" I say.

"Because they're cheaters and after reading through The Scam List, I think The Raffle Ruse is perfect for them," Darby says. "At the last competition, friends of theirs were the judges and award-ed first prize to someone from their school over ours when we were clearly the winners."

"That's it?"

"Yeah, Boone, 'that's it.' Winning competitions means more business. And I don't like how they do things here," Darby says and narrows her eyes. "Why are you looking at me like that?"

"How am I looking at you?"

"Like you think this is stupid."

"Not stupid," I say. "I just didn't expect something to rattle you this way."

"I'm not rattled."

"No, of course you're not."

We get out of The Destroyer and head for the front door. Darby's holding three gold envelopes, and I have a clipboard with an official-looking paper on top. I pull out my pack of gum and offer Darby a piece, which she takes. Now we both have swagger. As we get to the door, I hold out the five-dollar bill.

"This isn't the time, Boone."

"Which makes it exactly the time."

Darby stops on the sidewalk and sighs.

"What's the bet?" she says.

I tell her.

"What does that even mean? It doesn't make sense."

"That's the beauty of it."

"You might be the most immature person I know."

"If you're defining 'immature' as hunky and intelligent, then thank you."

Darby doesn't respond; she just walks inside the building without holding the door for me. I don't take it personally. Not everyone can be as well-mannered as I am.

The inside of Viper Strike couldn't be any more different than Yin's Dojo. Darby's place is well-lit with mirrors and motivational sayings on the wall. Viper Strike is decorated as if the owners did their shopping at Medieval Torture Chambers R Us. The walls are painted black with swords and nunchucks and maces on them. Fake torches with electric yellow flames dimly light the room. A weird soundtrack of monks chanting plays from invisible speakers. I look around expecting to see a guy in a leather mask chained to the wall, but he must have the night off.

The owners, Mr. and Mrs. Viper Strike, see us from across the studio and come our way. Both are dressed in identical black uniforms with open-mouthed snakes with large fangs over their hearts. He has long dark hair in a braid and neck muscles swallowing his chin. She has spikey blonde hair and biceps that must be inflated by a tire pump.

"We just finished up for the night," she says, "but if you're looking for information on classes, we have pamphlets."

"No, it's nothing like that," Darby says. "We're actually here with good news."

"I think you forgot to introduce yourself," I say to Darby.

The look she gives me perfectly fits with Viper Strike's décor.

She looks at them and says, "I'm…"

"Yes?" I say.

"Clitoria Von Wang," Darby mumbles.

"I'm sorry, what?" the woman says.

"Yeah, you sort of swallowed your words there," I say.

"Clitoria Von Wang," Darby says again. "I'm here from the Tristate Martial Arts Commission."

"Wait, I know you," Mr. Viper Strike says. "You work at Yin's. Isn't your last name West?"

"You know, he's right," I say to Darby. "You never did tell me the story. Why did you change your name again?"

I can almost hear Darby mentally listing the ways she may kill me once we leave. And look, I get it, the bet's immature. And stupid. And easy. I own that. But it's also awesome because Darby is the one doing it. Then the light in her eyes changes, and she shifts a little, standing straighter.

"My great-grandmother, Clitoria, was a Swedish woman who married a Chinese-born German named Victor von Wang. They suffered discrimination and many hardships because of their mixed heritage, and when my parents left me, I decided to honor my great-grandparents' legacies by renaming myself after them because I felt like we had a lot in common. It's brought a lot of questions and jokes, but I can handle it because my ancestors did."

Holy shit, Darby's so good.

Both the owners smile and nod approvingly at Darby, who believes the lie so much her eyes are tearing up.

"But as I was saying, I'm here representing the Tristate Martial Arts Commission, and I have great news," Darby says, holding up the three gold envelopes. "Do you remember entering a raffle at last month's regional exhibition?"

The couple looks at one another, both shrugging.

"Well, one of you must have," Darby says, "and the good news is, you won. Congratulations!"

I reach into my pocket and shower a handful of glitter onto the Reids. Darby reaches her arms out wide and gives both a giant a hug.

"What did we win?" Mr. Reid says.

"That's the really exciting part," Darby says. "You're about to win one of three prizes—an all-expenses-paid, weeklong vacation to Disney World courtesy of Stingray Travel; a brand-new

Super Sport motorcycle donated by Honda of Batesville; or the $5,000 prize."

"Oh my gosh," Mrs. Reid says. "I can't believe this!"

"And this is from what?" Mr. Reid says.

"The fundraiser raffle at last month's regional exhibition," Darby says. "We raised over $16,000 for underprivileged children to receive self-defense training. I'm sure you know there's a direct correlation between poverty and child abuse and neglect."

"I do, and it's awful," Mrs. Reid says.

"It is," Darby says. "But hopefully with the money we raised, we can reduce those statistics.

"Let's hope so."

"So which of the prizes did we win?" Mr. Reid says.

"That's the fun part," Darby says. "Each envelope contains one of the three possible prizes. You'll choose your envelope here tonight. Isn't that exciting?"

I toss the remainder of my glitter onto the Reids. They'll be finding the pieces in their hair for the next decade.

"So we pick?" Mrs. Reid says.

"Well, first you have a decision to make," Darby says. "Hugo?"

First Reggie, now Hugo. Nice.

I hold out the clipboard that has a paper with the IRS logo on top, followed by a small print you'd need an electron microscope to read.

"According to the IRS, you have to pay taxes on any prize you win over $500. Like if you win a car on a TV game show, it's not really free—"

"Because you have to pay the sales tax," Mr. Reid says. "Yeah, we know."

"I figured you did. I'm just explaining it so you understand everything before you make your decision," I say. "As you probably also know, the amount you pay is based on what you win. The three prizes here are of different amounts, from $14,000 for the Disney vacation, to the $5,000 prize."

"So you're just telling us we need to pay taxes on what we win?" Mr. Reid says.

"Not exactly," I say. "Because the Martial Arts Commission is a nonprofit organization, you can pay us a straightforward $1,000, and we'll file for you."

"But if you choose not to do that, then you're responsible for the taxes on your own," Darby says.

"Why would anyone choose that?" Mrs. Reid says.

"Because some people aren't comfortable paying a third party, which I understand," I say. "But you're right, paying the nonprofit directly makes a lot more sense. It's cheaper."

Mrs. Reid glances at the IRS form, then at Darby and me. If she smells a rat, I may be about to witness World War III as she and Darby go nuclear on each other.

"Aren't you both a little young to be handling this?" she says.

"Which is exactly what I told them," I say, and point to Darby, "but she—"

"—wanted to be the one who awarded the prizes, so we agreed to go through the training," Darby says.

"That lasted two stupid days," I say.

"Plus homework."

"And a test."

"Which he barely passed," Darby finishes. "But it was worth it to get to see people receive their prizes."

Mrs. Reid holds our eye for a second, then turns to her husband.

"I think the decision is obvious," she says. "Is the checkbook in the back?"

He nods.

"Then what do we do? Just fill out this form?" she says.

"Not even that," I say. "You just need to sign and date. We'll take care of the rest back at the office."

"Then let's do this," Mrs. Reid says, excited now, and to her husband, "Go get the checkbook."

She signs her name at the bottom of the form and writes the date beside it. The whole form will be in flames on the side of the road in fifteen minutes. It's important to always destroy any evidence of a crime.

"And that's it?" Mrs. Reid says.

"That and the check," Darby says.

"Made out to the Tristate Martial Arts Commission," I say, which will easily be cashable once I set up a bank account under that name.

Mrs. Reid's hard-eyeing the three envelopes Darby's holding. Maybe she's dreaming of getting out of town on a vacation. Or riding the streets on the motorcycle. But she's not getting either of those because all the envelopes contain the $5,000 prize. Not $5,000, a $5,000 prize. There's a big difference. In this case, that means thousands of dollars in coupons they'll never spend. Looking for $600 off on solar panels for your home? Or to save $300 on neon running lights on your car? Both of those discounts and others are in the coupon booklet. They're also all available in the local newspaper.

Mr. Reid appears out of the back, and you can almost hear the "Hallelujah" chorus from the heavens. Subtract another easy thousand dollars off the money I lost. Even Darby can't help smiling, a rare moment of breaking character. Then her smile disappears as we see the little girl, ten years old or so, come out too. She's the perfect combination of her mom and dad, a little powerhouse with spikey hair. Fortunately, she's missing her father's goatee.

"Pick the Disney trip, Mom!" the girl yells.

"That's my hope too, Bea," Mr. Reid says, rubbing the girl's hair. "We could all use a vacation."

"Especially one completely paid for," Mrs. Reid adds.

Bea hugs her mom's leg, and says, "You can do it!"

Mr. Reid, smiling from ear to ear, holds the check out to Darby, who looks at it, then at the little girl, before her shoulders drop just a fraction. I don't need to be a psychologist to know Darby's looking into a mirror. Other con artists, like my dad, can detach themselves from any personal feelings that might bubble up during a play and take a mark for their cash regardless of who it hurts. Darby's not that way, though. I'm not sure where I fall on that spectrum, but since I'm with Darby, I'll follow her lead.

"Clitoria, is everything okay?" Mrs. Reid says.

Darby flashes her eyes at me long enough to give her a *whatever-you-want* nod.

"Clitoria?" Mrs. Reid says again.

"No, nothing's wrong," she says. "Hugo, did you bring your stamp?"

Now it's my turn to let my shoulders drop. I go all hangdog, letting my neck go limp.

"Oh god," I say.

"You're not serious," Darby says.

"I brought the clipboard."

"Which was half your job. The other half—"

"Was a notary stamp?" Mr. Reid says helpfully.

Darby shakes her head, annoyed.

"I'm so sorry," she says. "I told you he barely passed the test."

Bea's no dope; she understands this means no prize tonight. What she and her parents don't know is that it really means no prize ever. Darby begins berating me in front of the Reids, and I offer a genuine-sounding apology. The Reids are quick to forgive us, especially after we promise to come back as soon as possible. By the time Darby and I are leaving minutes later, The Raffle Ruse officially called off, we're all such good friends I'm surprised we're not going for matching tattoos.

Back in the safety of The Destroyer, Darby says, "Thanks for that."

"No problem," I say.

"I just couldn't…"

"I get it."

"It was a lot of money to pass up."

"We'll make it up somewhere else."

I hand Darby the five-dollar bill, and she says, "Maybe you should keep it."

"Why? You won it fair and square, Clitoria."

"Yeah, but you're probably going to win it back tomorrow night."

"What's tomorrow night?"

"We need a night off," she says. "So you're taking me out. Plan big."

And for probably the first and only time in my life, I can't think of anything to say in response.

CHAPTER 17

Am I a Psychopath?

Here's the lesson for today—good things come to those who are as good-hearted, selfless, and humble as I am. That galactic groan you must've heard last night was the cries of millions of girls who've had their dreams of dating me dashed forever. They'll all just have to chase after the number two most eligible bachelor out there, whoever that schlep is, because Darby West wants me bad. But would she want me much if she could see me right now fulfilling my agreement with Kay and doing a two-hour shift dressed as Bongo the Hatcheteer from an anime show I've never seen? The answer is yes. Yes, she would.

I'm fine with the constant ribbing about my outfit from bored booth owners, but I'm not sure if I'll ever recover from Kay's suggestion that we put a rolled-up tube sock down my spandex tights. I never expected to hear the phrase "realistic engorgement" in my life, but now that I have, I wish I hadn't.

Whatever the people in Batesville are doing in an attempt to keep cool today, it's certainly not visiting Golden Mountain for its free air-conditioning. I could fire a cannon down any one of the aisles and not hit a single customer. Some people have wisely suggested Mom shut down on weekdays and focus on drawing customers on the weekends like most flea markets, but she said that would be admitting defeat. Say what you want about the McReedys, but you definitely can't accuse us of strong decision-making.

After my Bongo stint, I spend the rest of my afternoon putting together a patio set for Vernon of booth twenty-three's Tool Shed. Vernon's a well-known no-talker, a wrinkly old man who only speaks when he absolutely has to, which is more than fine with me. While he watches an idiot on TV explaining how the Democrats are ruining the country, I think out the battle plan for the night, which involves being undeniably charming to the point where Darby forces me in a wrestling match I will inevitably, and enjoyably, lose. Mostly, though, I'm thinking about how we walked away from a thousand dollars last night. Would I have done the same thing if Darby hadn't been there? My dad sure wouldn't have. I understand why Darby suddenly wanted out, but man, we could have used the money. Does the fact I'm now on the fence about this mean I'm an asshole? Or worse, my bigger fear, that I'm a psychopath like Dad?

It's close to three when I complete the table and chairs. Vernon's still being brainwashed by his news channel and barely looks my way when I stand up and announce I'm finished.

"I didn't know you were going to start selling outdoor furniture," I say.

"I'm not," he says. "This set's for me."

Great.

"Well, I'm glad I could play a small part in your comfort."

On my way to the apartment, I check the foreign account Ink set up for us. The current balance of $1,117 in just over a day proves once again you can never lose money betting on the number of horny guys in the world. I check one other thing on my phone that I'm not going to go into specifics about and feel a combination of euphoria and guilt. I'm not made to handle such complicated conflicting emotions. I'm close to home when I see Dr. Meg sitting alone knitting in her LifeHack booth. Dr. Meg's pushing forty and wears weird flowy dresses like she's a dropout from fortune-telling school. Her stall's draped in tapestries and soft lighting with low music playing from what has to be Pandora's Sensitive Crap station. Who better than to discuss my issues with than an unlicensed flea market therapist?

"Can I ask you a question?" I say.

"Of course," Dr. Meg says.

"How do you know if someone's a psychopath?"

"Wow, you just get right to it, don't you?"

"You just looked so busy, I didn't want to take up much of your time."

Dr. Meg smiles and points to the chair across from her. I take a seat and try to ignore the new age music burrowing into my brain and the incense scorching a hole in my masculinity.

"So before I answer your question," Dr. Meg says, "do you know what being a psychopath means?"

"Yeah, it's someone who's egotistical and doesn't have the ability to feel remorse."

"Okay, that's close enough. Are you asking because you feel like you're a psychopath?"

"Me? No, of course not. I'm asking for a friend."

"And does this friend work at a flea market and have a father who's currently in prison?"

"Most people also find him adorable and insightful," I say.

"Yes, I hear he's those things too. It's amazing how we connect with people who share so many similarities."

A potential customer shows up at the booth, and Dr. Meg tells him to give her five minutes. I'm not sure whether to be optimistic or pessimistic about how long she'll need with me.

"First, what you need to understand is only about one percent of the population would be classified as psychopaths, so while it is possible, it's highly unlikely."

"But still, one out of a hundred…"

"And there is an actual test that can be administered to see if a person suffers from psychopathy, but I can probably do a quick determination right here without the official test."

"By testing me and having me then apply it to my friend?"

"Obviously," she says. "Now, this isn't remotely official, but it is an example of a question asked to determine psychopathy. Have your friend answer as quickly as possible. Here it is: Two sisters are at their father's funeral, and one of the sisters meets a man who she determines is her soulmate. The next day, she kills her sister. Why?"

"Because she's afraid her sister will get the man before her."

"Wow, you're dark," Dr. Meg says.

"So I'm a psychopath?"

"No, it's actually the answer most people give, but psychopaths look at it another way. They say she killed her sister so she could see the guy again at her sister's funeral."

"Oh my god, who would say that?"

"Someone cold and narcissistic."

"Then you're saying I'm not a psychopath. I mean, if my friend says what I did, it means he's not a psychopath."

"Probably, but he's probably not anyway. I don't know your friend, but if he's like you, I'm guessing it's likely he's felt remorse in his life or worries about other people. Maybe he even worries about his mom a lot or the people who work for her."

"My friend does."

"Then I think he's fine," Dr. Meg says. "He probably just tends to overthink things, especially considering what his father did. If his dad wasn't in jail, he'd probably never worry about something so unlikely. He's not his father."

"But his dad is a part of him."

"But not as much as he thinks."

"How do you know?"

"Because we're our own people who have our own morals and philosophies and beliefs. We're not just copies of other people's DNA."

I hope she's right.

"Are you feeling better about your friend?"

"Much."

Maybe. Because if I'm unofficially not a psychopath, then I have no medical excuse for the way I am. I guess that means I'm just an asshole. Or maybe I'm overthinking things like Dr. Meg says. I guess there's a first time for everything.

After a quick wash-up, I head to meet Mom for a home-cooked meal. For the McReedys that means dinner at the Batesville Bob Evans. I find Mom seated at a middle table in the restaurant, which is crowded with old people gumming their grits and pretending The Grim Reaper isn't standing right behind them. Apparently, these people prefer clean tables and quality ingredients to the promise of the mystery hair you're likely to find in your food at Holtzmiller's Diner. I swear chain restaurants are going to be the ruin of this country.

"You're all dressed up," Mom says.

"Only the best for you."

"Or maybe you have a big date after mandatory quality time with your mom?"

"I'm not sure I like being so transparent."

"Boone, all moms know a lot more than they let on."

A waitress brings us waters, and Mom orders a salad, so I decide to eat healthy too and go with the 2,200-calorie country fried steak and eggs. God bless the teenage metabolism. We make small talk, Mom asking about my friends, me asking about a possible new renter. Soon our food arrives, Mom's in a salad bowl, mine on a platter the size of a sewer lid. If an entire NFL team sat down to help me eat right now, there'd still be enough for each of us to take home leftovers.

"So how's your father?" Mom says.

I almost cough gravy all over her.

"Huh?" I say.

"Don't 'huh' me. I know you go to see him."

I do a quick calculation, but no, the exit's too far away for me to make a clean getaway.

"He's fine," I say. "He had a black eye yesterday."

"Probably that mouth of his."

I don't correct her.

"I don't want you seeing him, Boone. He's not a good influence."

"And the people at The Mountain are?"

"They're not convicted felons."

I give her a look.

"Okay, not all of them are," Mom says. "But I still trust them more than I trust your father."

"How did you even end up with him?"

"You know that story."

"I don't mean how you met. I'm talking about how you ended up marrying him. Couldn't you see what he was?"

"No, I couldn't, which is a blessing and a curse."

"Why both?"

"If I had seen through him, you wouldn't exist, and that would be terrible. But at the same time—"

"Look at the trouble he brought us," I finish.

"Exactly," Mom says. "There are times I think I should have seen who he really is, but I was young, and your father was good looking and charming and dangerous in a safe way, if that makes sense."

"It does."

"You're both alike in that way."

"Are there other ways?"

"Too many to count, and not all of them good," she says.

"I agree."

It makes me think of Darby's declaration that I'm not good to girls. I haven't thought about it directly in a few days, but her words have never been far from my mind.

"Was Dad good to you?" I say.

"You mean besides the constant lying?"

I nod.

"Without the lying, I give him a C+. With the lying, an F."

"Did he ever cheat on you?"

"Of course he didn't cheat on me. You know that for two reasons. One, I mean look at me," she says, winking. "Who'd be crazy enough to cheat on all of this?"

"And two?"

"If he had, he wouldn't be in jail right now; he'd be at the bottom of the ocean in a barrel filled with cement."

"That's extreme."

"No, it's true," she says. "You keep your promises you make to people. Your father's lucky the police got to him for the lying before I did. Once trust is gone, it's never coming back. At least for me it's not."

"I'm not sure I can stop going to see him," I say.

"I know. He is your father, after all," she says, then adds, "Unfortunately. But just please be careful around him. He's a liar, and I don't want you believing things about yourself that aren't true."

"Like what?"

"I don't know. I'm not there in the visiting room with you, and I never will be. I just know he has a way of confusing things in a person's head, mine included."

"That's me too."

"That's why it's good he's in there and we're out here."

At the table next to us, a ten-year-old is ripping open sugar packets and creating a white mountain while his mom sits hypnotized on her phone. I give the kid a look, and he knocks off his destruction. I should just go all-in and buy one of Kay's outfits since I'm clearly a hero for saving our country's sugar supply.

"So who's the lucky girl you're seeing tonight?" Mom says.

"Darby."

"Did you guys already try that once?"

"It'll be different this time."

"Why do you say that?"

"Because I'm different," I say. "At least I'm trying to be."

"That's good, Boone. I'm proud of you."

Now if only I can get Darby to see that difference. If she doesn't, the night might be over fast. But if she does? Well, I'll do lip-relaxing exercises on the way to her place and hope for the best.

CHAPTER 18

My Date with Darby

"No cons tonight."

"Got it."

"I mean it, Boone. This is our night off. And all other previous rules apply too."

"No lying, no touching. Check."

"I'm impressed you remember."

"Do you have to follow the same rules?"

"I already told you, whoever makes the rules can break the rules."

"I like the sound of that."

She sighs impressively.

"Please try not to ruin this before we even get started."

Darby must not be planning on participating in a spontaneous MMA match like usual because tonight she's in a pair of simple red shorts and a multicolored top. Me, I'm in jeans and a vintage short-sleeved button-up from Miss Laverne's. We both look so good we should prepare for the inevitable swarming by the paparazzi. The date plan is a night at Xtreme Entertainment, a massive two-story complex with go-karts, laser tag, climbing walls, bowling, putt-putt golf, and other expensive ways to keep whiny kids busy on rainy days. There's also a full bar and restaurant with overpriced food if you're really determined to drain your wallet. Tonight, the parking lot's full, and I'm driving The Destroyer through the maze of cars when Darby points at a blue Dodge Challenger near the front of the building that's deliberately been parked to take up two spaces.

"What a jerk," she says.

"'Jerk' sort of implies you think it's a guy."

"Women can be jerks too, but in this case, you know a guy drives that car."

"How would I know that?"

"The parking job. It has 'I feel inadequate as a man' written all over it. Do you still carry that sign in your trunk?"

"I thought you said no cons tonight."

"This isn't a con," Darby says. "This is about righting a wrong."

"Like the vigilante conmen we are?"

"Exactly."

"You're the boss."

"It took you long enough to realize."

I pull into a parking space and pop the trunk. We've never done this together before, but we play our roles like we have. I grab the sign, and Darby digs through the junk littering the trunk and comes out with a ball-peen hammer. On our way over to the Challenger, I pull out my phone.

"Roadie?" Darby says.

"He'll know who to call."

Roadie picks up on the first ring. I tell him what I need, and he says he'll take care of it. It's good to know people who know people.

"Would you like the honors?" I say.

"Such a gentleman," Darby says.

I hold the handicap parking sign in place while Darby hammers it into the ground. And if you're wondering how I came to have this sign, or why I drive around with it in my trunk, you clearly have no understanding of who I am.

"There's our good deed for the night," I say when Darby's finished.

"The night's young," Darby says. "Who knows what else may come up?"

The inside of Xtreme Entertainment is a full sensory assault of beeping, buzzing, ringing, and neon. We step up to the front counter where a woman who might have been created right out of my most embarrassingly awesome dreams welcomes us. I ask for the Ultrapass game card, and as she types, I say, "You guys are busy tonight."

"Not any more than usual, but it's a rowdier crowd for some reason."

"Well, I hope they're paying you a lot."

"I'll send my manager over and you can mention that to her."

"I'd definitely do that for you," I say. "Just say the word."

The woman smiles, does a quick look to the left and the right, and punches a few additional buttons on her screen.

"I'm going to upgrade you for free to the Xtreme Ultrapass card. It'll give you a hundred extra credits to play on and fifteen percent off any food you buy."

"Wow, you're awesome," I say. "Thanks."

Darby and I head to the game area, which roars with video-game explosions, gunshots, and tires squealing. Thankfully, the area is lacking in small children tonight.

"Do you flirt like that with everyone?" Darby says.

"What? I wasn't flirting with her."

"Oh, you definitely were."

"I was being friendly. There's a big difference."

"And what's that difference?"

"Flirting has a romantic angle to it. There was nothing romantic about that."

"Maybe so, but I doubt you'd be," and here she does quote fingers, "'friendly' to a guy worker like that. Or someone who didn't look like her."

"Oh, was she good-looking? I didn't notice."

I speed up before Darby can give me a concussion, and soon we're standing at a row of Skee-Ball machines, their wood platforms and ramps scuffed and faded from years of use.

"I'm not sure we should start here," I say. "I wouldn't want to beat you so badly you want to go home early."

"Shut up and swipe the card."

Darby proceeds to destroy me, rolling the balls up the ramp and into the holes with scary precision. It's possible she's either related to the inventor of the game or secretly practices here eight hours a day.

"Again?" she says.

I swipe the card.

And this time the beating's so bad I almost need a supercomputer to determine how many points I lost by. Next to us, a college guy with his baseball hat on backward tips his beer bottle at Darby.

"How are your Skee-Ball skills?" she asks him.

"Nothing like yours," he says.

"How could they be? But I'm available for private lessons. It's pretty expensive, though."

"How expensive?"

"For you, I'd give a discount."

The guy smiles, saying he'll keep it in mind before I take Darby's arm and drag her away.

"He was nice," she says, practically purring.

"Uh-huh."

"What?" she says, grinning. "I was just being friendly."

"Okay, I get your point."

"I'm just a friendly, friendly girl."

"Stop."

I need an ego boost after my humiliation at Skee-Ball, so I angle us toward a nearby claw machine filled with stuffed animals. Darby may have said no cons tonight, but I need to weaken the rules set in place.

"How about a small wager?" I say.

"On this? A claw machine's a sucker's game."

"Not for me it isn't."

"Our usual bet?" Darby says, taking our five from her pocket.

"No, I was thinking if I win, we relax the whole 'No touching' rule for tonight."

"As long as you understand that *relaxing* the rule doesn't mean your hands get free rein."

"Of course not."

"And if you don't win?"

"Name it."

Darby thinks it over a second.

"You assist me at the dojo next week."

"Will Killer Kimberly be there?"

"Are you scared of her?"

"You're damn right I am," I say. "But I'll still take the bet."

"You sound pretty confident."

"Step aside."

Here's what you need to know about claw machines. For the most part, Darby's right—they're a sucker's game. The new ones are, at least. They run off a computer chip that determines just how often the machine will pay off. The older machines, however, like this one in front of me, have a set claw strength setting that makes winning a little more possible if you know what you're doing. And I do. It's just another benefit of having a felon for a father.

I walk a circle around the machine, looking in all the windows for the easiest win. You want a prize on top that isn't trapped by any of the others. I find a penguin in a top hat that was likely made in a factory by a kid earning three cents an hour. I swipe the card and grab the joystick, but come over to the side of the machine to play the best angle. Then I make sure the center of the claw is directly over the penguin in such a way all three claws will reach around it as far as possible before retracting.

"You have five seconds remaining," Darby says.

"Time to spare," I say, and hit the red button, dropping the claw.

As we're walking away with Darby holding her new sleep buddy, I put my hand on her lower back. I'm proud to say there's no shudder or immediate elbow to my nose.

"Just so we're clear," she says, "I don't bet on things where I don't already know what the outcome will be."

"Of course you don't."

"But I'd still like you to come help out at the dojo."

"I'm in, as long as you have a suit of armor I can wear."

We try out other games—I win at Whack-a-Mole, she at Pop-a-Shot—before playing a round of miniature golf that ends with me strategically losing the scorecard on the eighteenth hole before Darby can be declared the winner. On the way to the restaurant, we pass a Test Your Strength punching bag game surrounded by would-be punchers.

"You know what's weird?" I say. "I've never actually seen you fight."

"What's your point?"

"It could all just be one long con you're running. You have everyone thinking you can beat them up, so they don't mess with you. But maybe you can't really fight. It's brilliant."

"And you believe that?"

"I'm not saying it's true. It's just a theory."

"Would you care to test it out?"

"Not particularly."

"That's probably the smartest decision you've ever made."

In the restaurant, we're seated by a window, which is nice because we have a perfect view of a tow truck loading the Challenger onto its flatbed, while a guy with his sunglasses on backward argues with the driver. The truck drives away with the car, leaving the man shouting in the parking lot. Darby and I exchange a hard high-five over the table.

"No evil deed goes unpunished," Darby says.

"If we open a business, that could be our slogan."

"One thing at a time. Let's see if we make it through the night before we start making long-term business plans."

We order Diet Cokes and an appetizer sampler with enough fried foods on it to clog the arteries of every citizen in Batesville. Our conversation is relaxed and comfortable, with a good deal of ribbing on Darby's part, mostly about my grades after I make the mistake of telling her my overall GPA. As I mentioned earlier, banter is a potent aphrodisiac for me.

"So why did you decide we should do this?" I say.

"Because I think you're making an effort to be better. And you seem like you sincerely want to know about me. That goes a long way."

"And I wasn't making an effort the last time?"

"If you had, it wouldn't have ended."

"So that's why you ghosted me?"

Darby finishes off the last fried pickle and takes a drink while I wait. It takes a minute of her looking out the window before she finally answers.

"How do you remember the times we went out before?" Darby says.

"Like what did we do?"

"No, I know what we did. I'm wondering how you thought it all went."

"I thought it was great," I say. "We had a lot of fun."

"And I agree with that. Like I told you before, you're not very good at trying to really learn about a girl, but we could have worked on that."

"So why did you disappear on me?"

Darby doesn't answer right away.

"Do you remember our last date?" she asks.

"Yeah, The Monkey Joint."

When I picked her up that night, Darby wouldn't tell me why she was in a bad mood. I decided she needed cheering up, so I took her to The Monkey Joint, a truck stop outside of town that once housed a chimpanzee that smoked cigarettes. In the parking lot, I showed Darby a phony Pick 3 lottery ticket I'd printed that day with the previous day's numbers. Inside, the two of us sat close to a couple and Darby loudly berated me for losing all of our money and stranding us hundreds of miles from home. It didn't take long for the man and woman to come to our aid. After hearing about the winning lottery ticket we had but couldn't cash because we were underage, they offered to do it for us. We didn't take their money though; Darby wouldn't let us.

"You were unbelievable that night," I say. "It was probably your best performance."

"Right. That's the problem."

"How so?"

"Because, Boone, I'm good at running cons. Really good."

"The best."

"Exactly. I'm good at being bad, and I don't like that. Talking people into giving me their money? That's not me. But when I'm around you, it's what I want to do. I can't help it. It gives me a rush I don't get anywhere else. It's a different feeling from anything I do, even karate. It's not good for me, though. We were ready to take $500 from that couple for absolutely no reason. I can't be that person. So, I had to back off from you completely because I knew what would happen if we went out again—we'd make another play. And I'd love it in the moment, then hate myself later."

"And what we're doing now with the cons we're running?"

"This is different. At least I've made myself believe that. Deep down I know I'm lying to myself. If I really thought about what we're really doing, I'd probably back off again completely, but I can justify it to myself by saying we're doing this for a good cause and only taking money from people who we think deserve it. That works for me.

"I don't expect you to understand that."

"Oh, I understand it all right."

I tell her all about my recent psychopath concerns, and my worry that deep down I'm just my father. How I can see a life where down the line I'm in prison like him. How I understand the rush she talked about, and how I'm addicted to it. And how I justify what I'm doing right now just like she is. It's probably the most open and honest I've been with anyone. It's scary and makes me uncomfortable, but for whatever reason I have no problem doing it with Darby.

"You're definitely not a psychopath," she says, taking my hand.

"I mostly know that."

"And I'm happy to hear you struggle with this like I do. It makes me feel like we're in this together. That type of honesty goes a long way with me. We need to keep it up."

"I can do that."

"Let's make a deal right now—if either one of us is feeling uncomfortable with a play we're making, we need to let the other one know like we did with the Reids the other night. We both know what we're doing is shady, so we have to be each other's moral compass."

"I can do that too."

Darby takes the five out of her pocket and slides it across the table to me.

"What's this for?"

"I was concerned tonight was a mistake, so I made a private bet with myself—if I was right to worry, I'd keep the money, but if it turned out I was wrong, the money was yours."

"Well, I'm glad to take it."

"And I'm glad to give it to you," Darby says. "Now, if you don't mind, I'm ready to get out of here. The noise in here's giving me a headache."

"You want to go home already?"

"Eventually, but I think first we should take advantage of the 'no touching' rule being on pause for the night."

"Is that just you," and I do quote fingers, "'being friendly'?"

"No, that's me being flirty."

Which is how Darby and I ended up in The Destroyer making out, which I won't give you details about since I'm a gentleman. But I will say it's wonderful, and my connection with Darby makes it light years better than anyone else

I've ever been with. That's part of the problem, because after a while my goddamn conscience gets to me and I pull back, saying, "In the spirit of our new honesty, there's something I need to tell you."

Now Darby pulls back too.

"Why do I get the feeling I'm not going to like this?"

"No, it's nothing like that," I say. "Well, okay, it is sort of like that."

"Tell me."

"First, I just want to say this happened after I saw my dad the other day, so he had me a little confused about things. Then I was worrying about money and The Mountain and—"

"Boone."

"I ran The Grandparent Gouge."

Instantly, Make-Out-With-Boone-Bigtime Darby is gone, replaced by Your-Life-Is-Over Darby. And for good reason. On the list of cons you can run, The Grandparent Gouge is the worst. Only the shittiest people run it. I knew that going in, but I did it anyway. It's so bad I'm not even going to give you specifics on how it works. Let's just say it involves calling old people and pretending to be their grandkid who needs money. Feel free to call me an asshole. I absolutely deserve it.

"How much have you taken in?" Darby says.

"Almost a thousand dollars."

"In just two days?"

"I'm really good at it. Old people like me."

Darby turns and looks out the passenger-side window. The temperature in The Destroyer has dropped thirty degrees in the last minute. This won't end well, but I don't regret telling her. I should at least get credit for that.

"Take me home," Darby says.

"Look, I'm planning on giving the money back. I just wanted to be honest with you. I didn't have to do that. I could have given it back and you wouldn't have known about it at all. But I told you and—"

"Home."

Darby doesn't look at me as I pull out of the parking lot. All she does is give me the back of her head as she looks out her window. And I get it. I broke every rule she laid down on the night we teamed up. But there's this other part of me, the part growing louder in my brain, that's sort of pissed about what's going down. I mean, I told her the truth, something I didn't have to do, and something we just agreed we would do, and this is what I get for it? How is that remotely fair? But as irritated as I am inside, I like my arms attached to my body, thank you very much, so against all desires, I'm not saying a damn word. I could, though. I so totally could.

That's when Darby says, "You know what your problem is?"

And now it *so* on.

"Oh, please tell me," I say. "I'd love to hear the extensive list of my flaws you've been keeping."

"No, it's not a list, it's one thing—you can't turn off the conman side of you. And you know, I don't think you really even *want* to. You say you don't want to be your dad, but that doesn't stop you from making plays all the time. Everything you do is a con."

"Like what?"

"Like how you run cons behind my back after you promised you wouldn't. Or how you say you won't lie to me, then you do. Or how you sweet-talked the woman at the desk into upgrading our card. Even getting me into your car so we could make out—"

"You're the one who said we should leave!"

"After you scammed me into thinking you'd really changed. But you haven't. Not at all. I'm right, and you know it."

"Of course you're right, Darby," I say, having a hard time keeping the car on the road. "You're always right. And always good. It has to be exhausting being so right and so good all the time. Because I know how exhausting it is for all of us to be around you."

"Keep digging that hole, Boone."

"Just look at you—you don't swear; you constantly judge people, especially me; you don't have sex—"

Darby laughs so hard I stop talking.

"You think I'm a virgin?"

"Well, I—"

"Because not that it's any of your business, but I'm not. I'm just not like that with you. That should tell you something. And even if I was a virgin, why would that be a problem?"

"I didn't say it was a problem."

"Oh, you certainly did. You can't talk your way out of this one. So please explain to me how the fact I won't have sex with you is a character flaw. Because I don't think it is. Why do you?"

I don't say anything because there's nothing I can say.

"Well?" she says, not letting me off the hook. "Answer the question."

"It's not a flaw," I say. "I'm sorry. You're right."

"Uh-huh, but my being right about that just makes me even more exhausting, doesn't it?"

Game, set, match.

Darby turns away from me for the rest of the drive. When I pull up to her house after fifteen excruciating minutes, she opens the door and climbs out. Before she shuts the door, I say, "Here's your five back."

Darby gives me a look that makes me wish I hadn't said anything.

"No," she says, "I'm done playing games with you."

Darby goes to close the door but then leans in.

"You know what? I'm not even mad at you, Boone. You are who you are. That's not anything I can get angry at. But it's sad. You're sad. And I can't be around you."

Darby closes the door and walks into her house without looking back. That was my second chance with her. There won't a third. That's the cost of selling the lie.

I pull back onto the road, feeling as low and shitty as I possibly can. Maybe I *am* my father. Maybe I can't change. What are you supposed to do when you come to that terrible realization? I drive aimlessly for a while, then head for Garbage Mountain. Who knows how much longer it'll even be there? Add The Mountain's impending doom to how things went tonight, and I'm pretty sure the night can't get any worse.

That's when Ink sends a text proving how wrong I can be.

Come to The H. You need to see this.

CHAPTER 19

On Full Tilt

In poker, being "on tilt" means playing recklessly after a series of bad losses or hands. Players on tilt make stupid, emotional decisions that never work out, usually leading to them losing even more money. That's the best way to explain why I'm sitting in The Destroyer outside Parker Briggs' McMansion in Batesville's only gated community. I'm on full tilt, and have been ever since talking to Ink last night. What's worse is that even though I'm aware what I'm about to do is stupid, I'm doing it anyway.

Tonight, Parker is throwing a party he invited me and Darby to, so it's not the best time to come. But I had to work all day, and ruining a party might help my mood. I sent Darby a text that I needed to talk to her about what I'd learned from Ink, but she didn't respond. She also didn't show up to work her family's booth. It's likely she'll find a way to never see me again.

The Briggs' driveway isn't paved in gold like you'd expect, and the bushes aren't sculpted into dollar signs, but the doorbell has a loud, echo-y *bong* that announces "Rich people live here" for anyone who still needs convincing. If I remember right, there are six bathrooms in the place, each with its own private phone line. Still, it's really just your average three-story, four-car garage, foreign sports car in the driveway, $2.7 million house. Rumor has next year they're downsizing to the Taj Mahal.

I wait a solid thirty seconds before a girl in a yellow tank top and white tennis skirt appears the foyer. I rap my knuckles on the glass, and she stops and looks up at the ceiling. I knock again, and she does a full 360. Finally, after my third assault on the glass, this time with my keys, she squints at the door and shrieks an "Oh!" that's so high-pitched that dogs for miles are probably having spasms. She stumble-bounces her way to the door and spends a confusing minute giggling her way around the locks. It's probably a good thing Darby isn't here.

"Pizza guy?" she asks.

I glance down at my empty hands.

"I sure am," I say. "Where do you want them?"

Her wobbly head turns first, followed by her body, and then she's staggering through the foyer. Parker's house is just as I remember it—cavernous, sterile, and uncomfortable. All you'd need to make this place a museum are velvet ropes and an old security guard asleep in the corner.

At the back of the house, the girl opens a door unleashing an atomic blast of noise and music. In most houses this would be called a basement, but here it's another house entirely where Parker spends most of his time. Tonight, the basement's been transformed into a mini-casino, furnished with all the table games you might see in Las Vegas—blackjack, roulette, three-card poker, and craps. There's even a bank of six slot machines along the back wall, ringing and jingling over the crowd noise. So gambling, free drinks, and good-looking girls—it's possible I died on the drive over and this is heaven.

I spot Parker near the roulette table, where he's glad-handing everyone like a mini-version of his dad. Parker's wearing a black and white tuxedo, complete with an unfortunate top hat making him look like a life-sized Monopoly guy. He sees me and smiles, clapping the back of the guy he's talking to in a see-you-later way before coming over.

"Nice hat," I say.

"It's my party hat."

"It's something, all right."

Parker laughs and holds out a hand and we shake. I'll have to soak mine in gasoline later.

"Good turnout," I say. "Are your parents hiding?"

"Mom's off on a girls' vacation. Dad's upstairs. Did Darby come with you?"

"I'm flying solo tonight," I say. "Actually, I have a little business to discuss. Is there someplace we can talk?"

"Why am I not surprised?" Parker says. "Come on."

We weave through the crowd, which is made up of a combination of kids I recognize and those I don't. Near the stairs, I spot the two Darby and I saw going at it in the Moonville tunnel. Tonight, they're grinding to the music like they're trying to repopulate a dying planet. Oh, to be young and in love.

I follow Parker through a door into a room that's a different world than the one we just left. This is much more "rich man's hideaway" with a long oak bar on one end, a TV the size of a drive-in movie screen, vintage pinball machines, and furniture that could finance a four-year degree at an Ivy League school. A nice cloud of pot haze hangs in the air across the room where Marlana Hobbs holds court from a love seat surrounded by Batesville High's ruling class.

"Who invited him?" Marlana says.

"It's good to see you too," I say.

"Not working at the dirt mall tonight?"

"Dirt mall—that's actually pretty funny."

"I don't mean it to be funny."

Marlana's hot in a too-much-makeup kind of way, and along with a shiny party outfit that probably costs more than our monthly rent, she's wearing a tiara with "Princess" on it. Flashforward twenty years and Marlana's internet famous after being recorded shouting at a store employee who's refused to pierce the ears of Marlana's four-day-old daughter. She's tolerated me over the years because of my onetime friendship with Parker, but once we bought Garbage Mountain, she made her dislike of me clear. She holds it in mostly, though, because I once privately pointed out to her that her name spelled backward is "Anal Ram." You have to love anagrams.

Parker says, "Let's talk at the bar. What are you drinking?"

"Thanks, I'm good."

"You're good?"

"Habit-breaking's my new habit."

"Same old Boone."

Parker pours something gold from one of the dozens of bottles, and we take seats at the end of the bar. A smaller TV in the corner shows a soccer match, but the teams are only identified by their country's flag, so I have no idea who's playing. God bless the geography education of the American teenager.

"So what's up?" Parker says.

I pull my phone from my pocket and pull up the video file Ink forwarded me last night while we sat at a table in The H. I shouldn't be showing Parker this, but like I said, I'm on tilt. The video's in color, but because it's nighttime and the parking lot is flooded with fluorescents, everything has a dark tint to it.

"This is the security cam footage from the Megamall last week when $15,000 of Golden Mountain money was stolen from my car," I say. "That's me coming out of the building with Leyla, the girl who took it."

We watch as I walk an unsteady line toward The Destroyer with Leyla in her black and white striped tights. We stand at the back passenger door longer than would be expected, probably because I'm drunk and fumbling with my keys. Then finally, I open and door and climb inside and shut the door. Leyla then comes around to the driver's side, opens the front door, and disappears inside before coming out fifteen seconds later.

"That's the money pouch in her hand," I say.

Parker doesn't move as we watch the video. We both know what's coming. A car six rows over turns its headlights on, then pulls alongside Leyla. She gets in the passenger side before the car drives away, and the video ends.

"And that's your car," I say.

Parker smiles thinly.

"Almost a clean getaway," he says.

I've wanted to hit Parker for the last twenty hours, but now that the perfect time has arrived, I'm not interested. Punching him won't make me feel better. Only ruining him will do that.

"Why did you do it?" I say.

"Why do you do what you do?"

"What are you, a philosophy professor? Just answer the question."

"You're the one who wants answers, not me. Play along, Boone. Why do you do it?"

Scratch that—maybe punching him *would* make me feel better.

"Darby and I talked about this last night," I say. "Cons are something I'm good at, but lately I'm only doing them to people who deserve it."

"That's exactly what I'm doing," Parker says.

"You can't be serious."

"I'm totally serious. I took money from someone who deserved to lose it."

"Me?"

"Yes, you," Parker says. "Boone, you scam people out of their money. That makes you a bad guy. Maybe not to yourself, but definitely to your marks. You justify it by saying they deserve it. But it's still wrong."

"But you did the same thing to me."

"I did, but I'm not sitting here trying to make myself out to be innocent. That's where we differ. Besides, it's just business."

"You stole $15,000 from me, someone you know. That's not business; that's personal."

"We see things the way we want to see them."

"I still don't understand why you took the money," I say. "It's not like you need it."

"You're right. I don't need the money," he says. "Do you really want to know why I took it?"

"I wouldn't have asked."

"Then come on."

I follow Parker as we leave the rich man's bunker and fight the party crowd to get back upstairs. We pass a bathroom, and I say, "Give me a second," and head inside to do some business and calm myself down. When I come out, I say, "So who's Leyla?"

Parker laughs. "Leyla. That's funny," he says. "I made up that name for her. I figured you'd like that one. And how she was dressed. You're pretty predictable."

"Who is she?"

"A girl from Asheville who drank too much here one night and said she'd do anything if I didn't share the pictures I took of her."

"I never pegged you as a blackmailer," I say.

"I make use of the tools available to me."

It's too bad Darby isn't here for this. It'd be nice to witness Parker's legs torn from his body. We head down the back hallway toward a closed door. Parker knocks and waits before opening it. Cullen Briggs sits with his feet up on an oak desk, a copy of Donald Trump's *Art of the Deal* in his hands.

"Boys!" he says. "Is your party so boring you have to come to me for entertainment?"

"The party's fine, Dad," Parker says. "Boone wanted to talk to you."

"I did?"

"Go ahead," Parker says to me. "Tell him what you came here to talk to me about."

"Sure, have a seat, Boone. Like I said the other day, I've missed having you around."

I sit down across from Mr. Briggs. He's smiling at me, but now that I know what Parker's capable of, I don't see any friendliness in it. As you know, I'm a big believer that apples don't fall far from the tree. But maybe I'm wrong. I tell Mr. Briggs about the missing money, Parker's role in it, and the video I have. The entire time I'm talking, Mr. Briggs sits with teepeed fingers. He doesn't take his eyes off me until I finish, and then it's to look at Parker.

"I'm guessing this is all true?" he says.

"It is," Parker says.

"What did you do with the money?"

"It's in my safe deposit box at the bank."

Mr. Briggs nods and turns back to me.

"So what can I do for you, Boone?"

"Well, telling him to give me the money back would be a start," I say.

"I can have him do that," Mr. Briggs says. "But probably not in the way you're hoping."

"What do you mean?"

"I'm sure you know all about the business conversations your mom and I have been having?"

I nod.

"When she agrees to sell, the money you lost to my son will be part of my payment to her when I buy the property."

"But it's that stolen money that's forcing her to have to sell," I say.

"And while I may not fully agree with what my son did—too many risks involved—I have to give him credit for creativity. I told him it was time to play a more active role in the family business, and that's what he did. Nice work, son."

"Thanks, Dad," Parker says.

"Wow, this is one screwed-up family," I say.

"You would know screwed-up families," Parker says to me.

"I do, but the difference is I'm not screwing mine up even more by trying to impress someone who's part of the problem."

"No, the difference is your dad's in jail, and mine's right here. And I don't think you can stand that."

Mr. Briggs gets up from his chair.

"Enough, boys," he says. "Boone, I know you don't like any of this, but maybe try to see it from a different perspective. In a way, Parker did everyone a favor. He's speeding up the inevitable. Your mom was going to lose the business anyway, and this allows her to move on with her life faster than she would have if she continued trying to keep Golden Mountain alive. After we buy her out, the two of you can stop worrying about money, and I get what I want. Everyone wins."

"You're not going to get away with this," I say, and feel immediately stupid as soon as the bad movie line comes out of my mouth.

"Of course we are, Boone. What proof do you have? A low-quality video? You can't go to the police with that. They'd laugh you out of the building," he says. "If I were you, I'd look at the big picture. I'm going over in a day or two to make one final offer, and your mom will take it. She's a smart businesswoman. In fact, there's a good chance I'll offer her a position. I like having the best people under me."

Parker chuckles, and I have to fight the urge to go over the desk at Mr. Briggs.

"Now, you boys should get back to your party, if there's nothing else," he says.

There is nothing else.

The money's gone.

Darby's gone.

Soon Golden Mountain will be gone.

And there's nothing I can do about any of it.

CHAPTER 20

Darby in All Her Violent Glory

"Okay, the game's called Nim," I say. "Here's how you play."

I'm sitting at the bar in The Underground holding seventeen pennies. On the stool next to me is my accomplice for the night. Before I tell you who it is, you're about to lose whatever respect you still had for me. But in my defense, Mo and Arlo are busy tonight, Darby's out of the picture, and doing this will save me a beating. Desperate times call for desperate measures, and all that baloney. So, yeah, I'm with Gompers. Feel free to call me pathetic. I won't argue.

I spread the pennies out in a cluster on the bar. Gompers and I practiced the game earlier, so he doesn't need to hear the rules. But they're not for him. They're for whatever sucker decides he wants to play too, and The Underground is full of them tonight. Everyone's inexplicably here to watch the four-piece onstage that's made up of two keyboardists, a bassist, and a drummer. They're attempting to play upbeat dance music but are only succeeding in making the crowd jerk back and forth like it's suffering a group seizure.

"On your turn, you're going to either take one, two, or three pennies," I say. "Then it'll be my turn to take one, two, or three pennies. The way you win the game is to have the other guy be the one who takes the last penny. If you're the one to take it, you lose."

"Sounds simple," Gompers says.

"It is. Want to play for five bucks?"

Gompers puts a wad of crumpled ones on the bar. I have Darby's five on me, but I won't use it. Call me an optimist. Instead, I take a different five from my wallet and put it beside Gompers' money. We play a few games straight, the two of us exchanging wins. I order us beers from the bartender, who looks like he spends his off hours prowling the city in a van with "Free Candy" spray-painted on its side. The cans he gives us are so warm he must've been sitting on them earlier. When a guy steps up behind us, Gompers and I ignore him and play another round, this time with him winning.

"What are you doing?" the guy says.

I get a good look at the guy and then wish I hadn't. He has a snake tattoo wrapped around his neck and long hair that's so oily he must shower in Valvoline. Flashforward twenty years and he's nineteen years into a life sentence for murder. This isn't the mark we want, but Gompers apparently doesn't fear death as much as I do.

"Playing this stupid game," Gompers tells him. "Sit down. I'll show you."

The guy takes a seat beside Gompers and tells us his name is Randy. Gompers does a surprisingly concise and accurate explanation of the rules, only dropping the F-bomb three times in his instructions. He then challenges me to a game and asks if I want to go first or second.

"Second," I say, and Gompers takes away three of the seventeen pennies.

I take one.

Gompers takes two.

I take two, leaving nine pennies.

Gompers takes three.

I take one.

And now Gompers is screwed. There are five pennies left. Any number he takes gives me the ability to leave him one penny, which means he loses. He takes two pennies leaving me three. I take two. Gompers is stuck with the last penny.

"Goddammit," he says.

"The game's not so hard," Randy says. "You just screwed up."

"Where?"

"In the beginning. I'll show you. Five bucks, right?"

I tell him sure, and then we're off.

Here's the trick to winning Nim. If you let the other person go first, you can't lose. Any number of pennies they take, you take an amount adding up to four. If you start with seventeen pennies like we did, and you make sure four pennies go away each round, you'll end up leaving the last penny for the other guy.

I don't do this, though.

Even though he chooses to go first, guaranteeing me the win, I take pennies in such a way that in the end, I'm stuck with the loss. He gloats by grinning at me with mossy teeth that haven't felt a toothbrush's love in years.

"See?" Randy says to Gompers. "Easy."

"Double or nothing?" I say.

"Sure," he says. "You go first this time."

This is where a little cheating's involved. If you want to win Nim when you go first, have a penny hidden in your hand. On your turn, pretend to take one penny from the pile. Now the pile is still at seventeen pennies, and it's the guy's turn. Then, like before, you just follow his lead and take the number of pennies so each round adds up to four. You can't lose. But I do anyway on purpose. I'm letting him win to build his confidence. It's called baiting the hook.

"Crap," I say. "Again?"

"Hell yeah," Randy says. "Want to make it ten bucks?"

A minute later, I'm down another ten.

"I think I figured it out," I say.

"Sure you did," Gompers says.

"Again?" I say to Randy.

"How about for real money?"

Usually, it takes a while to get to this point, and some back and forth on losses with the mark, but he's making it easy for us tonight. It's nice when the con gods smile upon you.

"Sure," I tell him. "What are you thinking?"

"Fifteen hundred?" he says.

And other times the con gods don't just smile upon you, but they hand you the dumbest mark on the planet.

"Holy shit," Gompers says.

"That's a lot more than I was thinking," I say to Randy.

"You don't have it?"

"Well, I do because I got paid today, but I can't lose it."

"But you said you'd figured the game out," Gompers says.

"I did, but I'm not going to bet big money like that."

"But if you figured it out, you'll win big money," Gompers says.

"Yeah, come on," Randy says. "To win big, you have to bet big. Don't be a wuss."

I don't need to push this any further. Randy's a fish on the hook. He's dreaming of big money, and I'm about to double what I've brought in for Golden Mountain. It may be too late to stop a Briggs takeover, but with $3,000, I might be able to do pull out a miracle.

"Okay," I say. "Fifteen hundred. But let me see your money first."

"You don't trust me?" Randy says.

"I don't trust anyone."

Randy laughs and, after pulling out a Velcro wallet with a bulldog on it, fans out fifteen $100 bills. I match his money, and we both agree to let Gompers hold it for us.

"You want to go first or second?"

"It doesn't matter to me," Randy says. "You pick."

I choose first because there's just something satisfying about winning a bunch of money from palming a penny. And it just so happens I pulled one out of my wallet when I took out the cash. It's safely hidden in my fist as I reach for the pile of pennies.

"I'll take one," I say, and reach into the cluster, only pulling out the one penny already in my hand. Now we're still at seventeen pennies, and all I have to do is go in groups of four all the way down until he's stuck with one.

"I'll take one," Randy says.

"Three for me," I say.

He takes one.

I take three to end the round at four pennies taken.

He takes one, again.

I take a swig of beer, barely paying any attention because I know how this is going to end. It's actually a good thing I have Gompers here with me because once this beast realizes he's lost, he's going to be pissed.

"Three," I say.

"Tough luck," he says, and smiles at me so hard I know something's terribly wrong. I look down at the pennies left, and my body goes hot. By my count there should be five pennies left, but there are six.

"I'll take one," he says, leaving me with five.

There's nothing I can do. Whatever I do, he'll take the number of pennies that adds up to four, leaving me with one. I have no idea in hell how this happened.

"Go," he says.

I take two, hoping he'll screw up, but of course he doesn't.

"Two," he says.

Leaving me the final penny.

He says to Gompers, "My money."

My head's ready to explode. I do a quick count of the pennies on the bar. Counting the penny I palmed, there should be eighteen. But there aren't. There are nineteen. And it doesn't take me long to realize what happened—he palmed a penny too.

"My money," he says again.

Gompers looks at me, unsure what to do. I don't know either. I can't accuse Randy of cheating because he probably knows I did too.

"How about double or nothing?" I say.

"Do you have the cash to cover a bet like that?" Randy asks, and when I shake my head, he says again, "So my money. Now."

Gompers does the only thing he can.

"Nice doing business with you," Randy says, and walks away with my $1,500.

"What the hell happened?" Gompers whispers me.

"He cheated," I say.

"How in the hell didn't you catch him?"

"I wasn't paying attention. I thought I had him."

"Well, you didn't, dumbass," Gompers says, standing up. "Jesus, McReedy, you're such a goddamn loser."

I haven't felt this nauseous since I discovered the money gone from The Destroyer, which was only a week ago. I see a terrible pattern forming. There's only one thing to do in a situation like this—get hammered. I order another beer and try not to think about how everything's gone down the toilet in less than twenty-four hours. I down the beer, order another, and spot a girl on the other side of the room who, from her scowl and hunched shoulders, looks like she's having just as bad a life as I am. When I catch her eye, her sneer only grows. The two of us are going to get along beautifully.

I buy two more beers and take them over to Miss I-Hate-Everyone. She takes my peace offering without a thank-you, and we stand and watch the embarrassing display onstage. So many things make this girl not my type—her looks, her attitude, her cigarette smell—but I'm not picky tonight, and she doesn't seem to searching for Mr. Right either.

Over the music she shouts, "What's your name?"

"Lance. Lance Steele."

"Shut up."

"No, really, I'm an international model."

"Uh-huh. And I'm the next queen of England."

"Well, Your Highness-To-Be, should we try to dance to this noise?"

She grabs my hand, and we join the small crowd in front of the stage. The music never gets any better, but I don't care. We drink, dance, drink more, and jump around like we're trying to bounce our heads off the ceiling. Then the girl looks at me in that special way that says *Kiss-me-you-sexy-god*, which is exactly what I should do.

But I can't.

Because I know I shouldn't.

"What's wrong?" she says.

"Sorry," I say, and walk off.

She calls me a jerk, which I am, but not as much as I would be if I'd kissed her. I may be a loser. I may have lost Garbage Mountain. And I may have lost Darby too. But I'm not someone who acts this way. At least I'm trying not to be.

I'm heading for the exit when I see Randy walking into the bathroom. And guess who's following right behind him? Gompers.

I see it all then, exactly what happened tonight and how. Feel free to add *idiot* to my list of stellar qualities. I enter the bathroom just as Randy is handing Gompers his share of the take.

"Let me guess," I say when they look at me. "You met at the same MENSA meeting?"

"You're the idiot who fell for it," Gompers says. "Now you know how I felt."

"I do. So how about we call it even and you give me my money back?"

"Get lost, Boone."

"What if I beg?" I say. "I've gotten really good at it by listening to your mom beg to me."

This is why I should never drink.

Gompers punches me in the stomach, doubling me over. The beers I've guzzled almost reappear on his shoes.

"That's the best you can do, Gompers?"

This is the very definition of self-hatred.

Gompers watches me with eyes that are half-angry, half-confused. When he doesn't throw another punch, I throw a lazy right that has no chance of landing. Gompers steps back, shaking his head.

"You started all of this, Boone. Remember that."

This time his punch is higher, hitting me in the chest right about where my heart is. I've heard of pitchers getting hit by a baseball in the chest at exactly the wrong time and dying. Unfortunately, that doesn't happen to me.

"Nice one," Randy says. "Kick his ass."

The next blow is a shot to the side of my head rocketing me into the piss-wet bathroom stall. A buzzsaw rings in my ears, drowning out the electronic music nightmare happening outside. Gompers squats down beside me and grabs the back of my shirt, hefting me up. I'm on my knees before my beer-addled mind realizes what he's about to do.

"I'm done," I say.

"Too late for that."

Gompers forces my head toward the toilet. I fight against the oncoming shit shampoo, but Gompers has leverage, and there's no way I can hold on long. Really, there's something poetic about it—all of this started with the two of us in a bathroom, and now it's going to end with him killing me in one.

I try to stand, but he punches the back of my head with his free hand. My vision supernovas. I'm holding on to the edge of the toilet, my elbows locked, but it's no use. As Randy cheers Gompers on, my face is inches away from the stagnant cesspool. The smell is so bad I'm gagging hard. Gompers puts all of his weight on my back now. I'm a goner. I shut my eyes and mouth and pray the afterlife is kind to me.

Then, from behind us, a crash.

Gompers lets up a bit, but I can't turn my head.

Randy shouts, "No, wait!" followed by another crash.

Gompers says, "Huh?" and the two of us are yanked backward. I'm out of the stall lying on my back.

The first thing I see is Gompers next to me.

The second is Randy dazed against the wall.

The third is Darby standing over all of us.

She holds out her open hand to me and raises her eyebrows.

"You're charging me?" I say.

"You know the price."

I try to stand, but my legs wobble. I give Darby her five from my spot on the floor. Gompers gets up and takes a threatening step toward her.

"Back off, Billy," Darby says.

"Screw you," he says. "He had it coming."

"He's had enough."

"I'll kick both of your asses. I don't give a shit."

Gompers takes another step at Darby. Randy's on his feet now and, unsatisfied with just one beating tonight, comes up beside Gompers. I really should get up, but the beer won't let me. Gompers and Randy each take a step forward. They don't get any closer.

Darby's a blur—a whirling, spinning tornado of fists and feet. Her eyes are wide and wild as she kicks and hits, smashing Gompers and Randy repeatedly, bloodying their faces and bruising their bodies. They groan and whimper and plead over the keyboards and drums screaming away onstage. I'm witnessing something primal, something supernatural. I've never seen Darby in full action before, but what's happening in front of me is a ballet of brutality. Every moment is controlled and calculated. Darby isn't Darby anymore; she's something else, something animalistic and evolved. When she stops moving, she's barely breathing hard as she stands over Gompers and Randy, who groan and twitch on the floor. I've never seen anything so savage and terrifying and beautiful.

"Wow," I say, struggling to my feet. "You totally fight like a girl."

Darby, looking positively maniacal, says, "You're goddamn right I do."

CHAPTER 21

Dad Justifies His Existence

Ten minutes later, Darby and I are sitting on the curb outside the Megamall. My body aches in ways it never has before. Across the dark parking lot, cars on the highway speed away from Batesville. Too bad I'm not in one of them.

"Well, you wanted to see me get beaten up," I say. "Was is it everything you dreamed it would be?"

"I don't have the sense of satisfaction I thought I would have. But I do reserve the right to ask Gompers if hitting you was as wonderful as I've imagined."

"That's fair," I say. "And who knows? You might still get your chance to hit me."

"A girl can dream."

The door opens behind us, and two people laughing and talking and holding hands walk past us. Oh, to have a simple life.

"I thought you were done with me," I say.

"I should be."

"But?"

"I told you—I'm working on forgiveness."

"I'd think you'd want to start somewhere easier than me."

"I like to make things as difficult as possible for myself."

Darby's rubbing her knuckles, which are red and scuffed from playing superhero. Beyond that, there's not a mark on her. I can't say the same for myself.

"You hurt me, Boone. You broke rules that were important to me."

"I know. I'm sorry."

"Trust is everything with me. Even admitting that to you was hard. My parents have lied to me so many times I have a hard time believing anybody. And then you went and ran a con behind my back after promising me you wouldn't."

"Because—"

"No, let me talk," Darby says. "I know why you did it. You told me. In fact, a part of me even understands your thinking and on some level agrees with it. That's not the issue. What is the issue is you did it without telling me. That's the lying I'm talking about."

"It was more a lie by omission."

"But it's still a lie, and I get why you didn't tell me—you figured I would have talked you out of it, which maybe I would have. At least it would have been a decision we made together. Instead, you didn't trust me enough to let me in. But that's what partners do. That's what people in relationships do. They trust each other."

As much as my body aches and how exhausted I am, I feel worse about letting Darby down like I did. This guilt's been nonstop from the second I started The Grandparent Gouge. Like I've said, the con itself is terrible, but betraying Darby's even more rotten.

"I should have told you," I say. "I mean, I did tell you, but only after."

"Oh, believe me, the only reason I'm here is because you told me. If you hadn't and I'd found out by myself what you were doing, you'd probably be dead in that toilet right now."

"Well, thanks for not letting that happen," I say. "How did you even know I'd be here?"

"Where else would you be?"

"I'm that predictable?"

"Just like I knew you'd let me down when we first teamed up."

"I can't promise I won't do it again."

"Believe me, I know," she says.

"But I'm trying."

"That's probably the other reason I'm here—you're trying. Most people don't."

"And most people aren't as irresistible as I am."

"Keep it up," Darby says. "I can always take you back to Gompers."

We sit in the peace and quiet. Darby rubs her knuckles while I pretend my ribs and face aren't one giant exposed nerve. A few people walk past us on their way out of the Megamall. Either the show's over or they could only take so much bad electronica, which is pretty much a redundant phrase.

"I shouldn't have said you're exhausting," I say. "You're not at all."

"And you're not sad," she says. "You are infuriating, though."

"It's a skill I've honed over my seventeen years."

"You should teach seminars."

Darby takes out her phone and taps it against her leg.

"You sent a bunch of texts I ignored. Some of them you marked 'Urgent.'"

"They were," I say, "but I'm not sure they are anymore."

"What happened?"

I fill her in on Ink's video and how Parker admitted to the con. I barely get into the story before Darby's on her feet.

"We're going to the police," she says.

"It's pointless. You haven't seen the video. The quality sucks and it really doesn't prove anything. Nothing the police could act on anyway."

"Who says?"

"Roadie."

"Well, he would know," she says, sitting back down. "We'll just have to figure something out. It's what we're good at, right?"

"It might not be easy," I say. "I sort of did something stupid. I told Parker and his dad I'd be coming for them."

"Of course you did."

"I was having a bad day."

"That's the story of your life," Darby says. "What's our total?"

"A thousand, give or take," I say.

"Plus this."

Darby hands me the $1,500 I lost to Randy. I don't have to ask what the red spots on it are. It brings our total to $2,500, well short of the $15,000 lost.

"I took it from him while you were washing up," she says. "He didn't argue."

"Probably because he was too busy trying to stop the blood pouring out of his nose."

"Don't forget his mouth and ears."

"I'll be seeing that in my nightmares for the next decade," I say. "I want you to know I shut down The Grandparent Gouge."

"I thought you would."

"I returned the money too."

"Good. So what are we going to do?"

"I'm not exactly sure, but I have an idea of where to start."

"Wait. Before you tell me," Darby says, "I need you to promise we're going to do this together. All of it. Every decision, every play, we do it together."

"I can do that."

"Promise me."

"I promise."

"Good," she says. "Now what's your idea?"

Which is how Darby and I end up in the visitation room at Perrysburg Correctional the next day. Dad's black eye is now a yellowish-purple that will match nicely with his orange jumpsuit if there's a prison costume party and he goes as a rainbow. The three of us are at a small round table near the Coke machine. I'm not as nervous as I usually am because there's safety in numbers and I've now witnessed Darby's protective abilities firsthand.

"You brought a date to the prison?" Dad says.

"She's more like moral support," I say. "This is Darby."

"I know you, right?" Dad says to her. "From The Mountain."

"My aunt and uncle own Ancient Artifacts."

"I see the resemblance to your aunt. She's quite a striking woman."

Darby turns to me.

"Now I see where you get it," she says.

"Like there was any question," I say.

My body still throbs from my beating, but nothing like it did. Thankfully, my face isn't bruised up because I don't need any more similarities to my dad. Darby says the pain will go away eventually. I know I could kill it with beer, but after last night it's going to be a long, long time before I drink again.

"So what brings you two out?" Dad says. "Knowing Boone, I'm guessing it's not to announce your engagement."

"We're here on business," I say.

Dad's eyebrows twitch. It's the same thing that would happen when we'd be out and he'd spot a mark.

"If it's business, then what's in it for me?"

"Helping your family? Personal redemption?" I say.

"I'm going to need something a little more concrete."

Darby sighs. She's lucky she's never had to witness the Thomas McReedy Show. It's too bad she has to witness it at all.

"How about twenty dollars in your commissary account?" I say.

"Make it fifty, and we can get started."

"Deal," I say, and we shake. "So you know, I was willing to go to a hundred."

"You lowballed me knowing I'd have to take it. Nicely done," he says. "Tell me the situation."

I explain to him the how and why of Parker setting me up, my confronting him, and how Cullen Briggs laughed it off when he found out. Dad listens the whole time, getting more annoyed the longer I talk. It's a good thing I don't include Gompers setting me up last night or Dad's whole face would swallow itself.

"Wow, you've really screwed this whole thing up," he says.

"Believe me, I know."

"I mean, falling for the con is bad enough, but then talking to him about it—"

"That's not why we're here," Darby says, cutting him off.

"But he's my son, and I—"

"No, you said this is business, and you're getting paid," she says. "We're here for solutions, not criticism."

Dad actually shuts up at this. This is why I brought Darby.

"Fine," he says. "If you want my advice, I think you run everything you've got against anyone you can—the Briggses, their boothers, their customers. All of them. It's the only way."

"The boothers and customers didn't do anything to us," I say.

"They're guilty by association. That's what matters. Do you want to get back at these people and save The Mountain, or don't you? Because that's what it's going to take."

"We're not doing that," I say. "We want ideas on how to take down the Briggses. They're our marks. No one else."

"You're being shortsighted. You need to send a message. If you don't, people are never going to take The Mountain seriously. You want my advice, go after all of them. It's what I would do."

"But he's not you," Darby says. "So do what we're paying you to do."

"Oh, I like her," Dad says to me.

"Just what every woman wants to hear from a convict," Darby says.

"Scratch that," Dad says. "I like her a lot."

"Great," I say. "Now do you have any ideas for us?"

Dad leans back and stares at the ceiling. I could have brought The Scam List, but he wouldn't need it. His brain is an encyclopedia of cons, mostly short ones, and bar bets. There are also long cons in there, but we don't have the time to run those.

"There's a lot working against you," he says. "Your ages, your looks, the fact that they know you and how you'll be gunning for them. It's an impossible task."

"We know that," I say. "It's why we came to you."

"In a situation like this, there's only one thing you can do. I mean, if they know you're coming…"

He waits.

It takes me a while, but then I get it. I don't know why I didn't think of it myself. Then again, I'm sort of happy I didn't. It's just another way we're different.

"I've never run anything like that," I say. "It's way too complicated."

"There isn't anything else you can do," he says.

He's right.

"And the specifics?" I say.

"You'll have to come up with those yourself. You know the details. I don't. You know the players too. And I think you've got a good partner here to help you work everything out."

He's right again. Together, Darby and I can get our money back from the Briggses. I just needed to be pointed in the right direction.

"Are you ready?" I say to her.

"If you are."

We get up while Dad remains seated.

"I'm glad to know I can still be helpful," he says.

"Yeah, you're Father of the Year."

"Probably not, but maybe in the top hundred finalists?"

"Make it the top five hundred."

"I can live with that," he says. "You'll let me know how it works out?"

"You bet."

We leave him behind in the visiting room, and when the door closes behind us, Darby says, "You are so not him."

"That's nice to hear from an impartial party."

"I'm not exactly impartial," she says.

"But you also don't hide the truth."

We stop by the commissary where I deposit fifty dollars into his account. Then it's back to processing, where we're given back our phones and the keys to The Destroyer. It's not until we're in the car where we have privacy that we get down to business.

"We're going to have to run a Kansas City Shuffle," I say.

"I don't remember that in The Scam List."

"It's not in there. It's more a concept than an actual con."

It takes me five minutes to explain the idea of a Kansas City Shuffle to Darby and how we can use it to get our money back.

"How are we going to pull something like that off?"

"I'm not sure," I say, "but I do know one thing—we're going to need to use all the tools available to us."

CHAPTER 22

Selling My Biggest Lie Ever

Three days later in her office at Garbage Mountain, Mom and I have a sit-down with Parker and his dad. Mr. Briggs arrives all smiles, shaking our hands like we're all good friends, while Parker's smirk has me fantasizing about digging his embedded teeth out of my knuckles. But I'm excited about what's about to happen, and if it's any clue, I'm chewing gum. Once phony pleasantries are exchanged, the four of us take seats around the termite-gnawed conference table Mom brought in just for this occasion from booth forty-one's Next Stop, The Dump.

"I'm happy we're finally doing this, Liann," Mr. Briggs says. "You've had a nice run here. We'll do our best to take care of the place."

"I'm sure you would, Cullen, but that's not exactly why I've asked you here."

"It isn't?"

Parker shoots me a look, and I give him my *I-know-something-you-don't-know* wink and smile.

"Boone filled me in on recent events I wasn't aware of," Mom says. "And without getting into awkward specifics or pointing fingers, I want you to know I'm angry. There's business, there's personal, and then there's criminal. What was done to us falls into the criminal category. We may not be able to prove it happened, but I want you to at least acknowledge we've been wronged."

Mr. Briggs hesitates just long enough that I can tell Mom's shaken him.

"I'm not happy with how things went down," he says, "but I think we both know neither of our children is perfect. You know as well as I do we're only responsible for our own actions. What other people choose to do is up to them. I've spoken to Parker about what he did, and I'm happy with his version of the events."

"That's not really what I'm looking for," Mom says.

"But it's what I'm willing to give you. You're a clever family. Who knows? Maybe you're recording this and are hoping for an admission of guilt."

"That would be clever, yes, but you're giving me more credit than I deserve," Mom says. "I'm just looking for recognition that we're the injured party here. It makes the possible sale of Golden Mountain more tolerable knowing its failure isn't entirely my fault."

"I can concede that," Mr. Briggs says. "And for what it's worth, I'm sorry."

"Thank you, Cullen," Mom says. "That's all I'm asking for."

I feel bad for Mom. None of this is an act. She's poured years of her life into Golden Mountain, and now she's facing its end. In our planning for today, there was no mention by her of asking Briggs for an apology. Of course, knowing Mom, it's possible that getting any sort of admission from him, no matter how lame, would help her justify to herself what she's about to do.

"I've decided you're right," she says, "it's time for me to sell Golden Mountain."

At this, both Parker and his dad smile hard.

"But before I do that, I'd like one final hurrah, a chance to prove to myself that on a level playing field, I could have beaten you."

Both of their smiles fade.

"What do you have in mind?" Briggs says.

"I propose a contest," Mom says, "a one-day event to see whose business can bring in the most money."

"And when I win?" Briggs says, smiling.

"I'll agree to sell you Golden Mountain," Mom says. "But when I win, you compensate us for the loss of our $15,000. We can call it a charitable deed—just one business helping another during a rough time."

"Why would I agree to a contest when Golden Mountain is going to close down soon enough anyway? I'll just wait until the bank forecloses, and then snatch this place up."

Mom nods, saying, "You could absolutely do that. But you're taking a great risk assuming Golden Mountain will be available."

"Why wouldn't it be?"

"Because I have another interested buyer, and if you don't agree to the contest, I'll sell to them."

"Who's the buyer? What's his name?"

"It's a her," Mom says, "and her name is none of your business. I will tell you, however, she's offered me less money than you. Far less. However, I'm ready to sell to her and take less money if you don't agree to my proposal."

Mr. Briggs stares at Mom, trying to get a read. She stares right back at him, her face showing nothing. A poker game between the two of them would be brutal.

"I think you're bluffing," Mr. Briggs says. "I don't think you have another buyer."

"Then turn me down and see what happens."

Mr. Briggs smiles and goes back to staring. Parker's fidgeting in his seat like he's sitting in poison ivy.

"Don't do this, Dad," he says. "They're up to something."

"He's right; we are up to something," Mom says. "I want a chance at beating you in sales just once and earning our missing money back. Think of it this way: It's a no-lose situation for both of us—regardless of who wins, we're both going to do great business that day, especially after the advertising we do."

"Advertising?" Mr. Briggs says.

"Of course," Mom says. "Both of us will have to promote it. It'll be the can't-miss event of the week. All of Batesville will turn out. They get to be part of something fun, and both of us make money. Everybody wins."

"What's the catch?" Mr. Briggs says.

"There's no catch," Mom says.

"Oh, there's a catch; I know that. We both know what Boone is capable of. Just the other day at my house, he threatened to ruin Treasure Palace. He's playing an angle here, and I want to know what it is."

"Boone?" Mom says.

I've said to sell the lie, you have to believe the lie. And before you can do that, you have to get into the right mindset so you don't break character. It's not an easy thing to do. I mean, it's easy for me, obviously, but for mortals it's hard. Regardless, though, I don't need the right mindset this time because this time I'm not selling the lie. No, this time, I have to sell the truth.

"Mr. Briggs, I swear to you I'm not pulling a con here. I know what I said to you the other day, but I was emotional at the time. I apologize for that. Mom and I have talked a lot since then, and she's made me see I can't be doing anything illegal. I want to do whatever possible to save this place, but I can't end up in jail like my dad. So I promise you I won't do anything illegal with this contest. No shutting down your building so you don't have any customers. No closing the road so people can't get to your place. No tricking your boothers into giving me their money. Nothing like that. I swear it. I'll even sign a contract if you want me to."

"What a load of crap," Parker says.

But it's not. All of it's true. Shocking, I know. Believe me, I'm as surprised as you.

"Boone's telling you the truth, Cullen," Mom says. "He gave me his word. I know he doesn't have a spotless record, but he's assured me he'll play the contest straight, and I believe him."

Mr. Briggs thinks for a moment and then nods.

"Well, even if I don't have the faith in him that you do, I see no downside to the contest," he says. "Even if you were to win, you'll still be out of business in six months, at which point I'll be there to buy this place. So I accept your challenge."

"You're not serious?" Parker says.

"Sometimes you have to just trust people, son," Mr. Briggs says.

"But that's exactly what Boone wants," Parker says.

He's right about that. I throw him a quick wink no one else sees. I'm no doctor, but the shade of red he turns can't be healthy. There's a quick discussion on rules, but really nothing worth talking about. It's all on the up and up. In the end, both Mom and Mr. Briggs agree to promote the event for Saturday and to come together in this office at the end of the day to report on what they've earned.

As they shake, Mr. Briggs says, "You know you won't win, right?"

"Maybe," Mom says, "but it'll be fun to try."

They spend some time discussing ways to promote the event, so Parker and I get up to leave. I may want to save the family business, but that doesn't mean I want to listen to actual business talk. I'd rather have to sit through accordion night at The Underground. On the way out, we hit the door at the same time, bumping into each other hard. The awkward tangle of bodies almost takes us to the floor.

"Same old Boone," he says.

"You go first," I say. "I forgot something anyway."

Parker exits, and I lag behind in the office before heading through the door again.

Back outside the office, I hand Parker his phone.

"You left this on the table," I say.

He snatches the phone from my hand, inspecting it.

"Jesus, I didn't break it or anything," I say. "Relax."

"I'm not stupid enough to relax around you."

He's gearing up for another attack on my stellar reputation when Darby marches up.

"Tell me you and your mom didn't do what I think you just did," she says to me.

"It was her call."

"But you were for it?"

"Yeah, but I—"

A thousand bees sting my face as Darby slaps me. It takes all of my strength not to lose my footing. Or not to start crying.

"I won't be involved in this."

"Darby—"

But she's already gone, stomping off down the aisle. I rub my cheek, but it's too raw. Next to me, Parker shakes his head.

"All of this is bullshit," he says, "even that fake scene right there. I'm not stupid. You're up to something, and I won't let it happen. Treasure Palace is a vault. We're going to win your dumb little contest."

"Whatever you say, man."

I wait until Parker's heading for the exit before I call his name. He stops and turns.

"A vault?" I say.

"Impenetrable," he says.

"Yeah, well, my people tell me the security at your place isn't nearly as strong as you think it is."

Parker's jaw dropping and the huff he expels as he walks off tells me all I need to know—I've successfully sold my lie.

CHAPTER 23

The Art of Inducing Paranoia

If you want to make someone paranoid, act suspicious. Be semi-successful, and they'll start pulling out chunks of hair. But if you're completely successful, they'll end up in a strait-jacket rocking back and forth in a rubber room. That's my goal for Parker, so today I'm standing in front of a dozen friends and Garbage Mountain boothers. In the Treasure Palace food court. Saying this:

"Today we're going to talk about pickpockets."

Parker's standing nearby trying to look calm and cool, but his bloodless face and hands jammed deep in his pockets give him away. I heard him tell the security guard beside him to toss us out if we do anything wrong. We're not stupid, though.

"Pickpockets are everywhere just waiting for an easy victim, so the easiest way to protect yourself is to never, under any cir-cumstances, keep anything in your back pocket," I say. "It's in-credibly easy to steal from someone's back pocket. Mo, will you come up here?"

Mo high-fives Arlo and works his way through the small crowd that's gathered to watch.

"Do you have anything in your back pocket?" I say.

"No," Mo says.

"Okay, do me a favor and put your phone back there."

While Mo transfers his phone from his front pocket to his back, I say to everyone, "This is a good time to mention the importance of setting a password on your home screen. If you don't, you're just asking for trouble. A pickpocket can do a lot of damage to an unlocked cell phone."

People in the crowd take their phones out and begin setting a screen lock. So does Parker. He watches me while he does it, and I can almost hear the gears grinding in his head. Something's wrong, but he doesn't know what it is. Or maybe nothing's wrong and I'm just messing with him. He's not sure. It sure is fun to watch.

"Now, Mo's got his phone in his back pocket," I say, and start backing him up to the onlookers. "If your wallet or phone is in your front pocket, it's almost impossible for someone to get a hand in there."

I've got Mo up against the crowd when I reach to pat down his front pockets. The two of us may have been friends since second grade, but he still flinches at my hands groping his groinal area. He smacks my hand away, and I step back in surrender.

"There's no way I could have taken anything from him," I say. "He'd either see me coming or would feel it. His back pocket, however, is another story. Mo, let me see your phone."

Mo reaches into his back pocket, but his hands come up empty.

"Where's my phone?" he says, laughing.

"Where, indeed?" I say. "Anyone?"

Arlo steps out of the crowd near Mo, holding his friend's phone. He hands it back and gets a middle finger in return.

"Most pickpockets work in teams," I say. "One to distract the mark, the other to do the lift. Sometimes you'll even see a team of three. The third person takes the item from the lifter and walks in the opposite direction. It really is a thing of beauty."

A woman in the crowd says, "Can someone do it by themselves?"

"Oh, it would take a pickpocket truly talented, truly gifted, to pull something off like that."

I smile at Parker then, and now he's feeling himself up, expecting to find his phone, wallet, or keys missing. Everything's there, though, at least as far as I know.

"You know, with everyone here like this, it would probably be a great time to practice protecting yourself. Why don't you team up in groups of three and work the scenario I showed you. That way you can see what it feels like when someone's trying to steal from you. I'll be around to help if you have questions."

The crowd breaks into groups without questioning me. I could get drunk on this power fast. Now I understand why people become teachers. You tell a bunch of dopes to do something, and they do it. What could be better?

I break off from the would-be pickpockets and walk over to Parker. Batesville girls may say he's the best-looking guy in the junior class, but if they could see him right now in all his splotchy glory, he'd drop out of the top ten.

"What the hell is all of this, Boone?"

I shrug and say, "We came over to check out the competition and support the local economy. Plus, I told them they absolutely had to try these cinnamon rolls. Is there anything wrong with that?"

"It looks like you're teaching them how to steal from people."

"Seriously? No, I'm doing the community a service. There are criminals everywhere."

"And you just happened to choose this place to run your seminar?"

"What can I say? You have to act when inspiration strikes. But look, man, I promise you this has nothing to do with Saturday. We're all here today as customers, nothing else. It's not like we're casing the joint."

"It wouldn't matter if you were. We have this place on lockdown."

"Like you told me."

"It's not bullshit," he says. "Come on, let me show you something."

I follow him to a nearby booth called Jean Therapy, filled with designer jeans with massive holes in the legs, selling for over $200. At Garbage Mountain this place would have tumbleweeds blowing through it, but here it's filled with people hoping to wear what only the most fashionable dog attack victims wear in the big city. Parker calls over one of Treasure Palace's roving checkout clerks and asks him for the scanner he's holding.

"Do you know what this is, McReedy?"

"A portable blowup doll?"

"No, it's an upgrade to our credit card readers. Only three stores in the whole country have them. Profit Protector brought them over yesterday after I called them. So if you're thinking of pulling some sort of lame scam like your dad would do, think again. It won't work."

"Darn," I say, snapping my fingers. "You figured me out."

"Maybe, maybe not, but whatever you're up to, we'll be ready."

"I noticed more security than usual."

"We tagged you and your little field trip coming across the parking lot on our cameras. They let me know the minute they picked you up. Security's been trailing you around the building too. If you're dumb enough to step foot in here on Saturday, I'll be right there with you. You won't do anything in here now or in the future, but definitely not Saturday."

"Wow, you've certainly thought this through, Parker, but I've gotta tell you, you're going overboard. I'd have to be the ballsiest guy on the planet to pull something in the middle of the day with the whole public here."

"Whatever," he says. "I know you're trying to screw with me, coming over today with everyone. But I'm smarter than you. I have the GPA and ACT scores to prove it. There's nothing you can do to stop us from making more money than you. It just won't happen. Darby's aunt and uncle accidentally guaranteed it."

"How?"

"Oh, don't pretend like you don't know. But you should see it. Dad's gone all out for them."

Parker and I walk away from the food court toward another section of the building. Along the way, he points out all the decorations they've put up in the last two days, bragging about the super-secret special deals that'll bring in lots of customers and make them spend more than they normally would.

"What have you done at your place?" he says. "You might as well tell me. I definitely won't be going to see. Rabies isn't on my wish list."

I don't mind telling him because it's no secret. Mom's put up banners and signs out front and even paid for a radio ad. She also hired a professional cleaning crew who would have been more successful trying to sweep the ancient pyramids free of sand. Our biggest investment is for the stage being erected in the parking lot for My Demonic Foreskin and seven other bands Mo knows who'll perform. I feel pretty good about everything because even if things don't work out, it'll all be okay. At least that's what I'm telling myself.

"There's your girlfriend," Parker says, pointing to Darby standing outside the Ancient Artifacts booth. Her aunt and uncle made the move here on Monday, and by the number of customers, it was a smart business decision.

"Darby's not my girlfriend," I say.

"She'll probably be mine after a few days here."

"I wouldn't count on it."

"I have people watching her. She's not acting normal."

"How so?"

"She's talking to a lot of our boothers, asking questions, being friendly," Parker says.

"What's weird about that?"

"This is Darby we're talking about. She's not the most outgoing person."

"Maybe she's decided to change."

"Or maybe she's planning something."

I don't respond because not addressing his worry will make him even more paranoid. From the booth, Darby sees us but doesn't come over. She's busy with a guy who's trying to decide whether to buy the red or the blue kimono. It doesn't matter, though. If he's already decided to buy a kimono, the color won't matter because he's going to look stupid in it.

"I don't get it," I say. "How's this going all out for Darby's family? It looks like the booth they had at The Mountain."

"Not that," Parker says. "That."

He points to a massive blue and white banner hanging across the aisle—*BATESVILLE MARTIAL ARTS TOURNAMENT & EXHIBITION*, Saturday at noon.

"It's being thrown together at the last minute, but Mr. West says it'll bring in at least two hundred people. Whatever you're planning to pull, all you've done is guarantee there will be lots of people here. And those people are going to need to eat, and most of them will shop."

"Or maybe our plan is to turn all the ninjas loose in here to beat up your customers."

"Laugh all you want, but in a month you won't have a place to live and your mom will be working for us."

It's a possibility I try not to think about. I have a lie to sell, and that means no hesitation. Not that it's easy. My family's home and livelihood are on the line. For all the paranoia Parker's feeling, his smugness has me second-guessing everything, and I don't have time. Besides, it's too late to turn back now. The plan's in motion.

Two of The Mountain's boothers walk by, one of them taking pictures of the security cameras, the other writing notes on a yellow legal pad. Parker's eyes go as big as DVDs. He's about to chase after them, but before he can leave, I catch Darby's eye.

I pull at my earlobe.

Darby pulls at hers.

And Parker catches all of it.

Just like we want him to.

CHAPTER 24

The Kansas City Shuffle

Yoshi the Astronaut Vampire is the costume for the day.

If you've never had the privilege of seeing the show, it's about—oh, who really cares? He's an astronaut and a vampire—what else do you need to know? Yoshi's costume's a silver space suit with a black cape and round astronaut helmet with reflective glass that lets you see out but no one see in. It's the final piece Kay fits into place, and when she's finished, she steps back to admire her work.

"Can you see?" she says.

"Yeah," I say.

"How's the sound?"

"Perfect."

"Then my work here is done."

"More like just getting started."

"I look forward to it."

Kay has a right to be optimistic. Golden Mountain's only been open for an hour, and already the aisles are full of customers here for the deals and entertainment happening today. Outside the costume booth, Andy Alexander, the freshman whose big mouth sicced Gompers on me, is dressed as a four-armed space knight. Either Kay has him wearing a sock down the front of his spandex like she had me do or the future Mrs. Alexander is one lucky lady.

It's slow going to get outside the building because the aisles are so packed with people and families. Most are wearing yellow hats with the Golden Mountain logo, free today from booth ninety's Hatters Gonna Hat. The cleaning crew Mom hired worked around the clock for the last two days delousing the entire building. The whole place now smells like the world's largest doctor's office. It might be the first time I've ever seen customers walking around without holding their nose.

But while the inside of the building is busy, the real show's outside. The parking lot has a real carnival atmosphere to it if the carnival in question was owned by people who live under bridges and hang out in alleys at midnight. Members of Roadie's motorcycle gang—err, motorcycle club—are taking people for free rides on their bikes. Nearby in a small fenced-in area, an anorexic Shetland pony gives rides to children. Tables offer face-painting, balloon animals, and even fortune-telling. Bolan's open for tours to anyone willing to climb up into his mouth to take a picture. There's even a line of people waiting to risk their lives on a rickety merry-go-round and mini-Ferris wheel. And at the far end of the property, My Demonic Foreskin's playing its first of two sets of what's been promoted as an all-day music event. At the moment, Mo's wailing away on a cover of the MC5's "Kick Out the Jams" while kids from all over the area jump and dance around. Eventually, they'll all need food, and our fifteen food and drink booths inside will be more than willing to meet their needs.

Next door at Treasure Palace, there's no carnival outside. It's a good thing for them too because they'd have no room for all of the cars currently filling the parking lot. The inside's even more crowded like each car brought in a dozen people or maybe bused them in from out of state. But by the way these people are dressed, there's no way they'd set foot on a bus unless it was made of gold. You can almost smell the money on them, which is different from The Mountain, where everyone smells like fried food and regret. The booths in Treasure Palace are filled, while the roving clerks check out customers with their technologically superior credit card readers. I only get to witness three minutes of economics at its finest before Parker's walking up to everyone's favorite astronaut vampire.

"Really, McReedy? That's the best you can do? You didn't think I'd recognize you costumed up? I told you we'd be watching for anything suspicious."

"Nothing gets by you, Parker."

"You're wasting your time here. I'd think you'd be over enjoying Garbage Mountain's last hurrah. We have double the customers, and it's still early."

"It's okay," I say. "I'm not worried."

"And why's that?"

"Because we've already won."

Parker laughs.

"I've seen your place. It's a nice crowd for you guys, but nothing like we have. And these people spend big, unlike your customers."

"Exactly."

"What does that mean?"

"It means Golden Mountain will be around longer than you think."

Parker's smile fades. I'm so deep in his head he's probably been waking up at night drenched in sweat and screaming my name.

"I knew you'd be here today," he says, "so I got you a present."

"Oh, I love surprises."

"But probably not this one."

He waves his hand past the astronaut helmet, and a couple seconds later, Gompers is looking into the reflective glass. The fact it doesn't immediately crack is a testament to Kay's craftsmanship.

"He's private security just for today," Parker says, "and you're his only client."

"Lucky me," I say. "But you might want to watch out, Gompers. Darby's around here. Remember her? The girl who kicked your ass?"

Gompers snarls so hard the glass fogs up.

"I'm going to go check on some things," Parker says to Gompers. "Watch him. He may be here to pick some pockets."

"With those heavy gloves on?" Gompers says.

"Just watch him."

Parker goes one way, likely to go watch Yoshi the Astronaut Vampire from the security room, while Gompers follows me on my walk through Treasure Palace. We wade into a massive circle of people surrounding the foam mats in the middle of the aisle where Darby's leading an exhibition on self-defense with her mini-warriors. The audience cheers as they attack the air with terrifying intensity.

"I suggest staying away from that little girl right there with the red hair," I say to Gompers. "She has the foot of an NFL kicker."

"What's your play here, McReedy?"

"Do you really want to know?"

"Yeah, and I won't even tell Parker. I don't owe him anything."

I lean in as close at the helmet will let me.

"Okay, then," I say, "the play is that there is no play."

"Bullshit," he says. "You're a prick, McReedy, but you're not stupid."

"That's the sweetest thing anyone's ever said to me."

Gompers grabs the spacesuit.

"You know, someday I'm going to catch you out when your girlfriend isn't there to protect you, and I'm going to finish that beating I was giving you."

"I wish you were smart enough to know just how pathetic that sounds."

Nearby, a line's formed at a table outside Ancient Artifacts, where people are signing up for classes at Yin's Dojo. Further down the aisle, booths sell high-end kitchen equipment, designer clothes for dogs, and body soaps and creams the customers at Golden Mountain would probably mistake for food. It's another half-hour of browsing with Gompers playing tagalong before Parker catches up by the food court.

"Aren't you getting hot in that getup, Boone?" Parker says.

"I don't know."

"How can you not know?"

"Ah, just another of life's mysteries," I say. "Did you spot any shenanigans while you were gone?"

"Why do you think that's what I was doing?"

"Because it's all over your face and how you can't stop moving. You look like you haven't slept in days."

"I do not," he says.

"Gompers?" I say.

"McReedy's right, man. You look like shit."

Parker really shows himself then. There's a brief moment where his face relaxes and his body drops. The guy's exhausted, and it's all because of me. I've almost ruined this guy with paranoia. And to think my ninth-grade English teacher told me I'd never accomplish anything worthwhile.

"In all seriousness," I say to him, "I'd feel bad for you, but you brought it on yourself by stealing our money."

"It'll be worth it when this is all over and Garbage Mountain is ours," he says. "I'll sleep fine then, while you're wide awake wondering where you're going to live."

"And while I like that idea, I have a better one—do you like games?"

"I'm not going to do one of your dumb bar bets, Boone."

"No, you'll like this a lot. In fact, if you get it right, I'll tell you everything that's going on. There might even still be time for you guys to win the contest."

"And if I don't get it right?"

"There's a consolation prize. You really can't lose. It's no risk."

Parker looks at Gompers for help, which is sort of like asking a pineapple for career advice.

"Fine," Parker says. "I'll play your stupid game."

"Gompers," I say, "do you see the zipper on the front of this suit? In there's a folded piece of paper. Take it out, but don't show it to him."

Gompers does what he's told and holds the paper down at his side where Parker can't see it.

"Okay, here's the game; it's a simple question—what state is Kansas City in?"

"That's it?" Parker says.

"That's it," I say. "Gompers is holding the answer in his hand."

Parker's eyes go from me to the paper, then up to the ceiling. He's working out the angle, tying his brain up in knots.

"There are actually two places called Kansas City," he says finally. "One in Missouri where the Royals and Chiefs play, and the smaller city in Kansas. The question is which one you'd think I'd say. I've known you for years, and you think you're smarter than everyone even though you're not. So you're probably counting on me to say Kansas, thinking you could fool me. Because that's what most people would say. But I'm not most people. You wrote Missouri on the paper."

"Is that what you're going with?" I say.

"Yeah," he says. Then to Gompers, "Show me."

Gompers unfolds the paper, looks at it, and smiles before revealing it to Parker, who immediately frowns.

"You're too clever for your own good, man," Gompers says.

"Don't beat yourself up over it, Parker," I say. "You fell for the Kansas City Shuffle. You think you know the trick, so you try to outsmart the conman when really he's counting on you to do just that."

"Yeah, you're a genius, Boone. So what my consolation prize?"

"I'll give it to you, but I don't think you're going to like it."

"Christ, Boone, just give it to me."

I've been waiting all day for this. Even if Parker had guessed right and said "Missouri," this would have been his reward. I almost wish I was there to see it live in person. Because one second Parker's looking at me, and then Yoshi the Astronaut Vampire's helmet comes off, and all I can see is the ceiling flash by and then a solid shot of the Treasure Palace floor. The camera in front of the helmet may have me blind now, but the microphone in the antenna has no problem picking up sound.

"Hi, Parker," a girl says.

In the seconds of silence that follows, I imagine Parker's re-attaching his lower jaw.

"Wait, who are you?" Gompers says.

"Where's Boone?" Parker says, his voice shaking.

"Are you panicking right now?" she says. "Because it sure looks like you're panicking. Now you know how I felt when you sent that picture of me."

"Where in the hell is Boone?" Parker shouts.

"What's going on?" Gompers says. "Who are you?"

"I'm Angela," she says.

Maybe to the rest of the world she's Angela, but to you and me she's known by a different name—Leyla, the mystery girl.

"Angela," Parker yells, "I said where is Boone?"

Suddenly, I'm not looking at the floor anymore, but into the face of the girl who was blackmailed into conning me out of $15,000 just over two weeks ago. She smiles into the camera and says, "Should I tell him?"

"I don't know," I say. "Do you feel like you've tortured him enough?"

"For what he did to me? Not even close."

"Then go have your fun. We'll talk later. But if you're hoping to make out with me again, I'm sorry. I'm sort of spoken for."

"I'll have to live with the disappointment," Leyla/Angela says, and the screen blacks out.

The last thing I hear before the speaker goes too is Parker shouting for the fourth time, "Where is Boone McReedy?"

CHAPTER 25

The Awesomeness of Ruining Someone's Day

I wish I had a fun answer to Parker's question.

Like at this very moment I'm heisting diamonds and gold out of Treasure Palace's vault so Mom and I can leave the country and put flea markets out of our lives forever.

Or that I'm currently in bed with Parker's mom, brainwashing her with my sex god ways so she'll leave her husband and marry me, all so Parker will have to call me "Dad."

But the real answer isn't anything close to those.

No, instead, I'm currently in Golden Mountain working my butt off. Or at least working as much as I can while monitoring Leyla's/Angela's time at Treasure Palace on this handheld monitor and microphone gizmo courtesy of Vintage Tech.

It turns out finding Angela wasn't difficult once I knew she was from Asheville and that Parker had incriminating pictures of her. My buddy Wheeler's from Asheville and had heard the story. It would be an understatement to say she was more than happy to help me screw with Parker today. Begging and pleading for the opportunity is more like it.

I stop by Vintage Tech to return the monitor, then head up the aisle toward America Rocks! Overall, the crowd here is probably the best we've had since our initial opening, but I'll admit it's nothing like what's happening over at Treasure Palace. Our free hats, pony rides, and discounts on taxidermied parakeets just can't compete with their newer facilities and products that don't break once they leave the property. It's not a battle we could ever win. Everyone here realizes that now. Not that it's affecting anyone's mood. All the boothers have made good money, and the events going on inside and outside the building have brought an energy that's been lacking. Can we keep it up after today? I don't know. All I know is we're going to be around a lot longer than Parker or his dad are hoping. They've made sure of that.

After five minutes of swimming upstream, I reach America Rocks!, where today Roadie's offering a twenty percent discount to any customer who brings him a Photoshopped picture of the president in an embarrassing position—the dirtier, the better.

Roadie's finishing pinning up a picture of our commander-in-chief getting extra friendly with a dolphin when he sees me.

I tug at my earlobe.

He tugs at his.

Then he's heading down to Kay's Costumes.

Booths away, Mom's talking with a small crowd of customers. She's smiling and talking with her hands, having a good time, but when she sees me, she breaks away and comes over. Her hug squeezes all the air out of me.

"Isn't this great?" she says.

"That's exactly the word I would use."

"I really think we can build off this, Boone. I've talked to a lot of people who have never been here before today, and they said they'd definitely be back."

"Enough to keep us alive for a few more years?"

"That's not my worry at the moment. I'm just enjoying the day. You should too."

"Oh, I'm definitely doing that."

"And our friends from next door?"

"They'll be here soon, I think."

"Good," Mom says. "Until then, I have a bunch of jobs that need done."

I take a mental note of the work she lists, then fight my way into the customers clogging the aisle until I get to the food court. The crowd grows heavier here, not just in numbers, but in weight too, because it's impossible to eat flea market food without pushing the limits of yoga pants' stretchiness. I spend the next hour cleaning tables, emptying overflowing garbage cans, and restocking cups at The Leaning Tower of Pizza. I'm about to mop up my one-thousandth ice cream scoop spill of the day when Parker rushes in.

"What the hell have you done, Boone?" he yells.

"I'm sort of busy here, Parker. Maybe we can talk after close."

"No," he says, grabbing the mop from me, "we'll talk now. Why did you make me think Angela was you? What have you been doing?"

"Well, mostly playing janitor, electrician, and gopher for boothers who need something."

"You know what I'm talking about."

"Oh, you mean you? I've been screwing with you, that's all. And it's been a lot of fun."

"Whatever you've done, I'm going to make sure you go to jail just like your dad."

"I'm no lawyer, but I'm pretty sure that's not how the legal system works."

"And Garbage Mountain," Parker says, "this place will be torn to the ground. It's an embarrassment, just like your boothers and the losers who shop here. We wouldn't even let them in at our place. We have IQ and weight requirements at Treasure Palace that none of your customers could meet."

"And your customers?"

"Who cares?" Parker says, still fuming. "Our customers are terrible with their money, blowing it on crap they don't need, and thank god. We're getting nice and rich off our idiots, unlike your idiots who are bankrupting you."

"Hey now, watch it," I say. "They may be idiots, but they're our idiots, and we love them."

"Well, do it while you can because this place won't be here much longer."

"It'll be here longer than you think."

"Only if you somehow cheated, but I don't see how that's possible."

I check the time. Both businesses will close in an hour. Even if Parker figures out what's happened, or worse Mr. Briggs does, there's not enough time to do anything about it. So I might as well turn the screws on Parker a little bit more while I can since it brings me so much darn happiness.

"Do you know why people fall for cons, Parker? My dad used to talk about it all the time. It's because everyone thinks they're too smart to be a victim. Scams are something that only happen to other people, never to them. And because people don't believe they're vulnerable, they're actually more vulnerable because they're never on their guard. A lot of times, marks can't even admit to themselves that they've been conned. You'll even see times when a mark will actually help you with the con. Like the Auction Hustle at Moonville. Those kids were throwing money at us, thinking they were getting away with something. They did the work for us, and we just sat back and collected their money. A great conman can pull that off."

"So you're calling yourself great?"

"I'll leave that to the many biographers I'll inevitably have," I say. "Do you remember our talk about the Kansas City Shuffle?"

"What about it?"

"That's what's been going on all week."

"What are you talking about?"

"You're actually one of the people I know who's smart enough to see a scam coming because you know me. So you've been waiting for me to start some big con that only you could stop. But while you were focused on me—watching my little anti-pick-pocketing show, chasing Angela around in her outfit because you thought she was me, spying on Darby because we're a team, coming over here when you should probably be back at your place—I wasn't actually doing anything. I just had to sell the lie that I was planning something and let someone else do everything necessary for us to win."

"Darby?" he says.

I shake my head.

"Mo and Arlo?"

I shake my head again.

"Angela?"

I keep shaking my head.

"Then someone I don't know?"

"Oh, it's someone you know," I say. "But it's the last person you'd ever expect to screw you over."

Parker's face is so strained his head might pop off. I could put him out of his misery, but I'm enjoying this too much. And Parker's no dope. His eyes are staring at a place between me and the ceiling, replaying everything we've been talking about. It doesn't take him long. His eyes go wide.

"No," he says.

"Yes," I say.

"You mean *I* did something. What did I do?"

"Big picture, you played the wrong family," I say. "Small picture, you behaved exactly as I thought you would."

"You didn't do anything?"

I pause to suck in all the glorious pain and suffering radiating from Parker Briggs, the son of a bitch who conned me for $15,000.

"No, I didn't need to do anything," I say, "because you did it all for me."

CHAPTER 26

Revealing the Big Con

At seven o'clock, once both Golden Mountain and Treasure Palace close and the outside festivities shut down, we meet with Parker and his dad again in Mom's office. We have Opal with us this time, and they bring their own version of Opal, a crusty, sour-faced man named Al who looks like he spends his free time swearing at kindergartners waiting for the bus. He and Opal will probably leave this meeting engaged.

In the time since he stormed out of here, Parker must've found a team of professional therapists who dosed him with confidence pills because he's sitting across the table looking smuggier-than-thou. My guess is he's heard preliminary estimates from the day and knows we can't beat them. Or maybe he knows something I don't? I guess that's a possibility. Mostly, I think it's that Parker's default setting is cocky. His dad's the same way. He's across from Mom looking as tired from the day as her, but he has a smile on his face that says he knows he won. I wouldn't be surprised if he brings out a tape measure to start early renovations to the room.

"Want a piece of gum, Parker?" I say.

"What? Why are you asking me that?"

"I'm just going to have a piece. I thought I'd be friendly and offer you one too."

Parker just huffs and shakes his head. I pop in a piece of gum. Now I'm ready.

"Liann," Mr. Briggs says to Mom, "how did the day go here? From what I saw, you looked very busy."

"Not as busy as you, I don't think, but we had a great turnout. Regardless of what happens, it was good for both of us. And for Batesville."

"Agreed," he says. "Now let's get into the numbers, shall we? I think we're all excited to hear the returns."

"Absolutely."

Opal forces herself to stop making googly eyes at her soul-mate-in-anger and opens her laptop, her fingers flying over the keyboard. Most jokes about old people being terrible with technology are true, but Opal's an exception. If an alien ship ever crashes here, the military should send Opal in to figure out how their spaceship works. She'd have E.T.'s light-covered ship flying again in no time.

"According to the numbers, we had approximately 1,200 visitors today, which I know for a fact is our most ever," Opal says.

Mom and I exchange big smiles. It's a great accomplishment, and it'll have Mom walking on air for the next week.

"As for how much we brought in," Opal says, "today's account shows a grand total of, wow…"

"How much?" Mom says.

"$28,731."

In a wonderful moment of parent-child bonding, Mom and I yell out, "Holy shit!" We also share a hard hug that has my eyes bulging.

"We've never made that much in one day," she says.

"I think we can beat it," I say.

"That's the McReedy overconfidence I love so much."

Mr. Briggs says, "That's an impressive amount. You should be very proud. It'll be tough to beat."

Parker chuffs at this, and all eyes turn to Al. He starts in on his laptop, and as he does, Mr. Briggs says, "We had approximately 1,600 visitors today. A lot of it was cross-traffic from your place. I saw a lot of the yellow hats you were giving away."

"We made sure to remind our customers of the deals you were offering," Mom says.

"You did?"

"Like they say, 'A rising tide lifts all boats.' If one of us is succeeding, the other will too."

Mr. Briggs' eyes narrow, and for the first time, doubt shows on his face.

"Al?" he says.

After some final keystrokes, Al hits Enter. He reads the screen much longer than Opal did, his eyes squinting harder with each passing second.

"This can't be right," he says.

"What is it?" Mr. Briggs says.

Parker looks from Al to me. I keep my face straight, but, man, it's not easy.

"There has to be a mistake," Al says. "We're well below our projections, especially considering the number of visitors we had today."

"How much did we make?" Mr. Briggs says.

Al swallows hard.

"$3,834."

Parker and Mr. Briggs both launch to their feet and come behind Al to see the screen.

"That's impossible," Mr. Briggs says. "With today's crowds, we should have close to $64,000."

"It's what's in the account, Mr. Briggs," Al says.

"Well, the account is wrong."

"But the account's all that matters," Mom says.

Mr. Briggs ignores Mom, but Parker doesn't. His head snaps to her, then to me. This time, I give in to temptation and wink.

"They stole our money," Parker yells.

"How could we possibly do that?" I say.

"I don't know how, but you did."

"Calm down, Parker," Mr. Briggs says. "We can settle this easily. It's a simple accounting mistake. Call Profit Protector and get them over here."

"That's a good idea," I say.

Parker gives me a *screw-you* face and pulls out his phone. He punches at the screen so hard I'm surprised it doesn't crack. Then he hits Send.

Outside Mom's office, a phone rings.

Everyone looks at the closed door except for me. I look at Parker.

"That's gotta be a coincidence," I say.

A second later, the door opens and in walks a man wearing a light blue Profit Protector jacket. The black goatee he's wearing courtesy of Kay's Costumes hides his identity some, but it's the short spikey hair that really sells the disguise. I still have no idea how Kay managed to get all of Roadie's long hair hidden up inside of that wig.

"Now that's the mark of the best security company in the state," I say. "You call, and they're immediately there. Amazing."

"You called, sir?" Roadie says. "You're not having problems with your new credit card readers, are you? They've been a bit glitchy lately, sending money to the wrong place. It's regrettable."

Parker's neck muscles are close to ripping.

"What have you done?" Mr. Briggs says to Mom.

"I didn't do anything, Cullen. Boone didn't either. Like we promised. But like you said the other day, we're only responsible for our own actions. What other people choose to do is up to them."

Mr. Briggs keeps his cool, which is more than I can say for Parker, whose hands are clenched into fists on the table.

"I expected more from you," Mr. Briggs says.

"One of your many mistakes," Mom says.

Parker pounds the table.

"Where's our money?" he says.

"Who knows?" I say. "Technology is really confusing. It could be anywhere."

"Where is it, Boone?"

"Relax, it's safe. For now."

Parker eases but doesn't sit down.

"You put a different number in my phone for Profit Protector, didn't you? And this guy brought over scanners that sent the money to a different account. That's what you did, isn't it?"

"Wow, that would really take a master conman to do something like that," I say. "Someone would have to come from a long line of criminals to pull that off."

Parker starts around the table at me, but his dad takes his arm.

"Sit down, son," Mr. Briggs says.

Okay, so look, I'll admit it—Mom and I lied to Parker and his dad and even you when we said we wouldn't cheat. But, technically, we didn't cheat. Roadie did it for us. We just told him what we needed him to do. But what did you expect to happen? That I would suddenly sprout wings and a halo and never lie again? Haven't you been paying attention to who I am? It's called selling the lie. And like the Briggses, you bought it.

Once Parker sits, Mr. Briggs turns to Al and says, "Please call the police."

"You might not want him doing that," Mom says, "because if he does, you'll never see your money again. You need to figure out what's more important—getting your money back or watching the police question us?"

"Why can't I have both?"

"Because even if they do come, you can't prove anything," I say. "You have no evidence anything happened here."

"We still have your fake scanners," Mr. Briggs says.

"No, you don't," Roadie says. "I switched them out with your original scanners around five. Now it just looks like you had a really bad day of business, minus that last hour when you had your previous scanners back. You probably made some money there."

"Almost $4,000," I say. "Imagine how much they made the entire day. If only we had a way of knowing."

"Where is our money?" Mr. Briggs says calmly.

I look at Mom, and she nods. Now it's my turn to make a phone call. A minute later, the office door opens and Darby and Ink come in. Ink, carrying his own laptop, sits beside me, while Darby stands guard behind him. I reach back, and Darby and I bump fists. Ink gets to work, wisely not looking at Parker, who's firing lasers at him with his eyes. After a minute's work, he turns the screen so we all can see.

"Whoa, $71,000," I say. "That's amazing. You're quite the businessman. Or, I mean, you would be if you actually had that money."

"I would like my money, please," Mr. Briggs says.

"I'm sure you would," Mom says. "And it can be yours. For a price."

Give Briggs credit. He doesn't shout or pound the table. Parker could learn a lot from him about how to do business.

"What it'll cost?" Briggs says.

"You mean besides declaring us the winner of the contest in radio, TV, and newspaper ads?" Mom says.

Briggs sighs. "Yes, besides that."

"$15,000."

"That's all?" he says.

"I don't want more than that. All I want is what's rightfully ours."

"For the record, I argued to keep all of your money," I say. "But she's the boss."

Darby coughs.

"Oh yeah, and her too," I say. "They outnumbered me on this."

Briggs says, "So we concede the contest in the press—"

"Which will help our numbers," Mom says.

"—and you keep $15,000—"

"Which was our money to begin with," Mom says.

"—and we get the rest of our money back?"

"Yes," Mom says.

Briggs doesn't think about it long.

"Deal," he says.

"Dad, don't," Parker says. "Let Al call the cops. We can get rid of this place forever."

"Maybe," I say, "but then I'd have to make this part of our new commercial."

Darby holds up her phone, and we get the pleasure of watching Parker's tantrum railing against Golden Mountain and the people who shop here, ending with him calling Treasure Palace's customers rich idiots. Parker slides down in his chair, trying to melt into the floor.

"It wouldn't ruin you," Mom says, "but it certainly wouldn't help."

"No, it wouldn't," Briggs says.

"Plus, I don't think your boothers would be too thrilled to hear their money isn't as secure as you make it out to be," Darby adds.

Mr. Briggs teepees his fingers and after a moment looks at Ink and says, "Transfer the money."

Parker doesn't argue this time.

Ink says to me, "All but $15,000?"

"Unfortunately."

He gets the account number from Al, who soon acknowledges receiving the transfer. I sure hope this doesn't stop him and Opal from falling in love. I'd hate to be the reason true evil couldn't find happiness. Briggs stands up and in an odd moment offers Mom his hand.

"You know this place is going to fail eventually," he says.

"Possibly," she says, shaking his hand, "but if it does, it'll fail legitimately. Not from having our money stolen."

Parker, his dad, and Al leave, but not before Parker gives me one final sneer. We wait until the door closes before silently cheering. Darby and I hug, and so do Roadie and Mom, which is about the most awkward thing I've ever witnessed. Opal and Ink don't hug, probably because she's pining for her lost love Al and because Ink has standards, however low they are.

"I still think we should've taken them for all of it," I say.

"You wouldn't have, though," Mom says. "That's something your father would do."

"Does the fact I thought about keeping all the money change that?"

"No, what matters is that you didn't go through with it."

"It was a lot of money."

"We'll earn our money fairly. I think I have a better idea of what this place is now."

She goes to talk to Opal, and I walk over to Darby, who already has my five dollars ready.

"You really didn't think it would work?" I say.

"Oh, I figured it would. Life is just more interesting with money on the line."

"You can say that again."

The six of us leave the office to the cheers of our boothers. We hadn't told anyone of our plan, but you can't keep secrets in a family like this. While Mom hugs Miss Laverne, Kay comes over to Roadie to help him out of his ridiculous disguise. Darby and I only get to enjoy the celebration a short time because Parker's standing outside the crowd, arguing with our friends.

"Some people don't know when to quit," Darby says.

"We should go save him before Arlo gives up his pacifistic ways."

When we get there, Parker's giving it not only to Arlo but also to Mo, Ink, and Angela, who are all trying their best not to laugh at him. A handful of Darby's self-defense students stand behind our friends like a troop of miniature personal bodyguards.

"Come on, man," I say to Parker, "you're embarrassing yourself. Be a good loser and go."

"I'm not the loser, Boone; you are, and all of your friends here who helped you."

"No one's a loser, really," Arlo says, diplomatically. "Boone just got back what he had taken from him."

"No, this is about a lot more than just money now, and you know it," Parker says. "Every single one of you—"

"Will pay?" Mo says.

"No, will—" Parker says.

"Suffer?" Ink says.

"No," Parker says, turning red, "will—"

"Feel your wrath?" Angela says.

Parker shakes his head. "You should have stayed out of this, Angela. I have a certain picture people are going to love seeing."

Her eyes widen.

"You promised me you'd delete it if I helped you," she says.

"What can I say? Good blackmail material is hard to come by. And now I get to share it with the world."

"You wouldn't."

"I would," Parker says, "and I will."

Darby steps in between them.

"No, you won't."

Parker moves back.

"If you touch me, I'll have you arrested."

"I'm not going to touch you," Darby says. "But if you don't delete that picture forever, I know someone who would be more than happy to deal with you."

"Who?" Parker says.

"Me."

The moment I hear Kimberly's voice, muscle memory has me tasting bile. She steps up to Parker, who laughs in her face.

"Don't mess with her, Parker," I say. "Seriously, I'm doing you a favor here."

"Yeah, right," he says.

"Say you'll delete the picture," Darby says.

"Or what?"

"Or this," Kimberly says.

This time, Kimberly doesn't do the flip-over-the-shoulder move she used on me. She's not that kind or forgiving. She rockets her foot into Parker's crotch, launching him into the air. He slams to the ground, writhing around, sucking air, his hands clutching his balls. Mo, Arlo, and Ink look like they may throw up.

"I tried to warn you," I say to Parker. "She's a maniac."

"And she'll keep doing it unless you delete the picture," Darby says. "You won't see her coming either. She'll just appear and then—"

"Dick detonation," I say.

"Which is now the name of the next song I'll write," Mo says.

"I'm not joking," Darby tells Parker. "Promise you'll delete it, or this will happen again and again."

Parker whimpers something, and Darby leans in.

"Louder," she says.

"I promise," he says.

Disappointment isn't a strong enough word for the look on Kimberly's face. Devastation is more accurate.

"Don't worry," Darby tells her. "There will be others."

It takes a good two minutes, but eventually, Parker struggles to his feet and stumbles for the exit. The celebration then moves to the food court, where Mom says the food's on her, giving all of us, boothers included, a chance to risk diabetes and morbid obesity for free. I down two slices of pizza, a cherry slush, and am considering a piece of The Mud Hut's Defecake when Darby comes over.

"How much did we make off our cons?" she says.

"Just over $7,000. That Phone Fleece Ink set up for us brought in a small fortune," I say. "When do you want your cut?"

"I don't. I have a better idea of what we should do with the money."

"Am I going to like it?"

"Probably not," she says. "But it'll be good for both of us."

CHAPTER 27

I Am the Most Selfless Person Ever

On Monday afternoon, Darby and I climb out of The Destroyer and walk across the hot parking lot to Viper Strike Martial Arts. I'm still wiped out from the weekend's festivities and spent the better part of yesterday sleeping. I would've liked to repeat my award-winning performance of a sloth today, but Darby had me pick her up at eleven. I'll just have to find a way to function on fourteen hours' sleep.

"You're right, I don't like this," I say.

"Every negative action calls for a positive one to even things out," she says.

"What have I done that's so negative?"

"I don't have enough time to list them all."

"What do you mean?" I say. "We're not back in school for two months."

"I love it when you prove my point for me."

The medieval insides of Viper Strike look even more ridiculous in the daytime. With the sunlight coming through the windows, the black walls and old-timey weapons seem like we've walked onto the set of a D-level movie. All three of the Reids— the parents and young daughter, Bea—are at the front counter, almost as if they haven't moved since we left over a week ago.

"Clitoria!" Mrs. Reid says.

Darby shudders.

I whisper, "That gift is going to keep on giving."

"Hi," Darby says to them. "Sorry it took us so long to come back. It turns out Hugo lost the notary stamp. He didn't find it until yesterday. He's not the best looker."

"But I am the best-looking," I say. "I've won awards."

"Maybe at the county level," Mrs. Reid says, "but definitely not at the state level."

Darby's eyes go wide.

"Oh my gosh," she says to Mrs. Reid, "you're my new best friend."

Bea's bouncing with so much excitement she might come out of her shoes. At the counter, Darby retrieves three gold envelopes from a leather folder and fans them out for the family.

"Now, where were we?" Darby says.

"Aren't we supposed to write you a check?" Mr. Reid says.

"Well, I have good news—because of the delay, the commission's agreed to cover the taxes for you."

"We don't have to pay anything?" Mrs. Reid says.

"Nothing at all," Darby says. "You just need to pick an envelope. Do you remember the three prizes?"

"The Disney trip!" Bea yells.

"Or a motorcycle," Mr. Reid says.

"Or $5,000," Mrs. Reid finishes. That's not entirely accurate, but it's nothing that needs correcting this time.

Bea looks up at her mom and yells, "Can I pick? Can I pick?"

"Sure, but no motorcycle," Mrs. Reid says. "We don't need your father breaking his leg."

"Shoot," he says, "you'd ride it more than I would."

Mrs. Reid waves him off.

"Go ahead, sweetheart. Pick away."

Bea bites down on a fingernail and considers the envelopes. She turns her head this way and that, looking at the envelopes from the bottom and the sides until finally her mom gently says, "Bea." "Okay, okay," she says and reaches for the middle envelope. Once her fingers touch it, though, she pulls her hand back and goes back to her investigation. I have to bite my tongue bloody not to shout that it doesn't matter what envelope she picks; they're all the exact same prize.

"Bea, come on," her dad says.

"All right," she says, and reaches for the envelope on the left, which she takes from the counter, this time without changing her mind.

"Can I open it too?" Bea says.

Her parents nod, and she tears into the gold envelope, her parents leaning over her shoulder. Bea pulls out the card inside, and all of them scream at once.

"Disney!"

Then there's a lot of jumping and screaming by all of them. It reminds me a lot of the celebrating we did at Golden Mountain on Saturday. I go to mention this to Darby but leave her alone once I see the tears forming in her eyes. When the whooping calms down, Mrs. Reid says, "This is for real, right?"

"It is," Darby says. "You just take that to Stingray Travel in Batesville and they'll schedule your trip."

"And it's all for free?"

"All for free," Darby says.

Free for them, sure. For us, it took every cent from our two-week-long con-a-thon to cover their roundtrip airfare, rental car, park tickets, hotel costs, meals, and "complimentary" souvenirs. But even I have to admit, it's fun bringing people such happiness, even if they'll never know we were really behind it. I have them sign a paper filled with legal speak acknowledging they received their prize, and then use the notary stamp I swiped from Opal's desk when she was at lunch. We tell the Reids goodbye and are on our way out when Mrs. Reid says, "Clitoria? Hugo?"

We turn and see the family beaming at us.

"Thank you," Mr. and Mrs. Reid say.

"Yeah, thanks!" Bea says.

"It was our pleasure," Darby says.

"Mostly yours," I mutter.

Darby elbows me, and when we're back in the parking lot says, "Now come on, that felt good, didn't it?"

"Meh," I say.

"Oh, shut up. I know you have a soft spot in there. If you didn't, I wouldn't still be around you."

"Speaking of which," I say, as we climb back into The Destroyer, "we haven't really discussed 'us.'"

"What's to discuss?"

"Are the old rules still in place? Are we going to go out again? What's the deal?"

Darby pauses but keeps her eyes on me.

"Do you know what the best part of the last two weeks has been?"

"Slapping me?"

"Definitely number two on the list."

"Seeing Gompers pound me?"

"Number three," she says. "No, it was watching you become almost human. It's been nice, like finally seeing some return on investment."

"That's what I am, an investment?"

"A risky one for sure, but one I'm willing to stand behind for now."

I give her my million-dollar smile.

"So…good," I say.

"Right," Darby says. "Good."

She settles into her seat, and I fire up The Destroyer. I should be feeling about as good as a guy can, but something's bothering me. We're not driving for long before I bring it up.

"There's one thing," I say. "I don't think I can be entirely…"

"Straight?"

"Right, I can't do it. Making plays is a part of who I am."

"And one of the reasons I like you," Darby says. "I'm not expecting you to stop."

"Because you like them too."

"As we've talked about. But only if it's justified. Like what we did today."

"And how we saved Golden Mountain."

"Exactly. We do a little research, add to The Scam List…we could do some real good for people."

"Like the vigilante conmen thing we've talked about."

"Make it 'vigilante con artists' and I'm in," Darby says.

"You got it," I say.

The rest of the summer's going to be great. Sure, The Mountain is going to be busier than ever now, and senior year's an approaching storm cloud, but I can handle both. I'm even looking forward to the next visiting day at the prison to tell Dad about our successful Kansas City Shuffle. But maybe that's because I plan to put a couple hundred dollars into his commissary account without him even asking. I know I can definitely afford it. And if you set up your own Phone Fleece and then call it using a private line in the Briggses' bathroom like I did, you can wrack up some easy money too. Say $4,000 in three days before someone in the house finally hangs up the phone.

Of course, like Darby said, money gained from cons should go to a good cause, and I'll make sure it does.

That's exactly what I'll do.

You have my word.

Would I lie to you?

THE END.

Acknowledgements

It took five chaotic years to get *The Scam List* finished. I won't bore you with the details, but I will say I'm a different (and hopefully better) person than the one who started writing this novel back in 2015. I couldn't have completed this without the help of the following people:

My wonderful wife Jen who's the best friend, champion, nurse (you should see her take out surgical staples!), advisor, and partner-in-crime a guy could ask for. You will always be the only one for me.

My kids Brody, Sam, Charlie, and Murphy keep me young, on my toes, and always ask about my writing. You awesome knuckleheads make our world a wonderful, albeit chaotic, place.

My agent Kerry Sparks believed in this novel more than I ever could've asked. Thanks for your guidance, support, and friendship.

In a just world, writers John Mantooth (aka Hank Early), Mindy McGinnis, and Kimberly Gabriel would be household names. These great writers helped shape this novel into what it became.

A quick thanks to: amazing cover artist and designer Claudean Wheeler; copy editor Erin Schneider; brilliant proofreader Olivia Walker; logo designer Aaron Roberts; website genius Michael Cook; Jim Marcum; Kerry Rudy; Sam W. Anderson; Jessica Strawser; Josh Penzone; super fans John and Kay Watson; Karen Brissette; Spotify playlist maker Mark Richardson; the Ohio Writing Project; The Cincinnati Public Library Foundation; the nurses and doctors of Cleveland Clinic and UC West Chester Hospital; the students and staff at Mason High School; and my parents.

And finally, thanks to my readers for supporting my work and helping me get my butt back in the chair to write. Hopefully, you won't have to wait as long for the next one.

Kurt Dinan is a high school English teacher living in Cincinnati with his wife and four children. His debut novel, *DON'T GET CAUGHT*, was a Junior Library Guild selection and winner of 2017 YALSA's Teens' Top 10 book. *THE SCAM LIST* is his second novel.

CPSIA information can be obtained
at www.ICGtesting.com
Printed in the USA
FSHW011647280520
70528FS

9 781734 912708